The Mythmakers

Miss Cuddlywumps Investigates:
Book V

By
Roby Sweet

Cuddlywumps Publishing

First edition
© 2017 by Roby Sweet

ISBN 978-0-9981555-4-8

Cover images via Adobe Stock: leaves background © Maksim Pasko; knife © bsd555; film © losw100; blood spatter © macrovector.

To
Mom and Ray,
with much love.

Books in the Miss Cuddlywumps Investigates series:

Find them all at www.CuddlywumpsPublishing.com!

A Note

As a classically educated cat, Miss C likes to drop the occasional classical reference into her conversations. Please consult the Cuddlywumps Classical Dictionary beginning on page 232 for definitions of terms that may be unfamiliar.

Chapter 1

Mid-November

This is not going to be okay, Rory Roberts thought as she squirmed in the back seat of the deputy's patrol car. The metal of the handcuffs felt cold and hard against her wrists and hurt as though it were pressing directly against bone. With her hands behind her back, she could not get comfortable. No matter which way she turned, some part of her body was scrunched or pulled. Her whole left side felt bruised from when that nutjob tackled her in her own backyard—at one thirty in the morning, no less—and her shoulders strained as she turned so she could see her little stone cottage, which the car was parked in front of. Then there was the fact that she was dressed only in her pajamas, robe, and L. L. Bean boots—perhaps not the most appropriate attire to be arrested in.

At a polite distance down the sidewalk, Rory's neighbors stood watching, their faces lit by the flashing red and blue lights of sheriff's department vehicles. They shuffled and whispered in the cool, fall night, stealing glances in at Rory. They must all think I've lost my mind, she thought. One next-door neighbor, Mrs. Crabtree, scowled at her. Odd that the old woman's husband wasn't there. But whether Mr. Crabtree was there or not, the Mrs. would tell the sheriff, the press, and anyone else who would listen that she'd seen this coming for a long time. She never had liked Rory, for reasons Rory couldn't comprehend. Laura Williams, Brooksford's biggest worrier, stood shaking her head. She'd say that she'd seen it coming too, but she would attribute Rory's sudden outburst of violence to stress and overwork rather than some defect of character. Madison Gunther, the town's mayor and one of Rory's best friends, stood alone among the crowd, a blank stare on her face. Was she having flashbacks to the night her husband had been arrested for trying to kill Rory? *Well, what goes around comes around, I guess,* Rory thought.

She turned her head to look up into the front window of her cottage, where her cat sat gazing out on the scene. The cat was a large, fluffy-tailed calico named Miss Cuddlywumps, though everyone called her Miss C. She was mostly white, with large patches of black and orange splashed over her head and back. Her tail had a distinctive white tip. Rory locked eyes with the cat. Who would take care of her? Frantically, Rory looked around for Lee Cooper, her other next-door neighbor and also her lifelong best friend. Ever since she had first come to this town as a little girl visiting her grandparents, she'd hit it off with the boy next door. Their friendship had lasted over forty years, but where was Lee now?

The driver's door was opened, and Deputy Sergeant Opal Washington slid into the seat. Before Opal could say or do anything, Rory was asking, "Who's going to take care of Miss C? My cat? I can't just leave without someone to take care of my cat."

Opal looked into the rearview mirror to meet Rory's eyes. The deputy's eyes were wide and kind, her skin caramel brown, and her voice was soothing when it came. "Don't worry about Miss C. Your friend Lee is in there, and he's said that he'll watch over her. I take it he has a key to your place?"

"Yes, but—"

"Then don't worry about it, Ms. Roberts. He'll take care of things for you."

After trying again to adjust herself to be more comfortable, Rory asked, "Could you just loosen the handcuffs? Please?

Come on, Opal, you know I haven't actually done anything wrong. I don't know what that girl's telling you, but I did not do anything to her friend." She thought it best not to mention that this friend now lay dead in her backyard, stabbed with a knife Rory had been found holding.

Opal's look hardened. "Sorry, Ms. Roberts. Sheriff Davis says everything is to be done by the book. No special favors for you."

No special favors. Well, what was the point of dating the county sheriff if you couldn't get any special favors when one of his deputies arrested you for something you didn't do? Rory huffed, her patience wearing thin.

"Where is the sheriff? If I can just talk to him, we can straighten everything out."

"I'm sure he'll be talking to you once we get you processed."

"Processed? You mean fingerprinted and photographed, like a criminal?" Rory's voice rose in pitch and volume as panic flooded through her.

"Everything is to be done by the book," Opal insisted.

"I want to call my father, before any of this processing." Surely Rory's dad, a retired prosecutor from a couple of counties over, would be able to make this right and get her released before they took the processing too far.

"When we get to the station, you can make your call. Until then, just sit tight."

Rory squirmed in the seat some more, prompting Opal to say, "I'm telling you, Ms. Roberts, this'll be a lot easier for everyone concerned if you just sit tight and calm down."

"But, Opal—"

"Just calm down. It's going to be okay."

No it's not. It's not going to be okay, Rory thought. Deep down, she'd known it from the start of this whole, weird episode.

Chapter 2

One week earlier

Rory perched on the edge of her sofa and worked the top off the jigsaw puzzle box, setting it aside where she could see the picture of a group of cartoon kittens climbing up a scarecrow. Cute. Also seasonally appropriate, just as she liked her puzzles. She rummaged through the box, inhaling the gray scent of cardboard, on the hunt for edge pieces. That was the way her dad had taught her to put jigsaw puzzles together: Find the corners, complete the edges, and fill in from there. Others may have their own methods, sorting first by color, for example. Craziness.

"Corner piece," Rory declared, setting the blue-sky piece near the corner of the coffee table.

The calico cat named Miss Cuddlywumps, who much preferred to be called Miss C, sat on the floor near Rory's feet. She snuck a paw up onto the table and snagged the bit of sky, pulling it to the floor.

"Hey! You give that back, cat. Criminy, it's too early to have you start stealing pieces already." Rory reached down to pick the piece up before the cat could damage it or run off with it. Every single puzzle Rory did—and she always had one going—ended up with several pieces missing and several others chewed and mangled beyond recognition. She and Mike Davis, the Monocacy County sheriff and Rory's boyfriend, took bets on how many pieces Miss C would hide or destroy. Lately the actual numbers had always been in the double digits.

Where was Mike anyway? Rory snuck a look out the living room window to the street outside. It wasn't even five o'clock, and already the light was fading. Fall was Rory's favorite season, the crisp, light air, the leaves in their riot of warm colors, the pumpkin spice coffee, muffins, donuts, pancakes. Rory loved the fall, but she was not a fan of the shortening days, the sun rising two hours after she got up and setting before she'd even eaten dinner. So much darkness was disheartening.

Outside, there was no sign of either Mike's department SUV or his personal car. Unusual. He was supposed to be there at five, and since he was habitually early, she'd expected him by now. If he was going to be late by even a few minutes, he always called to let her know. Didn't want her to worry, he said.

She reached for her cell phone, but it buzzed before she touched it. "Mike calling," the screen told her. When she answered it, he greeted her with, "Hey, hon. I'm going to be a little late. I just got into Brooksford, but there's a ... situation down here in the south end. Shouldn't take long."

"What kind of situation?" Rory asked, suddenly extra-attentive. She'd been involved in more than one "situation in the south end" in the past couple of years, and just the thought of another one set the hair on the back of her neck on end.

"Nothing big. Just some kids messing around taking video. I'll talk to them and find out what's what, and then I'll be on my way. This dinner smells too good to keep it waiting."

The dinner was chicken chow mein and kung pao shrimp, along with egg rolls and hot and sour soup. She could almost taste the soup already. Mike had picked it up at a Chinese restaurant they liked down in Westbrook. Brooksford, Maryland, a village of just 226 inhabitants where Rory's family had lived for generations, did not boast any take-out places, nor did anyone deliver there.

"Are you sure I shouldn't come down?" Rory asked, getting off the sofa and going in search of her shoes. "You know, to bring the food home and keep it warm?" That would be her way in, her excuse to head down real quick and just see what was happening. She did have friends in the south end, after all, and she wanted to be sure they were okay.

"No, no. You stay there. The food's fine. I'll just talk to these kids for a couple minutes, and that'll be it."

"Well, I'm on my way, so I'll see you in a sec," Rory said and ended the call. She could just picture Mike's exasperation, that little twist to his mouth, his blue eyes narrowing. He was adorable when he was frustrated with her.

Rory went into her bedroom and strapped on her fanny pack, making sure her keys and wallet were in it. She decided to forget about finding her shoes, opting instead to step into her L. L. Bean boots in the laundry/mudroom before she went out the back door. She wouldn't even bother to tie the laces, not for a quick trip like this. The weather was warm for November, so she left her heavier barn coat hanging on its peg and slipped instead into a lightweight fleece jacket.

Miss C followed her from the living room to the bathroom, where Rory checked her gray-streaked brown bob for general tidiness, then to the kitchen and mudroom. The cat meowed the whole way, even staring suggestively at the pet stroller.

"Forget it, cat. I'll only be gone a minute, and it's too much trouble to fit that thing in the car."

Rory turned on the outside light and went out the back door, down the couple of steps leading to the concrete slab that was her patio, and toward her Accord, which was parked outside her detached garage. Normally, if she wasn't in a hurry, Rory would walk to the south end of town. It was a walk she took frequently, usually pushing Miss C in her stroller. Brooksford was a perfect town for walking, with good sidewalks and generally light traffic. No time for that now, though.

Rory backed carefully onto Main Street and observed the speed limit all the way to the town's only four-way intersection, where she came to a complete stop despite there being no other cars or pedestrians. Now that Mike was in her life, she felt she had to set an example by obeying basic traffic laws. She continued into the south end and spotted Mike's department SUV parked outside the Brooksford Inn, the bed-and-breakfast operated by Frank Laser and his wife. The inn was also the only restaurant in town, and it had struggled for the past couple of years. Frank himself had been implicated in the town's first-ever murder, which happened right outside Rory's cottage, and later a guest had been killed in one of the inn's rooms. Restoration of the inn's reputation was an ongoing concern ... as Rory and the whole town knew because Frank brought the subject up at every opportunity.

Now, the innkeeper stood on his front lawn, talking loudly to Mike next to the hand-painted Brooksford Inn sign. Across the street, in front of the Miller house, two twenty-somethings, a guy and a girl, leaned against a dark-colored minivan that had seen better days. The girl was average-looking but for the dull red hair that hung listlessly to the center of her back. Rory felt like telling her she should brush that hair out to give it a little life, but then mentally kicked herself for thinking like her mother. If this girl wanted to have hair that looked like it only got washed every other month, that was her prerogative. The guy was even less remarkable—average height and underweight, with wiry arms protruding from a plain black T-shirt. A knit hat covered the top of his head. The side door to the minivan stood open, and judging from the jumble inside, it looked like the pair of them might be living in it.

Under the yellowish light on the front porch of the Miller house, Liza Cunningham stood with her stepdaughter, Grace, unabashedly watching the scene across the street.

Halloween decorations—poster-board pumpkins and a menacing black cat—still hung on the door. Grace had drawn them herself. She was something of a wiz at art.

Rory caught Mike's eye, and he sent her a warning look that said, "Not now," so she went toward Liza first, walking across the front lawn toward the white-painted farmhouse that Don Miller had willed to his mistress upon his death. Liza, however, was not his mistress but his ex-wife, living in the house in exchange for low monthly rent and doing some general upkeep while the mistress was serving time in the county jail.

As with so many things in Brooksford, it was complicated.

Fifteen-year-old Grace managed a smile for Rory even though she didn't have Miss C with her. Grace loved Miss C, and Rory suspected that the girl tolerated her mostly because of the cat. No matter, though. Grace was a standout at the computer arts magnet program she attended. She was smart and talented and polite, once you worked past her shyness. Who cared if parts of her hair were neon green? Actually, the green was a departure from the bright blue she'd been sporting last time Rory saw her, which was just a few days ago. The cut was as cutting edge as ever, with the hair shaved to a quarter inch except on the very top, where the inch-long green spikes pointed every which way. She wore faded, ripped jeans and an equally ripped flannel shirt over a T-shirt. Chunky black-framed glasses set off the look.

"Hi, Grace. Liza. New haircut?" Rory asked, knowing that Liza must be responsible for the cut and the dye job. Formally, she was Dr. Liza Cunningham, visiting lecturer in American folklore at Westbrook College, but she made money on the side as a hairstylist. It was Liza who answered.

"I tried to get her to change it when school first started, but she wanted to wait till after Halloween, didn't you, Gracie?"

Grace looked down at the lawn and shrugged. "Iguess," she mumbled, turning the phrase into a single word.

"It looks great." Rory stopped herself from saying more, though the words "you be stylin'" passed through her mind and almost made it to her lips. Surely something like that would only have earned her a well-deserved eye roll from Grace. "Any idea what's happening over there?" she asked instead, with a thumb over her shoulder toward the inn.

That did get an eye roll from Grace, though Rory sensed it was meant not for her but for one of the parties involved in the disagreement across the street.

Liza answered again, "These kids—people, I mean— these people showed up here and just started taking video of the road into town and some of the houses down this way, including the inn. Frank took offense and told them to stop, but I guess they told him to shove off, and the sheriff happened by while they were arguing. That's all I know." She folded her arms across her body and shivered.

At this point, Frank suddenly raised his voice, shouting, "Can't you get 'em for disturbing the peace or something?"

The two people in question remained near their minivan, waiting quietly. It seemed that, at least for the moment, Frank was the one disturbing the peace.

Mike raised his hands in a gentle "stop" motion, and Frank calmed down. Rory admired how he could keep his cool when everyone around him was losing theirs. It was one of those remarkable things about him, like how he could stand to watch the Weather Channel for hours on end or listen to country music or follow football.

He was off duty and not in uniform, wearing instead gray casual slacks and a creamy yellow sweater that emphasized all the right places across his shoulders and chest. A blue ball cap, designed to look vintage, covered much of his close-cropped blond hair. Rory felt her knees turning to jelly, as they still tended to do when she caught sight of Mike. How had she ever managed to land such a well-dressed guy? And would she have to up her own style game to match his? She hoped not, because she didn't just dress in t-shirts and comfortable old jeans out of laziness; that was what she liked.

"The sheriff sure is good at calming people down, isn't he?" Liza asked, watching the scene.

Frank now stood with his hands in his back jeans pockets, listening while Mike talked. He wore an insulated flannel shirt against the chill, a navy blue Rotary cap on his head.

Rory gulped. "Sure is," she said, hoping her voice sounded more or less normal. Grace made a sound that might have been a giggle, telling Rory her voice had *not* sounded normal. "So, uh, what did you say these guys were doing that got Frank all riled up?" she asked to change the subject.

"Filming, but we don't know what for. I thought I heard something about a school project, in all the shouting. I think these two might be Westbrook College students. I know I've seen them on campus before."

Now Mike was shaking Frank's hand, and Frank turned and walked up the inn's front steps. He didn't go inside, but stayed on the top step, watching as Mike made his way toward the minivan. To Rory, Mike called, "You must be getting hungry. Why don't you grab the food and go on home? I'll be there shortly. Don't wait though—go ahead and eat."

Rory nodded, took her leave of Liza and Grace, and retrieved the grocery bag full of take-out containers from the front seat of Mike's vehicle. All the while, she was thinking, *Bull, mister. You're not worried about me being hungry. You just don't want me hanging around here and getting involved in whatever's going on.*

Chapter 3

Tail held high, Miss C pranced back and forth in front of the coffee table while the Rory and Mike persons ate their dinner. Rory had arrived home before Mike, food in hand, but she hadn't eaten it right away, and she refused to answer questions about why she hadn't taken Miss C to the scene of wherever she'd been. When the pet sheriff—that was how Miss C thought of Mike—came knocking some fifteen minutes later, Rory greeted him by asking, "So what was all that about?"

Mike answered with, "What were you doing down there? I told you to stay put."

That had not gone over well.

"I was hungry, just like you said. I wanted to get the food," Rory had told him, her voice rising.

Her answer had prompted Mike's very sensible question, "Then why haven't you eaten anything? You were just sticking your nose in again, and I wish you wouldn't do that." Then Mike grabbed Rory in one of their too long and too frequent embraces, and he said, "It is kind of cute though," and kissed her.

"Stop that," Rory pretended to protest, not very convincingly. She kissed him back, and that was convincing.

Miss C had looked away. A cat can only take so much.

But now they were eating and talking, and the cat wanted to be in the middle of it, right where she should be.

"They're making a documentary?" Rory asked, inanely repeating what her pet sheriff had said, as she so often did.

"That's what they told us," Mike answered.

"About Brooksford?"

From his second's hesitation, Miss C knew that Mike preferred not to answer this part.

"Not exactly," he said.

"Well, what then?"

"Yes, tell us what, because we will only find out in the end," Miss C meowed, prompting Rory to say, "Hush, Miss C. You can't have any of this food." As if a cat of Miss C's quality would deign to put such goo in her mouth.

"Okay, you're probably not going to like this..." the Mike person began, pausing long enough to give Rory a chance to tell him she'd changed her mind; she did not want to know after all. Which of course did not happen.

"Mike, just tell me."

He took a deep breath and said, "They said they're taking some kind of creative storytelling class down at the college, and they're making a documentary about the Woldwomper for their term project. They were down there getting some dusk-time footage of the road into town and that new Historic Brooksford sign."

Miss C watched as Rory's face paled. "The Woldwomper?" she repeated, proving Miss C's earlier thought about her inanity.

The subject of this Woldwomper had first come up over the summer, when an archaeology project had uncovered one skeleton after another buried in several backyards around town. That had been a fascinating situation, actually, as it had furthered Miss C's understanding of the formation of myths. Some people had been murdered a long time ago, and other people gave the killer a colorful name. Over time, the truth had been forgotten and the colorful name morphed into a monster. Why, it was almost classical. Professor Eleanor, whom Miss C had lived with before Rory, and who had taught the cat all about Greek mythology, would have been proud. The professor had also taught Miss C all about mysteries, reading to the cat regularly from the likes of Agatha Christie, Dorothy Sayers, and even Ngaio Marsh, grand dames of the golden age of mysteries. This education had served the cat well since she'd come to Brooksford, where strange things happened with startling regularity.

Mike nodded and took another bite of food, assuming that's what it actually was.

"Does Madison know? I've got to call her," Rory said. She set her plate on the coffee table and started up off the sofa.

"Hold on." Mike reached out and caught her by the arm, pulling her across his body. How he did this while balancing a plate full of food in the other hand, Miss C was not sure. He was deft, this pet sheriff. With Rory now in his lap, he said, "I introduced them to Liza, since she knows so much about the Woldwomper. She'll let Madison know anything that needs to be known about what they're up to. In the meantime..." He tickled Rory's midsection, and she squealed like a little girl, squirming in his arms.

The tickling was too much for Miss C. She retreated to the living room window, jumping onto her two-story cat condo to gaze out at the dark, quiet street. Behind her, Rory giggled. *"Professor Eleanor never giggled,"* the cat meowed disdainfully. Then she realized her beloved professor, the one who'd raised her from a kitten, crossed her mind less and less often these days. Was that wrong? Would Professor Eleanor be disappointed? No. She would say something wise, perhaps something from Marcus Aurelius, the philosopher whom she called Uncle Marcus. Something like, "Each day brings its own gifts." And what this day had brought was the Rory person, her pet sheriff, and a new situation with the people making a film about a local myth. *"We shall see what this Woldwomper documentary brings,"* the cat meowed quietly.

Chapter 4

The next morning, Rory was up shortly after five to feed the cat and read the local paper. After the cat's breakfast, they sat together on the sofa, Rory reading from her e-reader and summarizing the stories aloud, the cat offering the occasional *mrrp* in response to the day's news. "There was a fire in a warehouse downtown that was being turned into apartments. Faulty wiring, they think."

"*Mrrp.*"

"The girls' basketball team from Westbrook High is on a winning streak."

"*Mrrp.*"

Most days, the cat would have more to say, but Rory couldn't blame her this morning. None of the news was very interesting, actually. Nothing nearly as interesting as the news Mike had delivered the night before: a couple of amateur filmmakers—very amateur, judging by their status as students in a storytelling class—had wandered into town with their iPhones, looking to shoot a documentary about the local bogeyman. Rory had already decided that Madison Gunther, Brooksford's mostly ceremonial mayor, needed to hear about this, and she needed to hear about it from Rory herself, in person.

She checked outside, where, at only a little after six, it was still dark. Gunther's General Store and Café would not be open yet, so there was time to shower and make herself somewhat presentable before going to deliver such unsettling news.

Showered and dressed in her T-shirt and jeans, Rory spread moisturizer on her face—her one concession to the beauty industry, and one she made only because her skin had started going saggy and dry several years ago, almost exactly on the day she turned forty. She sensed Miss C watching her, and the moment her hand touched the pet stroller, the cat jumped down from her condo and trotted over, meowing to be picked up and set inside. It seemed the cat was getting lazy, or maybe just overweight. She used to jump into the stroller herself, but now she rarely did so, preferring to let Rory lift her into it.

"What's up with you, cat? You getting old or something?" Rory asked, fully expecting the long meow she got in response.

"*Of course I am getting older. And you are no spring mousling yourself,*" the cat meowed, quoting something Professor Eleanor had often said. Rory, of course, understood none of it.

"At least you're leaving your collar on these days." She gently flicked the ID tag that hung from the cat's red collar, causing the collar's bell to jingle.

"*I have decided to give you this one victory in the small matter of the collar.*"

"I swear you're getting heavier though."

"*No, I'm becoming fluffier with each passing day.*"

"Must be time for a trip to the vet. You're due for your shots anyway." Rory zipped the stroller's front panel closed and wheeled her cat to the door.

"*I am perfectly healthy, except you do not feed me enough chicken,*" the cat meowed.

Outside, the recorded bells from the town's meeting hall began chiming the eight o'clock hour. The Brooksford bells, everyone called them. From seven in the morning until seven at night, they were a reliable way to keep track of time. Rory checked her fanny pack once more for keys and cash, and then they were out the front door and down the two steps to the sidewalk. The small patches to either side of the steps—Rory's front yard—were blooming with yellow and orange mums, which she had paid Grace to plant for her. It seemed that girl had a talent for gardening as well as art, and Rory had already decided to ask if she'd be willing to take on more of the yard work around the cottage. Since she'd inherited the house, her own brown thumb had not been kind to her grandmother's beloved garden.

Walking south toward the center of town, Rory breathed in the cool fall air and thought back to the summer, when this whole Woldwomper thing had first come up. She remembered being a child and hearing stories of the vampire-like creature that was supposed to haunt the woods around Brooksford, dropping out of trees to take the unwary. She'd been terrified of it back then, and for one summer she'd habitually searched the branches of the big sugar maple in her grandparents' backyard for any sign of the killer beast. But over the years the Woldwomper stories faded away, becoming something the old-timers talked about once in a great while. Younger people or newcomers to the area, meanwhile, had barely heard of it.

Until this past summer, when Brooksford's search into its own past had uncovered something that was just hard to believe. The Woldwomper was real.

Well, not real, exactly, Rory corrected herself. It was more "based on a true story," with lots of poetic license afforded those who recounted it. A murderous highwayman became more monstrous with each retelling, until he was so frightening, the families of his victims took extraordinary measures to ensure that their murdered loved ones—their children—did not become vampires.

This was not the sort of thing the modern Brooksford wanted to be known for, and so, if there were kids making any sort of movie about the Woldwomper, even just for a college course, the mayor needed to know.

A few minutes' leisurely walking brought Rory and Miss C to the door of a two-story yellow-painted brick building that stood on one corner of the intersection where Main Street crossed Old North Trace Road. Madison had the green-and-white-striped awning retracted this morning. Above it, a painted sign read, Gunther's General Store and Café. Hand-lettered poster-board signs in the large front window promised triple-certified coffees and locally made baked goods delivered fresh daily. To the right of the front door, on a post just in front of the window, stood a two-foot-high replica of the building, topped with a sign that said, Brooksford Little Free Library. Inside its glass-front door were two shelves full of mostly paperback books, free for the borrowing.

Even from the sidewalk, Rory could smell the aroma of fresh-brewed coffee. She had a taste for some pumpkin spice this morning, never mind that the pumpkin spice season seemed to start earlier and earlier every year, so that the flavor hardly seemed special anymore. As she pushed the door open, she saw she would not be getting Madison to herself as she'd hoped.

Liza Cunningham was already there, standing at the counter drinking a coffee.

"I told her," were the first words out of Liza's mouth once Rory and Miss C were inside. "I thought she'd better hear it in person."

There was no question as to what "it" was. Madison was already tugging at her earring the way she did whenever she was agitated about anything.

"I can hardly believe it. Someone's making a movie about the Woldwomper? Who'd want to do that?" she said from her stool behind the counter. She was ten years Rory's senior, with short hair that was more gray than brown these days. Her reading glasses hung from their chain around her neck, and the morning's newspaper lay spread open before her. Looked like Liza had arrived before she'd had time to finish reading it.

"I think it sounds interesting," Miss C meowed. *"Like modern Hesiods, they are creating a new mythology. It is all very classical."*

Before anyone could respond, Madison scooted off her stool, asking, "What can I get you, Rory, pumpkin spice?"

"Please," Rory said, parking Miss C's stroller at their usual table near the counter and watching as Madison turned to the wall behind her where a collection of handmade mugs hung from pegs, their owners' names written on bits of tape below them. Madison offered regular patrons, all of whom were Brooksfordians, the honor of purchasing their own mug to replace the paper to-go cups other customers got. Not everyone was given this privilege, and it wasn't one she extended lightly. Rory's mug was blue-green with a stout handle. She noted that Liza's was gray flecked with deep red. This was new, and it meant that Madison had finally decided Liza was here to stay.

Madison slid the full mug across the counter and collected the two dollar bills Rory had already laid there for her. "Liza said the sheriff had some words with these 'filmmakers,'" Madison said.

"I guess he talked to them for a little bit, just to find out what they were up to, but he didn't really tell me more than that," Rory answered, understanding that Madison had meant her statement as a question for her.

Liza took the other chair at Rory's table. "I'm not sure it's going to be any big deal. From what these kids, Katie and Spike, told me, they're doing a short documentary about a local legend. It'll be ten minutes long, max."

"Spike?" Rory interrupted, picturing the wiry guy with the knit hat.

Liza shrugged. "That's what he likes to be called, I guess. Maybe he has a really embarrassing name. Anyway, I know the professor teaching the course they're talking about, so I can ask and find out if they're legit, but I don't know why they'd make up something like that. I doubt it'll come to anything."

"Everything comes to something," Miss C meowed.

Madison had resumed her place on the stool. "You may be right. I just don't want this Woldwomper story told too far, you know? We managed to get through the Halloween season without any shenanigans, and I'd like to keep it that way."

The mayor had feared that stories of the Woldwomper might turn Brooksford into Maryland's vampire capital, attracting all manner of wackadoodles, as Rory would call them. Happily, nothing of the sort had happened, and they'd gotten through Oktoberfest and Halloween with hardly a mention of the region's old bogeyman.

"I really think you should just relax. They said they'll be filming a little more around town, and they even asked me to sit for an interview. They sound like a couple of kids who just want to get a good grade on their class project," Liza said. "I'll find out today."

"I would take nothing they say at face value," Miss C advised. *"I've found that most humans are dishonest about their true intentions, especially if they call themselves silly names like Spike."*

"We'll see," Madison replied, sounding sure of nothing.

Chapter 5

Knowing the day's mail wouldn't have arrived at the post office by this hour, Rory headed home to work. In the living room, she released Miss C from her stroller and watched the cat trot into the kitchen to see if any food had appeared in her food dish. A moment later, the cat reappeared to follow Rory into their home office, where several small editing tasks awaited.

Rory's work as a freelance editor paid her bills and allowed her to work from home and at hours of her choosing. These days, her work mostly came from existing clients and referrals. She rarely had to hunt for work anymore, she commanded higher rates than she'd ever dreamed of, and now that she lived without rent or mortgage in the family home where generations of the Roberts family had grown up, she'd finally been able to start a retirement fund. She was also able to make some upgrades to her business equipment, like the two new computer monitors that were due to be delivered this week.

An early morning email check had shown nothing pressing, but Rory had two short documents to edit and a few requested changes to make to a manuscript she'd edited the week before—it would be an odds-and-ends day, a day for clearing things up. It was the kind of day she enjoyed more than just plowing through one manuscript hour after hour. On those longer projects, she found it hard to maintain attention or interest from start to finish.

Rory settled into her desk chair and began her first task. Miss C jumped up and installed herself in the bed on the corner of the desk, near the window and the bird feeder suction-cupped to the glass. There, she'd watch for birds until she fell asleep.

At about noon, they were disturbed by the sound of shouting coming from the street. At least three voices. That couldn't be good. Miss C, pulled from a deep sleep, was fully awake in a second, head and ears cocked toward the front of the house. When the next shout came, she was up, out of her comfy bed, and jumping to the floor. She trotted into the hall and toward the living room. Rory saved her work and followed.

The shouting was much clearer from the living room.

"No! *YOU* get out of *OUR* shot!"

Looking out the window, Rory saw the beat-up blue van from last night parked right in front of her cottage. Standing near it were the redhead and the thin guy in the knit hat. They were facing off against two young men whom Rory judged to be athletic types—tall, well built, with easy good looks that she was sure must attract a lot of girls. The taller one had curly, sandy-blond hair and the kind of pretty-boy looks that she associated with quarterbacks. His sidekick—darker and a little shorter—must be his favorite wide receiver, she decided, impressed that her Sundays spent watching football with Mike were paying off. Across the street stood two more young men who were—not athletic. They looked to be about the same size as the football players, one tall, the other a little shorter, but they held themselves differently, without the swagger of physical confidence. Rory stereotyped them too, as the sort who could usually be found hunched in front of a computer. They looked a little grungy, their military-style coats didn't seem to fit quite right, and they frankly looked scared of the football players.

The knit-hat guy—Spike, Liza had said his name was—didn't seem to be afraid at all though. "We were here first. Besides, you're just copying our idea," he said—not yelling, but with a firmness in his voice that said he would not back down. Now that Rory was seeing him at closer range, she could see the angry red acne blemishes on his chin. Wiry black stubble dotted his cheeks, suggesting that he was trying, unsuccessfully, to grow a beard. His colorful cap was pulled low over his ears, and a mass of curly, light brown hair protruded from its front, covering his forehead.

The redhead, Katie, stood at his side, a clipboard in one hand, a pen in the other. Her red-orange hair fell in irregular strands around her face and over her shoulders, and her mouth was set in a frown. She gestured with her pen as she spoke. "You can just stay out of the way while we get our shots. Then it'll be your turn."

The quarterback laughed. "Our turn?" To Spike he said, "Hey, man, you let your woman make all the decisions for you?" Then, as he reached up with both hands to adjust the curls on either side of his forehead, he laughed again, with his receiver joining in.

"This curly-haired one reminds me of Narcissus," Miss C meowed. *"He is overly concerned with his appearance, physical and otherwise."*

Spike hurled some unsavory words at the quarterback, who gladly returned them, and moments later all four of them were shouting and gesticulating at one another. Even the two grungy guys across the street lobbed over a few insults, mostly aimed at the quarterback. Rory was wondering if the groups would come to blows before she could call the sheriff's department, but then a deputy's patrol car rolled onto the scene, red and blue lights flashing. The grungy guys noticed it right away and shut up, but the other four went right on arguing. The deputy sounded two notes from the siren, and all argument ceased.

Rory recognized Deputy Sergeant Opal Washington in the driver's seat, situating her smokey bear hat on her head before she got out. She left the lights flashing. Opal Washington was not a large woman, but her physical presence far exceeded her actual size. Mike had confided to Rory once that if Opal had been just half an inch shorter, she would not have made it into the department. As it was, though, she was one of his most trusted deputies, and she was the first African American woman in the department to hold a deputy sergeant's rank. It was just a matter of time before she made lieutenant, Mike said. Rory liked and trusted her too, so she was relieved that it was Opal coming onto this scene.

"What's the problem here?" the deputy asked the assembled group, being careful to include the two across the street. She pointed to them with her left index finger and then bent it inward twice in the universal "c'mere" sign. "You two involved in this? Come over here. I want the whole story, and I don't want to walk all over creation to get it."

The two grungy guys shuffled across the street, heads down, pushing at each other as they went. "It's your fault," "No, it's your fault," Rory imagined them sniping at each other. The quarterback and wide receiver looked cocky. Spike seemed to be in the same league with the grungy guys, backing down now that the law was here. Katie waited patiently, still frowning.

"Now, I think it's still ladies first, isn't it, boys?" Opal asked the group, though Rory knew she wasn't really asking. Nodding toward Katie, she said, "What's your story?"

Katie drew herself up to be an inch or two taller than the deputy. Then, looking slightly down at her, she said, "My friend and I are making a film for our class, and we're just trying to get a few shots without these turds getting in them." She gestured toward the football players. "All they have to do is wait until we're finished."

"So you want them to get off of the public sidewalk for your convenience?" Opal asked reasonably.

That prompted the quarterback to put in, "Yeah, it's public."

"But you're deliberately messing up our shots," Katie returned. "It looks stupid to have you buttheads in our story."

To Miss C, Rory said quietly, "Ooh, 'buttheads.' This is getting serious, Cuddlywumps."

In reply, Miss C meowed, *It looks rather ridiculous to me. Socrates never engaged in discourse at such a low level.*

"Just edit us out," the quarterback said.

"We can't edit you out of every single shot," Katie sneered.

That got Spike involved. "Yeah, we can't do that."

The football guys laughed. "'Yeah, we can't do that,'" the quarterback mocked in a singsong voice.

"This Narcissus is also a bully," Miss C observed.

"Listen, you—" Spike started to say, but Opal cut everyone off with her own raised voice. "Enough! Everyone just quiet down. I don't want any of y'all to talk unless I tell you to talk." Then, noticing that one of the grunge boys had raised his smartphone and started filming the scene, she said, "And what do you think you're doing?"

The phone dipped in his hand, but Rory couldn't tell if he turned it off. "I'm, like, filming. For our class."

"You all are in the same class?" Opal said, gesturing with one hand to include all six of the budding filmmakers. Each of them nodded and/or grunted in the affirmative. "What is this class anyway?" she asked the group.

Katie answered, "Creative Storytelling through Film."

"Uh-huh. And you all got assigned to come out here?"

"No," Katie answered again. "We choose our own topics. We're doing a documentary about Brooksford and the Woldwomper."

"Uh-huh," Opal said again. Turning to the quarterback, she asked, "And what's you fellas' story?"

The quarterback answered, "We're shooting a horror flick, about a vampire."

"Uh-huh. And you two?" She turned to the grunge boys.

The one who'd raised his phone said, "We're making a film about making a film. It's, like, meta."

"Meta," Opal repeated. "That why you're filming this right now?"

"Yeah," he said a little defensively.

"Uh-huh. Well, look here, people. This is a small town, and right now every single one of you is disturbing the peace. Now I can't tell you how to figure out your own schedules for your documentary or your horror flick or your meta-whatever. But I can tell you that if you disturb the peace again, I'll issue every single one of you with a citation, and don't you think for a second that I'll hesitate to run any of you downtown if it comes to that. We understand each other?" She gave a hard look to the quarterback as she said this.

The six filmmakers mumbled and suddenly became very interested in their own shoes, looking down intently. Even the guy who was doing the meta-whatever seemed to suddenly have decided to film his shoelaces.

"I'm sorry, I didn't catch that. I said, do we understand each other?" Opal said again, louder.

That prompted a rumble of assents from the group, though none of them looked up at her.

"Okay. Now. Work it out."

"Well, I want to film them, so..." the head grunge boy said.

"Okay then, meta boys, you go on back across the street, and stay out of everybody's way," Opal ordered. The two complied, still seeming to snip at each other on the way.

"And that leaves you all." Opal crossed her arms over her chest and adjusted her weight onto one leg. It was her "I can do this all day" pose, Rory knew. "I assume one of you got here first?"

"We did," Katie said quickly.

The quarterback uttered a particularly offensive slur toward Katie, prompting Spike to shout something slightly less offensive back at him.

"Quiet," Opal commanded, one hand raised in a "stop" gesture. Then, to the quarterback, she said, "Now, since these two folks got here first, maybe you could just exercise some common courtesy and stand back out of their way or go do your filming in another part of town until they finish up here."

"But this is the house," the wide receiver protested, gesturing toward Rory's cottage.

"Be that as it may, a little courtesy will take you far in this situation. In fact, if you had exercised it to begin with, we would not be having this conversation and I would not be on the verge of giving you a citation. How's a hundred dollars sound, each? 'Cause that's the fine for disturbing the peace in this county. Now, are you going to become courteous, or do I have to start writing? I've got my favorite pen right here."

At the mention of a possible hundred-dollar fine, Katie's face blanched, as did Spike's. Rory guessed they'd have a hard time coming up with that kind of money. The quarterback and wide receiver also seemed to think better of continuing the feud.

"Hey, man, let's go shoot over by that bridge. We were gonna do that anyway, right?" the wide receiver said.

The quarterback gave in, but he did not look happy about it. "I guess. So we can just go?" he asked Opal.

"Long as you do it quietly, yes," Opal said magnanimously.

The football players turned and strutted toward the center of town. Rory guessed they were headed to the intersection, where they would turn left and walk the thirty yards or so up North Trace Road to the bridge that crossed the West Brook.

Opal turned to Katie and Spike. "All right, you two, you're free to do whatever, but try to stay out of trouble, you hear me? I don't want to be riding up here again to untangle you bunch of budding Spielbergs or Scorceses or whatever you are."

Katie and Spike muttered something in response, and the deputy sergeant touched the brim of her hat in farewell and got back in her patrol car.

"And Deputy Sergeant Washington restores the peace once again," Rory said.

"Yes, but how long will it last?" Miss C meowed, her white-tipped tail twitching.

Chapter 6

Mike did not have plans to come up that evening, so after a scrumptious dinner of Swedish meatballs and noodles courtesy of a cardboard box from her freezer, Rory had some free time to work on her puzzle or read a book. It was chilly in the house, so she pressed the button to turn on her gas fireplace. She'd barely settled onto the sofa before she heard her back door opening and a voice calling out, "Hey, Ror! I've got cookies."

Lee, her next-door neighbor and lifelong best friend. They'd been friends ever since the days when Rory visited her grandparents as a little girl and Lee, who was exactly her age, became her default summer playmate. From the start, they'd understood one another as no one else did. Now, Lee lived with his mom next door and taught English at the local high school, the same one he'd graduated from. He was the only person who had the privilege of entering Rory's home without knocking. Not even Mike could do that yet.

"Bring 'em in," Rory called back to him.

"Should I start tea?" he answered, still in the kitchen.

"Yes, but let's not delay those cookies, okay?"

"Pepperoni neutrons," Lee said as he entered the living room with a foil-covered plate of cookies his mother had no doubt baked just that afternoon. The greeting was the super-secret battle cry he and Rory had shared for over forty years. Nobody else understood it, but that was mostly the point.

Rory returned the greeting and patted the table. "You can just leave those right here. What kind are they?"

"Molasses." He set the plate down and pulled back the foil to reveal a pile of dark brown cookies glistening with sugar.

"Mmm," Rory said, reaching for a cookie with one hand while waving Lee away with the other. "Go get that tea started. I'm gonna need it after I go all pepperoni neutrons on these cookies."

"Nice to see you too," Lee joked, on his way back to the kitchen.

"I am happy to see you," Miss C meowed from atop her condo, not that anyone was listening to her.

Rory had eaten two cookies in the moments it took Lee to fill her teapot and set it on the stove to heat. She was starting on the third when he came back into the living room. "I thought you were watching your figure," he said.

"Who, me? Why would I do that?" Rory answered, not sure if he was kidding.

"You know, for your man." Lee flopped onto the sofa next to her and reached for a cookie. Now she knew he was joking.

"Please," she scoffed, but then she had to wonder.... "Do you think I'm fat?" She half feared his answer. Lee was hardly a health nut, but he did make more of an effort than Rory did, what with his morning runs and his insistence on eating such things as carrots and lettuce. Meanwhile, she had recently made a move toward pants with "comfort stretch" waists. It just made life easier, she reasoned.

"No. I'm just teasing. You look fabulous, dahling," he replied in a horrible accent.

"Shut up." Rory gave him a playful punch on the arm. "Did your mom tell you about our local filmmakers?" she asked, knowing that certainly the Brooksford grapevine would have delivered news of their town being a bit player in one or three movies. They were efficient that way.

Lee nodded. "She did. A documentary, a vampire flick, and some artsy-fartsy thing. I wonder if we'll be able to see the finished product—the documentary, I mean. It would be cool if it could get incorporated into the historical society somehow."

Rory hadn't thought of it before now, but if this short documentary turned out to be any good, maybe it would be of some benefit to the town. The horror flick and the meta thing, on the other hand.... She was just going to say as much when the kettle whistled, a sound followed shortly by someone knocking on her door.

"Someone is here," Miss C meowed, too late to be of much use. She'd been distracted by talk of the films and thoughts of Hesiod and Homer and hadn't been watching out the window.

Lee headed for the kitchen and Rory pushed herself off the sofa. "Who could that be?" she asked.

"Maybe it's Mike."

"I'm not expecting him, and he hasn't called or anything to say he's coming by."

"It is not your pet sheriff. It is that Liza person and the half-baked girl with the funny hair. Something is wrong with them," the cat meowed, peering out the window.

The tea kettle's whistling stopped at about the same moment Rory opened the front door. On the other side of it stood Liza, with Grace on the step just behind her. Liza seemed near tears, and even Grace seemed agitated, shifting her weight from foot to foot, though she may have been only trying to keep warm. Why kids these days refused to wear coats when it got chilly out, Rory did not understand.

"Liza, what's wrong?" Rory asked in surprise. For a moment she thought that Grace's no-good father must have made an appearance, but she knew that wasn't it when Liza said, "She's back," as though the words were being wrenched from her throat.

Chapter 7

Rory ushered them both inside and installed them on the sofa, telling Lee to fix two extra cups of tea and offering them what was left of the molasses cookies. Liza refused a cookie, but Grace took one and nibbled at it quietly. Miss C had gotten down from her condo to sit on the sofa next to Grace. She purred loudly as Grace stroked her with one hand.

"Now, who are you talking about? Who's back?" Rory asked.

"Sephie Rennsfelder," Liza said.

"Sephie?" Rory repeated. "But she's—"

Miss C stopped purring suddenly. Rory thought she saw the cat stiffen, but that had to be imagination or coincidence, right? Surely she didn't recognize the name.

Meanwhile, Liza said, "Out on parole. She says she got released this afternoon—something about overcrowding and good behavior. Anyway, she just showed up at the house, expecting to move in right away. She kicked us out." Her voice shook as she finished.

Persephone Aurora Rennsfelder.... She'd once been a vice president of a local bank and was the mistress to whom the late Don Miller had left his house at the south end of town. But that was before she'd gone a little wackadoodle and, for reasons that still made no rational sense to anyone else, gotten obsessed with Rory and Miss C. It had been Sephie who'd attempted to target Rory in a hit-

and-run, Sephie who'd snatched Miss C from her stroller, intending to kill her. She'd spent roughly the past year in the county lockup on the hit-and-run and animal cruelty charges, and now suddenly she was free? Just the thought of her haughty, too-good-for-you attitude made Rory's skin crawl. And what were Liza and Grace supposed to do, if the woman had indeed tossed them out?

"I guess we'll go into Westbrook and stay in a hotel until we can find a place. We just had time to pack overnight bags, and—" Liza was saying, but Rory stopped her.

"No, you won't. You'll crash here with me tonight, and tomorrow morning we'll figure something out."

Both Liza and Grace cast a glance around the living room. Rory's cottage comprised a tiny two bedrooms, one of which was her office, plus just one bath, the living room, kitchen, and laundry/mudroom. By modern standards, there hardly seemed room for three people to live in it, even for a short time. "We couldn't. We'd be putting you out," Liza said.

Rory insisted, "You won't be putting me out, and there'll be plenty of space. You two can have the bedroom, and I'll sleep out here. It'll be fine."

"You will be putting me out a little, but I suppose I can allow it, if it is to protect the innocent half-baked girl from the Queen of the Underworld," Miss C meowed.

Lee had returned by this time, carrying two mugs of tea in each hand. "Hot tea coming through," he said, bringing a tiny smile to Grace's face. Rory suspected the girl had a crush on the teacher who gave her a ride to school most days. "Rory's right, Liza. We'll help you figure something out," he said. "No worries."

"You must have a lease or something, right?" Rory added.

Liza shook her head. "I know it was stupid, but we just had a verbal agreement with Sephie to stay there and take care of the house. I never thought I'd stay there this long, but I just haven't found a way to leave this town. The people are all so nice, and Gracie loves it here. But I guess we'll have to move on now."

And so soon after she finally got her own mug at Gunther's, Rory thought.

"Somehow it'll work out. Maybe you can rent from someone else in town," Lee offered.

That prompted a smile from Liza, but Rory saw that it was forced. They all knew that tiny Brooksford wasn't exactly rich in rental properties.

Lee stayed for another hour or so, helping calm Liza's and Grace's nerves. After he'd gone, Rory helped her unexpected guests get settled into her bedroom for the night. Then at the late hour of nine o'clock, she arranged herself on the sofa with Miss C on her lap and called Mike. He answered, clearly expecting some of their usual "how was your day" chit chat, and he sounded truly surprised when she opened with, "Why didn't you tell me Sephie Rennsfelder has been released?"

"Released? When?"

Before he could ask any more one-word questions, Rory cut him off and told him how Sephie had shown up in town and tossed Liza and Grace out of her house. He seemed flabbergasted.

"I don't know anything about that. I'll make a call to find out what's going on. Where are the Cunninghams tonight?"

"They're staying here. That's how I know what's going on."

"You gave up your bed again?"

"Yeah, well, you know..."

"You are a noble woman, Rory Roberts."

She heard the smile in his voice and met it with her own. "Well, it's just one night."

"Tell him about how the Queen of the Underworld is making my life extremely uncomfortable," Miss C meowed.

"I hear Miss C has something to say about it," Mike joked.

"So what else is new?"

"Sephie doesn't know that Liza and Grace are with you, does she?"

Now she heard concern in Mike's voice. "I don't think so." Although, if Sephie wanted to go trolling around town looking for them, she'd surely spot Liza's car in front of the little stone cottage in the north end.

"Are all your doors locked, including the back door?"

"Um..." Since the past couple of months had passed quietly, Rory had gotten lax about locking up. Brooksford was usually such a safe little town, and she liked that her buddy Lee could just walk in without her having to get up and open a door for him.

"Never mind. Just lock up after we get off the phone, please. I'm sure it's nothing, but if Sephie shows up there, don't open the door to her. Just call me, whatever the hour."

"I will," she said, wishing he had offered to drive up and personally protect her. They could cuddle on the sofa and have one of their long-ranging talks, or she could just lay her head on his chest and listen to the reassuring thump of his heart. And then what, one of them would sleep on the sofa and the other on the living room floor?

"Everything else okay?"

"Mm-hmm."

"Weather Channel says there's a front moving through late tomorrow, so get ready for it be colder—windy too. Your maple's going to lose the rest of its leaves."

"Oh, really? They mentioned my maple tree specifically?" she joked. Watching the Weather Channel was one of Mike's obsessions. Rory took a passing interest in it for his sake, but for the most part, she was content to just let the weather happen.

"Such a comedian you are. Listen, we'll talk first thing in the morning, okay? Love ya."

"Yeah," Rory answered, wanting only to be wrapped in his strong arms, where she always felt so treasured, so safe. "Love you too."

Chapter 8

Rory woke to an aching neck and back and a cat planted on her chest, tapping her face with a paw. "No," she moaned.

"Time to get up. Early cat gets the mouse." Tap tap tap. *"And one of our guests is already up."*

"We can't get up too early or we'll wake Liza and Grace. Now hush," Rory insisted, pushing the cat out of her face.

"Ms. Roberts?" a voice said from across the living room.

That brought Rory into a sitting position, as Miss C jumped out of the way. *"I told you."*

"Grace, you're up early," Rory said stupidly, eyeing the girl's silhouette there at the entrance to the hallway. The silhouette shrugged.

"Always get up early. Stuff to do."

"As do I. Have you ever heard the saying 'Early cat gets the mouse'?" Miss C meowed in the girl's direction.

Rory swung her feet to the floor. "C'mon, cat. Let's feed you so you'll quiet down. Grace, help yourself to the bathroom or whatever." She stretched, yawning loudly, and forced herself to her feet.

"I'm all done. Showered 'n' everything. Been up awhile," Grace said.

Stumbling toward the kitchen, Rory wondered just how early Grace actually got up, if she was already showered and ready to go. "That's admirable." She yawned again. "Tell me, Grace, what do you do this early in the day?"

Rory retrieved Miss C's food dish from its place mat on the floor and pulled a can of high-end chicken-dinner cat food from a cupboard, while the cat rubbed against her ankles, purring and meowing.

Grace folded her lanky frame into a kitchen chair. "Y'know, breakfast, study, finish homework."

Breakfast? Criminy. What was Rory going to feed her guests? She hadn't been expecting company and didn't usually keep much in the way of breakfast food in the house. She wasn't a big breakfast person herself, preferring to fuel up for the day with coffee and candy, and sometimes a muffin or brownie from Gunther's. Almost as though reading her mind, Grace grinned and said, "Mr. Cooper said w'could have McDonald's f'r breakfast."

Good old Lee. He knew Rory's morning habits, and it was just like him to offer to take care of Grace's morning meal on their way to school. From the shy way Grace revealed their breakfast plans, Rory guessed this was not a normal occurrence—maybe it was a first. Lee had been driving Grace down to Westbrook High to attend the county's magnet program for computer arts and sciences for over a year now, and Rory seriously doubted he'd ever treated her to anything from a fast-food joint before.

"Mmm ... that sounds good," Rory said in the midst of her thoughts. "I love their hash browns."

Grace grinned.

Measuring beans into the coffee grinder, Rory said, "I'm starting the coffee. You want a hot chocolate or tea or anything?"

"Liza lets me have a coffee."

"She does?"

"Sure," Grace said, as though there were nothing strange about it.

Well, and maybe there wasn't anything strange about it. Back when Rory was in high school, thirty-some-odd years ago, the only kids she knew who drank coffee were a couple of guys who sported full beards and looked to be in their early twenties. The bit of gossip their classmates dared utter about them centered on how many times they'd been held back in second grade. But these days, with kids downing all those energy drinks.... "Okay. You take anything in your coffee?" Rory asked, remembering a piece of advice Lee had given her once for communicating with Grace: *Just talk to her like she's a person.*

"Naw."

Rory pushed the button to turn the grinder on, and the whirring whine of the appliance filled the room. She'd never heard Grace say anything approaching "naw" before, and she wondered if it was a bit of dialect she'd picked up in school. She let the grinder work the beans into a medium-fine texture, and then dumped them into the filter, closed the basket, and set the machine to brew. Turning, she saw Grace seated at the kitchen table, a spiral notebook open in front of her and Miss C hovering at her feet. As the girl studied a page in the notebook, one hand reached down to scratch the cat's head.

"What'cha studying?" Rory asked.

"History. Got a quiz," Grace replied without looking up.

"Perhaps I could help you. Is the quiz on Herodotus?" Miss C meowed.

Rory leaned back against the counter, her hands behind her fidgeting with a drawer handle while she thought of a hundred different ways to say what she wanted to say. Well, best to just get it out, she decided. "Listen, I hope you're not going to worry about, you know, Sephie and the house and all."

Grace looked up at her but said nothing. She was waiting for more.

"Because it's going to work out," Rory fumbled. "Liza's going to take care of it, and we'll all help—me and Mr. Cooper and even the mayor, I'll bet. I just don't want you to worry."

"S'a nice town," Grace said then, her eyes puddles of tears.

Rory wanted to go throw her arms around her in a protective embrace, but she knew somehow that this would be the wrong thing to do, so instead she just said, "Yeah, it is." Then the coffee maker beeped, and she had an excuse to turn before she teared up beyond control. "Two coffees, coming up," she said brightly as she poured, cursing Sephie Rennsfelder under her breath. That scheming, selfish woman wasn't good enough for Brooksford. Liza and Grace, on the other hand....

At that moment, Liza wandered into the kitchen, still looking half asleep. "Oh, coffee," she said and intercepted the cup Rory had been taking to Grace.

"Hey!" Grace protested as Liza took a sip and made an exaggerated "mmm" sound.

"Sorry, kiddo. Age before beauty," Liza said. Then she set the cup on the table in front of Grace and kissed the top of her head. "Morning."

"Did you sleep okay?" Rory asked, thinking of her oh-so-comfortable bed and how it compared to the sofa. She handed the cup of coffee she'd intended for herself to Liza.

"Not really. Spent most of the night worrying about ... you know," she said. Then to Grace, "Only one cup, Gracie, okay?"

Pouring another coffee for herself, Rory said, "I'm sure it'll work out somehow. I called Mike last night, and he didn't know anything about her being released, so maybe it was a mistake or something. We'll find out this morning. It's weird that she just showed up here with no warning. Mike should've known if she was getting out."

"Could've escaped," Grace said.

The look that passed between Rory and Liza said that they had both thought the same thing. But it wasn't possible. If Sephie had escaped, Mike would know and the sheriff's department would have checked at her house first, where they would have found her and taken her back into custody. Of course, none of them had actually been at the house since last evening, so they didn't know what might have happened there overnight.

"Like I said, I'll talk to the sheriff," Rory said.

❧

As planned, Grace went out at 7:15 to meet Lee for the drive to school. "No more coffee," Liza reminded her as she went out the door, and Grace responded with a sound that left Rory with the distinct impression that she would be getting a second coffee from McDonald's. Soon after, Rory's cell phone sounded with the notes of a country song—her ring tone for Mike.

She answered right away, and he confirmed her worst fears. "Sephie Rennsfelder was released on parole yesterday afternoon. She was considered nonviolent, and she's had perfect behavior while in custody—"

"Nonviolent?" Rory interrupted. "She tried to kill my cat, and she planned to run over me with a truck!"

"I know, hon. But she's got a good lawyer. It's all on the up and up, though it should've gone through me, all things considered."

"You think?" Rory said, knowing that he'd understand her sarcasm was not aimed at him.

"My captain is going to get a good talking to this morning, believe me."

"So what now? Sephie's just out, free to do whatever?"

"Not exactly. She has to keep her nose perfectly clean for the next eighteen months, or she'll be back with us. She has to report, in person, to her parole officer once a month."

Rory relayed this information to Liza as they were getting ready to go out to Gunther's for a little breakfast and a chat with the mayor. Liza didn't have to be on campus that day, so she planned to start searching for a new living arrangement for her and Grace. Maybe Madison would know of someone else in town who was looking to rent part of their house. They entered the café to find Frank Laser there, already chewing Madison's ear off. His chocolate-brown Newfoundland, Clementine, was at his side. The dog wandered toward Miss C's stroller, sniffing in at the cat. Frank himself glanced at the new arrivals and nodded curtly at them to acknowledge their presence, but he did not stop talking.

"They were out there all night, I'm telling you. There must be an ordinance against that sort of thing, Mayor."

Instead of tugging at her earring, Madison had a firm grip on her reading glasses, squeezing until her knuckles were white. "I just don't know what you expect me to do, Frank," she said. "If they're in front of your property, it seems to me it's up to you to ask them to move on."

"But I want something official. Rory, I don't suppose you're hiding that sheriff of yours up in your cottage, are you?" Frank asked. "He could scare 'em off."

With a shake of her head, Rory replied, "No, sorry. What's going on?"

Waving his hand dismissively, Frank said, "Those kids who're making that stupid movie or whatever. They spent the night in front of my place in that old van. You believe that?"

Rory exchanged a look with Madison and saw that the mayor was already operating on frayed nerves. "You know, Lee was saying last night that this documentary could turn out to be a good thing for the town. If it's any good, I mean. Maybe the historical society could show it and then have our very own folklorist give a talk about it. Could we get a couple pumpkin spices, Madison?" she asked. Then, while Madison's back was turned as she reached for their mugs on the wall, Rory added, "I don't suppose you've heard the other news."

Madison spun back around, a mug in each hand, faster than Rory would have expected. "What other news?"

Liza started to answer, saying, "It's—" but before she could finish, the bell on the front door jingled and Madison's eyes widened.

Rory knew whose voice she was about to hear before the words were even spoken. "Ahh, good morning." Turning to the door, Rory saw Persephone Rennsfelder in something considerably less than all her glory. The woman before them seemed older, more tired, less beautiful than the banking executive they recalled. She wore black yoga pants and an old college sweat shirt, and her blond hair fell to her shoulders looking stringy and unkempt. Rory remembered the appraising look Sephie had given her once; back then, she'd come up wanting in Sephie's estimation, but now the situation was reversed. Rory, even in her T-shirt and comfort-waist jeans, could have looked Sephie over and delivered an insult, or at least felt superior. Only she didn't. Instead she felt a tugging of sympathy for this woman who'd fallen so far. Looking to the window beyond her, she spotted Sephie's black Mercedes parked at the curb. Well, maybe she hadn't fallen quite so far after all. The sympathetic feeling faded.

Miss C hissed at the new arrival, and Clementine growled, prompting Frank to admonish the dog, "Quiet down, Clemmie."

Sephie approached them warily. Clementine growled again, and again Frank quieted her. "I'm not here to cause trouble," Sephie said. "Liza, I don't know why you took off last night. There's room in that house for all of us, surely."

Liza retreated a step but said nothing.

Madison spoke up. "How can you even be here, Ms. Rennsfelder? Surely your sentence isn't up yet."

"Cost-cutting measures. Since I'm not violent, and I've had good behavior, they reduced my sentence to time served plus community service. Could I get a coffee, please? I have money, even after the fine."

Rory noticed that Sephie failed to mention the regular trips she'd be making to her parole officer. And the "not violent" part of the woman's statement—what a bunch of malarkey. How could she have fooled the jailers so thoroughly?

"You are still a liar, Persephone, Queen of the Underworld," Miss C meowed.

Part of Sephie's face twitched in response to the cat's meow, but she quickly tried to cover it. "I see you still have that … darling cat," she said to Rory, who took a step closer to Miss C's stroller.

"Yes," Rory said simply.

Meanwhile, Madison had filled two mugs with pumpkin spice coffee and slid them across the counter to Rory and Liza. "Was that a plain coffee, Sephie?" Madison asked, apparently not willing to turn away business, even if it did come from someone they all despised.

Sephie eyed the mugs on the wall—they all noticed the longing look she gave them—but the mayor held a to-go cup, ready to fill it for her. Resignation showed in Sephie's eyes as she replied, "Yes, just a large of whatever you've got that's strong. I need a kick to get me going this morning. Didn't sleep well."

Silence fell among them as Madison filled the cup. "Room for cream?" she asked, stopping the pour momentarily.

"No, thank you."

The cup full, Madison set it on the counter and collected her two dollars. Then, "So, what do you want?"

If Sephie was taken aback, she didn't show it. "Why, I'm moving in, Mayor. To my house." She emphasized "my" and shot a look in Liza's direction.

"You'll have to give me a few days to get Grace's and my things together and figure out a place to stay," Liza said.

"Oh, but I don't want you to go. I mean, you don't have to. I've got some ideas that you should be part of," Sephie said, with some of her old charm oozing through.

Clearly Liza didn't know what to make of that. None of them did.

"What sort of ideas?" she asked warily.

Sephie began to regain some of her former confidence. "I've had a lot of time to think in the past year," she said. Rory almost laughed aloud but restrained herself. "I've been thinking of Historic Brooksford."

"We're already creating Historic Brooksford, and we're doing just fine without your input," Madison said, in what Rory knew was her best fake-polite voice.

"Oh, yes. I saw your little sign at the edge of town, and I read about some of your goings-on in the paper. There've been some ... unfortunate happenings, from what I've heard." She smiled, the way a shark might just before it bites your leg off.

Yes, this was still the same Sephie they'd grown to know and loathe.

"We've had a few bumps in the road, but so what?" Madison challenged her. "We're getting there in our own way, in our own time."

"But, Mayor, don't you think it's time to put some oomph into these plans? Have you managed to get that old church on the National Register of Historic Places yet?"

Madison's armor cracked a bit. "No, but I understand Mr. Crabtree is working on it," she said, referring to the president of the Brooksford Historical Society and Rory's neighbor on the side opposite Lee.

"I'm sure he is." That condescending smile again. "What else have you got going on? I spoke to those two people who are making your little film—"

"It's not 'our little film,'" Madison interrupted. "They've got nothing to do with us."

"Oh, but, Mayor, you can't let this get away from you. A film about our town? It would be free publicity."

"It's not about Brooksford, exactly," Rory said.

Sephie waved her hand. "Oh, I know, it's about some monster in the woods. But that doesn't even matter. If this thing comes off, it could put Brooksford on the map in people's minds. They'd come by just to see. And what will they find when they get here? Any shops to go in? Any place to have a little lunch?" Sephie looked around at them. They all knew she had just stated Madison's dream exactly: to have their town grow into the sort of place that had quirky, atmospheric shops and a comfortable, inexpensive place to get a meal, the sort of place that would attract couples or families looking for a quiet afternoon.

Currently, they were nowhere near having any of those things.

Continuing her speech, Sephie said, "No. There's nothing but that little historical society, and that isn't even open most of the time. You're piddling along at building Historic Brooksford, but you need someone to drive it. Someone like me."

Rory could hardly wait to hear Madison's reply to that. Their mayor was sure to say that they could get along just fine without the input of a common criminal who should maybe think about moving to another town, thank you very much. At least those were the words dancing through Rory's mind as she watched Madison collect herself before answering.

The words that actually came out of Madison's mouth though were, "But you've lost all your influence. How could you possibly get funding for anything now?" If Rory had hoped for a cutting edge in the mayor's reply, she was disappointed. Madison couldn't be thinking about actually working with Sephie, could she?

"Forget that for the moment. The money will come. What this project needs is someone with initiative, with drive, like I said. That's me."

Sephie seemed to have grown as she talked, so that by the time she finished, she'd regained her former stature. Rory could almost forget that the woman was dressed in what Sephie would once have dismissed as rags. The clothes didn't matter. The woman wearing them was, for lack of a better word, ballsy.

"Well ...," Madison dithered, and Rory knew she'd given in, "it's not just my decision. The historical society would have to be involved."

"Of course. We'll set up a meeting. Till then. Oh, Liza, do you want a ride back to the house?"

Stunned, Liza said, "No, thank you."

"Ta-ta then." And Sephie swept out of the café and into her car.

"What just happened?" Frank asked when she'd gone. "Did that woman just take over our town?"

Nobody answered.

Chapter 9

Throughout the course of the day, it became generally known that groups of student storytellers would be wandering around town working on their projects. Katie and Spike had set up an interview with Liza to get background on the local folklore; the football players had gotten permission to film in the woods and field on the other side of the West Brook, with a few friends as actors; and the meta boys ... well, who knew what they were doing. Madison, since Rory had floated Lee's notion of at least one of the resulting films being a boon for the town, was encouraging people to cooperate. "Let's just hope some of these kids are as talented as they are insistent," she'd said to Rory.

So it was hardly surprising to Miss C when the blue minivan pulled up in front of Rory's cottage again. *"Company,"* she meowed from her spot in the window. *"It is those film so-called makers, these modern Hesiods and Homers."* She cast back, searching her memories for what Professor Eleanor had taught her about Hesiod. It had not been much. She knew more of Homer, the blind poet. If Homer were alive today, perhaps he would be wielding a cell phone with a camera like this Spike person. Or maybe, since he was blind, he would have an assistant who worked the camera while he himself provided direction. In that scenario, Katie was Homer. *"Well, why not?"* the cat chirped to herself. *"It is the twenty-first century."*

The Rory and Liza persons were in the kitchen eating and talking, and they paid no attention to the cat meowing in the window. Miss C watched as these modern mythmakers stepped out of their vehicle and looked around. The red-haired girl kept holding her hands at arms' length, the tips of her thumbs touching and her fingertips pointing upward as she spun slowly about, looking through the three-sided box she'd created. It was possibly the weirdest thing Miss C had ever seen a human do. She didn't understand what the hand-box thing was all about—perhaps it had something to do with being a blind mythmaker—but she did understand the camera in the phone that the boy wielded, and she held herself very straight and still as it passed over her. She would be the epitome of the cat in the window, the model for all others to follow. Everyone kept saying things like "if the film turns out to be any good." Well, now that they had footage of Miss C, surely it couldn't help but be good. They could probably just stop filming now, in fact. *"That's a wrap,"* Miss C meowed, quoting something she'd heard in one of Rory's television shows.

The cat stretched as the people approached the door and knocked. Once again, she informed the Rory person of who it was, but it did no good. Rory only muttered, "I wonder who that could be," as she shuffled toward the door. "Oh, hello," she said when she saw who was on her doorstep, though Miss C could hardly believe her person was surprised to see them. Everyone knew they wanted to interview the Liza person.

The young woman and man were invited in, and introductions were made. The woman, as they already knew, was named Katie, and her collaborator was called Reggie, though he preferred to be called Reg or, for reasons Miss C could not comprehend, Spike. Katie appeared to possibly be artistic. She had a brooding quality and dressed in the dark colors artistic people enjoyed. Actually, she reminded the cat a little bit of the half-baked girl Grace, only with less originality. Katie came in talking about lighting and sound quality. For all her apparent technical know-how, she seemed to be something less than half-baked, as though she'd spent a short time in a hot oven, leaving her exterior dark and crusty and her interior a warm, gooey puddle.

Spike's function, so far as Miss C could make out, was to hold the camera and drive the van.

Arrangements were made for two short interviews: one with Liza, and one with Rory. *"I'll just sit in on those,"* Miss C informed them, and no one told her no. *"I am an excellent interviewer, unafraid to ask provocative questions."*

Katie installed Liza on the sofa and made the box thing with her hands, scanning the room. Then she pulled a small device from her coat pocket and pointed it in all directions, looking for the best natural light, she said.

"The best natural light will be near the window," Miss C meowed helpfully.

Katie lowered her device and looked over at the cat in the window. "Um..." she started, and then chewed her lower lip—a common habit for her, judging by the state of her lips. "Does the cat have to be here? I mean, she's great, but she's kind of making a lot of noise. It might mess up the sound."

"On the contrary, my input will undoubtedly improve the quality of your short so-called documentary," Miss C countered. *"I am beginning to think you are not a Homer at all."*

Then the Rory person swooped in to pick the cat up, saying, "I'll get rid of her." She carried Miss C into the office and deposited her on the desk. "Just be quiet, okay? Get in your little bed and go to sleep." And she left, shutting the door.

"Unjust!" Miss C objected. She jumped down from the desk and trotted to the door, where she crouched down to hook a paw through the crack at the bottom, maneuvering her claws to scratch the paint on the other side. *"I am a prisoner of conscience!"* she wailed, as loudly as she could. When that brought no response, she sat back, considering

what other course to take. Yes, if she remained quiet, she could just barely hear what was being said in the living room, but a mere verbal record left out so much detail of body language, odor—nuances that Miss C could not afford to miss in what might be her only chance to see mythmaking in action. There remained only one thing to do.

"I am dying! Suffocating! Help! Help the poor, suffering kitty!" she wailed, while she stretched up to scratch at the woodwork surrounding the door. Surely the destruction of property would get the Rory person's attention, even if the cries didn't.

Somewhat predictably, moments later the cat heard hurried footsteps approaching and the Rory person saying, "I'm really sorry, guys. I don't know what's wrong with her."

Miss C settled herself so that, when Rory opened the door, it was to find her cat sitting regally in the middle of the room, her fluffy tail wrapped around her front paws. The cat looked up and blinked when Rory stuck her head in the door.

"What is your problem, cat? And what.... Aw, criminy.... Look what you've done to this woodwork. That's going to need repainting, if not replacing."

"Well, you should not have locked me in here," Miss C informed her as she sauntered past, tail high, while Rory was absorbed in inspecting her damaged doorframe.

The cat reentered the living room and resumed her place atop her condo. She turned to face Katie, who sat in the nearby rocking chair. Liza remained on the sofa, alone, while Spike slouched in a corner, his hands stuffed into the pockets of his jeans. Miss C wondered why he did not remove his knit hat inside, even though the temperature next to the fireplace was comfortably warm. Perhaps there was something wrong with his head.

Katie gave Miss C a dirty look. "So I guess we'll have to try it with the cat. There's no other place you could put her? Outside, maybe?"

"No," Rory said. "She doesn't go outside."

"Except when I want to, and today I do not wish to," Miss C meowed.

"It's just, she's gonna mess up the sound," Katie complained.

"If any of you say anything interesting, I shall be quiet."

Liza suggested, "We could go somewhere else."

But Katie shot that idea down. "No. I like it here. This house has—I don't know—atmosphere. We'll try to work around the cat. Spike, you ready?"

Spike said nothing, but he did remove his hands from his pockets. With them came his phone, which he now turned on and pointed at Liza. Katie said, "This is the interview of Dr. Liza Cunningham, local folklore expert. Dr. Cunningham, could you describe the story of the Woldwomper?"

The Liza person then proceeded to tell again the story that she'd told so many times in the past few months. Miss C listened quietly, hoping for some new details but getting none. She already knew all about this Wold so-called womper, otherwise known as the Forest Vampire.

"But what about modern times?" Katie asked. "Do people still fear the Woldwomper?"

Liza hesitated. Miss C looked at the Rory person standing nearby and knew that the answer was yes. People did still fear things that they knew were not real. Humans were so irrational, it was a wonder they ever accomplished anything.

After a few heartbeats, Liza said, "There is still some fear of the unknown, of the dark. That's why we have stories like this, to try to offer some explanation, even if it's not a comforting one. But the message is that, if you stay out of the woods, out of the dark places, you'll be safe."

"That's not true though, is it? I mean, you can get hurt even if you don't go in the woods," Katie said.

"Of course. Life doesn't always work out the way the stories tell us it should. But remember that uncertainty is part of the legend too, especially in later versions. You never know where the Woldwomper will strike."

"Hmm. Okay, let's wrap. Cut it, Spike."

Spike lowered the phone. Katie seemed pleased. "That was really great, Dr. Cunningham. Really interesting. Are you teaching your folklore class next semester? I'd love to get into it. I'm really into stuff like that."

"Perhaps if you were truly fascinated by folklore, you would not call it 'stuff like that,'" Miss C meowed, drawing another dirty look from Katie.

Speaking over the cat's meow, Liza said, "Not the intro course. That'll come around again next fall. But I'm putting together a seminar on animals in folklore. It'll be a lot of writing. No monsters, I'm afraid, but I can get you a spot, if you're interested. Stop by during my office hours or shoot me an email to remind me, and I'll approve it."

"Yeah, thanks."

"So you don't need anything else from me right now?"

"No. But thanks, really. This is gonna be so awesome, with your interview and all."

"You'll get a lot from Rory too. She spent a lot of time here as a child, and she knows a lot of the stories."

"And me," Miss C meowed. *"I know much more than people think I do."*

Katie seemed less than enthusiastic about interviewing Rory, but she could hardly refuse to interview the woman who'd let her living room be used as an informal set. "Yeah, sure," she said.

Liza then told Rory, "I guess I'll pop down to the house and talk to Sephie, see if we can work anything out."

"Do you have experience dealing with Underworldy beings? Perhaps I should come with you as protection," Miss C meowed. Seeing the confrontation between the Liza person and Persephone, in which Liza might possibly be turned into a pomegranate, would be so interesting. She walked casually toward the front door.

Rory warned, "Just remember that she's slick. She'll do whatever it takes to get what she wants."

"Oh, don't worry. I have no intention of trusting her. I just need a place for Gracie and me to live until I can find something else."

Coat on, Liza had her hand on the doorknob. Miss C waited for the door to open so she could scoot out it and accompany her to her meeting with the Queen of the Underworld. But Rory picked her up. "Move it, cat, so people can get out the door."

Miss C squirmed and complained loudly as she watched Liza leave, but to no avail. The door was shut, her opportunity gone. Well, no matter. She could participate in the Rory person's interview.

Chapter 10

Rory wished Liza hadn't suggested that Katie interview her on camera for the documentary, and she sensed Katie felt the same way, but it looked like they were stuck with it, neither of them wanting to back out. And so, prompted by Katie, Rory once again recounted the story of being a young girl frightened by Woldwomper stories told in her grandparents' backyard after a summer barbecue. Miss C had installed herself on the sofa next to her and offered the occasional meow. Katie decided the cat's presence added a certain touch of reality, so she didn't object—at least not verbally.

"Don't look at the camera. Just pretend it's not there," Katie kept reminding her. Rory tried to follow instructions, but it wasn't easy, what with Spike constantly moving the phone's focus back and forth between her and Katie, and then to other spots around the room. He hadn't done this during Liza's interview. At one point while Rory was talking, he turned around to shoot the family photos and mementoes on the mantel behind him. Had this kid ever actually seen a movie? Her own amateur photography attempts did not extend to video, but it seemed to her that the motion would be disorienting to viewers. Her inner editor objected to the setup.

"Shouldn't you have two cameras if you want to film both of us? And shouldn't you maybe film that other stuff separately?" she finally asked, right in the middle of the interview.

Katie looked disgusted. "It'll be fine. It's all in the editing. Whatever we use of yours will probably be just audio anyway." Here she shot a look to the cat at Rory's side. Miss C had not behaved well at all. She'd started out okay, just sitting and being mostly quiet, but then she seemed to be hit by a feeling of restlessness, and she walked repeatedly onto Rory's lap, letting her tail twitch up to hit Rory on the chin.

"Okay, let's go on. So, uh, it must have been scary when that skeleton turned up in your backyard, huh?" Katie asked.

"Yes, she was terrified," Miss C meowed. *"I remained composed, of course."*

But Rory answered, "Well, it was odd, but I don't know about scary."

"But rumors of vampires...?"

"None of us ever took it seriously," Rory insisted. "I mean, come on—vampires?"

"Liar," Miss C meowed. Professor Eleanor had taught her to always speak the truth, even when the truth was somewhat painful or embarrassing.

Finally, after Miss C jumped up onto the back of the sofa and began walking behind Rory's head, Katie said, "Well, we've probably got enough here. Cut it, Spike."

Without a word, Spike stowed the phone in the front pocket of his too-loose jeans.

"Do you have many more interviews to do?" Rory asked, much more comfortable asking questions than answering them.

Katie gazed out the front window for a moment before saying, "I doubt it. We'll get some more shots of the town, probably do some tonight. I want to get some night shots, with the moon. It was kind of cloudy last night. Then we'll just have to edit it all into something coherent. Spike's really good at that. Hey, you said that story that scared you happened in the backyard of this house? You think we could get some footage of that?"

"Sure. I'll show you through the back." Rory led Katie and Spike through the kitchen and the laundry/mudroom, taking them out into the yard, where Spike brought out his phone and started filming the tree until Katie suddenly said, "Gimme that, Spike. You're being too jerky. Here, do it like this." She held the phone steady and did a slow pan from the house to the garage.

"I want it jerky. It's a style," Spike insisted.

"It's a stupid style that gives people a headache, and I'm the director, so what I say, goes."

"Whatever," Spike said. He stuck his hands in his pockets and sulked.

Rory wondered if this was how Spielberg did it. She thought probably not.

Soon enough, Katie lowered the phone. "Guess that's enough for now," she said as she walked back toward the house. "Thanks, Ms. Roberts, for letting us use your house and stuff."

"Yeah, thanks," Spike chimed in with less enthusiasm.

Chapter 11

That evening, Rory had dinner next door with Lee and his mom, and afterward they played cards while they enjoyed tea and dessert. By the time Rory went out their back door to head home, the weather had turned suddenly blustery and colder, just as Mike had warned her it would. She wished she'd thought to bring a heavier coat, but the walk home wasn't very far—not far enough to get frostbite on a chilly, windy evening. In the moonlight, she could see the branches of the big old maple dancing with the wind, leaves rustling as they detached and fell to the ground. The tree would probably be bare by morning.

She found Miss C waiting for her in the kitchen, apparently hoping for some more food, which Rory did not give her. Instead she said, "Come on, cat, time for bed."

Amazingly, Liza had worked out a deal with Sephie Rennsfelder so she and Grace could stay on in the Miller house, at least for the time being. Liza and Sephie were like oil and water. How they were going to manage to live together, Rory did not know. At dinner, Lee mentioned that Grace had said on their ride home that afternoon that it might be kind of cool to live with a reformed convict. Had the girl forgotten her antipathy for Sephie? Surely she hadn't forgotten how Sephie had treated Miss C. Well, it wasn't Rory's business who Grace and Liza lived with, really. Tonight, the only thing that was her business was this episode of *Grey's Anatomy* being streamed right to her bedroom television. She fell asleep before the show was halfway over.

Some hours later, Miss C stirred from her place at Rory's side. The cat stretched in three different ways and sat up, licking at a front paw before jumping to the floor and padding out of the room.

Time for nightly rounds.

She went first to the kitchen, where she stopped for a drink at her water bowl and checked her food dish for any new additions. Finding none there, she went on to the living room. From atop her condo, she surveyed the street outside. In the depths of the night, all was quiet. No cars, no pedestrians. The place where she'd lived with Professor Eleanor had been busier, with at least some cars going past even late at night. That had always been interesting. The cat tried to recall her professor's face and couldn't, quite. She was sure the outlines were right, but the middle part was indistinct. Well. Miss C jumped to the floor and walked through the living room and a short way down the hall to the office, where she leapt onto the desk and stepped into her bed at the corner next to the window.

Out this back window, interesting things happened sometimes. It was probably too much to hope that something interesting would happen tonight though. The cat tucked her paws under her body and let her tail wrap around her, its tip twitching near her nose. She nestled down, preparing to let her eyes close. That was when she heard it. A slam, like a car door, coming from the street. Unusual, but not necessarily alarming. Nevertheless, in an instant she was wide awake and padding to the living room and the front window.

Yes, there was a car out there. In fact, it was the minivan driven by Spike and the Katie person. She'd heard the driver's door slam, she guessed, and now Spike was practically falling out the passenger door.

"I don't get why we have to do this in the middle of the night, and when it's so cold," he said, putting together the longest string of words Miss C had yet heard from him. He slammed the door, taking no care to try to keep it quiet.

"Shh," Katie responded. "You wanna wake up the whole neighborhood? Now get your gear and let's go. We get our shots here and we're done. Then you can put your delicate self in bed and get your precious beauty rest. God knows you need it."

Spike slid the van's side door open and rummaged inside a moment, emerging with his "gear," a single cell phone, which he stashed in his pocket. Why he'd had to keep it stored in the back seat, Miss C did not understand, but then, humans were often rather nonsensical. Spike closed the door with a sliding sound and a bang, and he and Katie headed up the sidewalk.

Where were they going? Hard to say. They'd mentioned "night shots" earlier, but Miss C hadn't realized they'd be getting these shots near her house. Well, no matter. Probably.

She waited.

All went quiet but for the wind, which still blew, but less-heavy gusts now. Miss C settled into a loaf position atop her condo, letting her eyes slide almost shut and preparing to meditate until the filmmakers returned. That was, until headlights pierced the darkness, lighting up the back of the minivan. It seemed that another car was parking on the street, but it was just out of her view. Miss C opened her eyes and sat up, pushing the side of her face right up against the cold glass of the window as she tried to see just a little farther down the street, but it was no use; she could see nothing of the vehicle or whoever was getting out of it. She did hear the doors closing—one, two of them.

Then, "That's Spike's ride, isn't it?" she heard someone ask in a voice much too loud for this time of night. "You think they're really back there?"

"Shh!" another voice, this one hushed, answered. "Of course they're back there. She told me they would be. Hurry up."

Footsteps. The newcomers seemed to be walking up the driveway. Friends of Katie and Spike? Perhaps, the cat decided. It sounded like they were looking for them.

Did these new developments warrant waking the Rory person? The cat listened and thought. Probably not. Not yet. Better to see what transpired. Waking Rory when something *might* be about to happen was likely to be unproductive. The Rory person did not usually grasp things until they were exploding all around her. She made for a rather inept investigator at the best of times, and when she'd been woken from a sound sleep, she was worse than useless unless there was a true, undeniable emergency.

Well, Miss C could see nothing more from this window, and since one of the newcomers had mentioned "back there," she trotted to the office and jumped silently onto the desk to survey the backyard. Peering outside, she could see two shadowy figures deep in the yard, near the maple tree. They'd be out of range of the motion-activated floodlights at the corners of Rory's house. One of them—Spike, she guessed—stood with his arms crooked at the elbows, no doubt holding the phone while he filmed the nothingness of the dark backyard. To the cat, the greenish night-vision glow of its view screen was like a small spotlight, many times brighter than what a human would see. Katie stood next to Spike, probably telling him what to do. But where were the newcomers? Miss C could not see them anywhere. Maybe they had gone somewhere else and had nothing to do with Katie and Spike after all. She was glad she hadn't woken Rory.

Then she saw the view screen suddenly turn, so the phone and its camera were pointed toward the house. Was this more of Spike's "style"? The camera shifted again, so now it pointed toward the dense shrubs behind the detached garage. The figures near the tree assumed defensive postures. Something was wrong. Katie and Spike were afraid, possibly expecting an attack. Miss C stilled her breathing, watching and listening.

"Who's there?" Katie called. Silence. She took a step toward the house. "Ms. Roberts?" she called, shining a flashlight in that direction. She got no answer.

Spike and Katie had an exchange that Miss C could not hear. Then the cat's ears twitched, picking up the sounds of movement near the garage. Clearly, Katie also heard this, as she swung her flashlight in that direction. "Hello?" she called again. Now she was walking toward the house, towing Spike with her, saying more words that Miss C could not quite make out.

Suddenly, two figures burst out from the opposite side of the garage, hooting, growling and lunging toward Katie and Spike, who both screamed.

Now was the proper time to wake the Rory person.

Chapter 12

Rory had no idea what was happening. Her cat had woken her from a deep sleep, in that frantic way Rory had come to know all too well. She'd swung her legs out of bed, noting that the time was 1:37, put her feet into her slippers, and pulled her robe on. Then she heard a distinct scream that seemed to be coming from her backyard. What the...? She grabbed her cell phone from her nightstand and took off at a run toward her back door.

Opting not to turn on any inside lights, just in case anything weird was happening out there, Rory peered through the glass of her back door. Miss C meowed at her feet. The floodlights weren't on, but there was definitely something happening out there, beyond the garage, near the tree. There seemed to be some sort of fight taking place among three ... no, four people. Rory distinctly heard laughter, and saw someone throw a lopsided punch. The four figures coalesced into a dark, writhing mass of arms and legs.

Rory dialed 911 on her cell and switched out her slippers for the Bean boots she kept at her back door. When the operator came on the line, Rory relayed her exact location—giving her address and letting them know there was a disturbance happening in her backyard.

"Ma'am, just stay inside. I'm sending a sheriff's deputy your way to check it out," the operator said, but Rory was already stepping out into the cold night, Miss C at her heels. The floodlights came on as she opened the door, but the sudden brightness near the house only made it harder to see into the depths of the yard.

"I think it's just some kids," she said. Then, "Hey, break it up out there!"

"Ma'am, for your own safety, I'd advise you to remain inside and let the authorities handle this," the operator was saying. Rory ended the call and dropped her phone into her robe pocket. This would not be the first time she had ignored the advice of the experts on the emergency line. Help was on the way, and that was all she needed to know.

For reasons she would struggle to explain later, Rory ran across her lawn toward the knot of people. As she got closer, she recognized Spike's hat, and yes, that was Katie's voice. The others, though, she couldn't identify. They were males, certainly, but they wore hooded sweatshirts with the hoods pulled close over their faces. Plus, it was dark, despite the moonlight and the floodlights. She should have known better than to get in the middle of that melee, she would say later, but at the time, adrenaline took over, she saw Katie's terrified face, and she inserted herself in the thick of it, yelling like somebody's mother for everyone to just break it up. She pushed one of the hooded strangers away from Katie, telling him to knock it off. He pushed her back. Then, apparently deciding the push wasn't enough, he tackled her to the ground, wrapping his arms around her and dragging her down sideways. Rory landed painfully on her left shoulder, her attacker's body pressing her down. "Stay out of it, old lady," he breathed into her ear. Then he was up. Despite the new ache in her shoulder, Rory struggled to her feet. "Who you calling old?" she yelled, pulling a stray leaf out of her hair. Spike was within grabbing distance, so she grasped hold of his sweater, intending to pull him away from the fight, but as she did so, he made a grunting sound and crumpled toward the ground. "Let's go!" a voice yelled, and just like that, the fight was over, with two figures running toward the street.

Rory knelt at Spike's side. He was trembling, from terror, or possibly a well-placed punch, she assumed. From the street, two car doors slammed, and then an engine gunned and a car sped away. Should she have taken the time to look out front at what kind of car the miscreants were driving? No, she decided. She couldn't have known that there was a car involved.

A siren sounded in the distance, no doubt the sheriff's deputy the 911 operator had promised her. Good.

And Miss C was right at her side, meowing up a storm. Less good.

Rory felt something under her knee, something hard and round, like a flashlight. Just what she needed.... She grabbed at it, picked it up, felt with her thumb for an on switch.

Nearby, Katie was collecting herself from where she'd been knocked to the ground in the melee.

"Spike?" she said. Then she turned the bright white beam of her phone's flashlight onto her friend's face. Rory really hoped it was mostly the whiteness of that light that was making him look so ashen. His eyes were slits, and he was beginning to tremble uncontrollably. "Spike!" Katie repeated, now with desperation in her voice. She moved the light toward his abdomen, where they could now both see blood seeping between his fingers as his hands pressed against a bleeding wound.

The light went next to the object Rory held in her hand, which was not a flashlight at all but a military combat knife with a blade at least six inches long.

"You stabbed him?" When Rory didn't reply but only stared mutely at the knife in her hand, the smears of dark red blood on its blade, Katie repeated hysterically, "You stabbed him? What kind of nut are you, out here with your cat and stabbing people?" she demanded, and then she threw herself at Rory, catching her off guard and knocking her over onto her sore shoulder again. That prompted Miss C to get involved, running in to take a swipe at Katie's face. It felt good to know her claws had found purchase in the young woman's flesh.

"It wasn't me," Rory said from where she now lay on her back. She was aware that the siren had wound down, and a new voice was making its way toward them.

"Everybody freeze!" the voice demanded.

Rory breathed a sigh of relief to hear Deputy Sergeant Opal Washington's voice. The only thing that would have been more comforting at that moment was Mike's voice.

"Ms. Roberts, that you?" Opal asked as she approached with both flashlight and gun drawn.

Before Rory could answer, Katie said, "She stabbed Spike! We need help—an ambulance! But look out for her—she's crazy, and she has a cat!"

Opal was close enough now to look Rory in the eye. "Ms. Roberts, please just set the knife on the ground," she said calmly, but with her gun still drawn.

Rory had not realized she was still holding the knife. She dropped it in the grass and started to get to her feet.

"Hold it!" Opal stopped her. "Stay on the ground. Roll over on your stomach, with your arms stretched out."

"What?" Rory asked in confusion. "But, Opal—"

"Right now, on your stomach." The deputy emphasized her point with her weapon.

Rory complied, insisting, "I don't know who those people were, Opal, but—"

"We'll discuss it later, Ms. Roberts." The deputy sergeant ran one hand along Rory's flanks, shooing the cat away as she did so. When she found the phone in the robe pocket, she removed it. Then she grabbed Rory's left wrist and slapped a handcuff on it, followed by the right wrist. Rory now lay on her stomach, face in the grass, with her hands cuffed behind her back.

"You are being arrested," Miss C explained, her whiskers tickling Rory's face.

"Opal?" Rory asked in confusion. The chill in the air and on the ground crept through her robe and pajamas, and she began to shiver.

"Later," Opal said, now kneeling at Spike's side. He had stopped trembling.

In the next seconds, Opal called for backup and an ambulance, she lowered her ear to Spike's mouth to listen for breath sounds. She tilted his head back and gave two quick breaths into his mouth before she started chest compressions, which weren't at all like the compressions Rory was used to seeing on her television shows.

Nearby, Katie sat cross legged in the grass, crying. More sirens were coming now, and Rory could only hope that one of them belonged to Mike's department SUV. Surely someone would have called to let him know that something was going on at her house. Other activity was happening too, other lights were coming on at her next-door neighbors' houses, and then she heard, "Ror?" Lee. "What's going on?"

"Mr. Cooper, stay back please," Opal warned him.

"Can I help you, Deputy? I know CPR," he said.

"Yes, thank you. Here. Take over compressions, but let me check for a pulse first." Opal stopped long enough to feel at Spike's neck, then she shook her head and Lee knelt to begin chest compressions.

Miss C lay quietly at Rory's side, near her face. Oddly, the cat wasn't making a sound.

Two EMTs arrived and took over Spike's care, leaving Opal free to deal with Rory, which she quickly did. "On your feet, Ms. Roberts," she said, yanking on her arm.

"Hey, that hurts," Rory objected.

Miss C hissed.

"Let's go." The deputy steadied Rory as she got first to a sitting position and then, one leg at a time, struggled to her feet. Miss C began circling around her legs. "Mr. Cooper, could you do something with the cat, please?"

Lee stooped to pick up Miss C. The cat objected verbally but allowed herself to be carried. "I'll get her inside for you, Ror," Lee said.

"Spike—he's going to be okay, right?" Rory asked stupidly. "He was just—"

"Not now, Ms. Roberts," Opal cut her off. "Walk." With one hand firmly gripping Rory's arm, the deputy led her toward the front of the house, where her cruiser was parked.

"Aren't we going in the house?" Rory asked.

"No. We're going to the cruiser. Now walk."

Opal escorted Rory across the lawn to the driveway and street, where they found a loose knot of Brooksfordians standing in their nightclothes, watching. Excited chatter skittered through the gathering when Rory appeared in handcuffs and was taken straight to the cruiser. Opal opened the back door and guided Rory's head as she maneuvered herself into the seat.

Chapter 13

Events had taken a turn that Miss C had not foreseen. She'd suspected the two intruders were up to no good, but the last thing she'd expected was for the Spike person to end up dead. No, that wasn't quite true. The very last thing she'd expected was for her Rory person to end up under arrest, suspected of committing the murder.

Who was going to feed her in the morning, if the Rory person went to jail?

Miss C meowed as much as she sat in the window, from where she could see the deputy's car with Rory in the backseat. Behind her, the Lee person and Rory's pet sheriff were talking.

"What happened out here tonight?" the sheriff was asking.

"I heard a siren, and when I looked outside, I saw Rory's floodlights were on. I thought something must be wrong with her, so I came over."

"And when you got here, what did you see?"

"Well, Opal was doing CPR on that kid, and Rory was handcuffed on the ground. The other one, the girl, was sitting nearby crying. Mike, you can't seriously think that Rory did anything to this kid, can you?"

"The report we have is that she was seen with the knife in her hand just after he was stabbed." Miss C understood from the sheriff's voice that he found this report as unbelievable as she did.

"Who says that?"

"The only eyewitness."

"But come on, Rory with a combat knife? She can barely cut a steak without help, you know that."

"Yes, it is true that the Rory person is not adept with basic cutlery," Miss C confirmed, though no one had asked her.

The sheriff went on. "Rory says there were two other people out here. You know anything about that?"

"No. The first I knew anything was wrong was when I heard the siren. You're not going to charge her, are you?"

The sheriff hesitated.

"I don't believe for a second that Rory hurt anyone out there, but I've got to do this by the book, Lee. I can't do anything that looks like special treatment. You understand, right?"

"Sure, I guess. But if I were you, I wouldn't expect Rory to be so understanding."

The sheriff made a sound that caused Miss C to think he was rather terrified of what might happen next.

Chapter 14

Rory was taken to the sheriff's department and put into a cramped interview room, brightly lit by overhead fluorescent bulbs. A small table was pushed against one wall, with three metal folding chairs scattered near it. When Opal brought her into the room, she pointed to the chair in the far corner. "Sit there, please, Ms. Roberts," she said. "But first, I'm going to remove your handcuffs. Any funny business and they go right back on, you hear me?"

Too terrified to speak, Rory nodded her head vigorously. She felt Opal holding her wrists while she released the handcuffs. The deputy sergeant's hands were warm, her touch gentle.

"There now," Opal said as Rory sat and began rubbing her wrists, relieved that the weight of the cuffs was gone. "That better? You want a coffee? It's nothing like Gunther's, but it's hot and it's strong."

"Y-yeah," Rory stammered. "Thanks."

Opal slipped the handcuffs back into the carrier on her gun belt. She reached behind her for the doorknob. "Just try to relax, Ms. Roberts. We're going to get to the bottom of whatever happened out there tonight." The deputy left the room then, closing the door behind her. It shut with a heavy *thunk* that indicated to Rory she was locked in.

She sat on the edge of the hard metal chair replaying the events of the night in her mind. She shouldn't have gone outside, but it had looked like Katie and Spike were in trouble. She shouldn't have picked up the knife, but at the time, she hadn't known it was a knife. She certainly hadn't known it had been used to stab Spike.

The room smelled of disinfectant and stale sweat. How many criminals had seen their hopes of getting away with their crimes end right here, at this table, in this chair, with their nervous feet tapping on this scuffed tile? Realizing her own knees were bouncing up and down, Rory forced them to stop. She spotted a bit of dried maple leaf stuck to the front of her robe and picked it off, looked for a suitable place to put it and, not seeing a trash can, laid the leaf carefully on the table. Would a murderer do that? No, a murderer would have flicked the leaf to the floor without a thought. She crossed her arms over her chest. *Just be calm,* she told herself. *Everything's going to be fine. Mike won't let anything happen to you.* Only, where was Mike? And for that matter, where was Opal? How long did it take to get one cup of coffee? Her knees began to bounce again, and again she stopped them. *Don't act guilty,* she thought. *They're probably watching.* Surely there was a camera somewhere in the room, recording her every move. Someone might be watching the feed right now. Rory looked up, trying to move her eyes while keeping her head still. Yes. There was a camera mounted in the corner near the door. *Don't act guilty,* she told herself again.

From down the hall, she heard footsteps echoing, coming closer to the room she was in. Then a key turned in the lock, the door swung inward, and there was Opal, carrying one disposable coffee cup balanced atop another.

"Here we go," the detective sergeant said as she set one of the cups in front of Rory. "As I say, it's not Gunther's, but it's better than nothing." She used a foot to pull one of the other chairs closer to her and then sat in it.

Rory grabbed the coffee cup with both hands and raised it for a tentative sip. As Opal had promised, it was hot and strong—too strong, actually, and yet it lacked the mouth-flooding flavor of Madison's brews. "It's not bad," she lied.

"Well, it's strong enough to cut steel, but you get used to it. Now"—she paused to drink from her own cup—"you realize everything that happens in this room is being recorded?"

"Yes," Rory said, her eyes flicking involuntarily toward the camera. She was surprised at how clear and strong her voice came out.

Opal nodded. "So, tell me what happened out there tonight. You have some kinda beef with this Spike fella?"

"Is he really dead?"

"For real and forever. Now, what were you doing out there?"

"It is my yard," Rory pointed out.

Another nod. "True that. They were trespassing—that why you went after them?"

"Yes ... but no. I mean, yes, they were trespassing, but no, I didn't go out after them. I went out because they were being attacked."

"Attacked by what?"

"By the other people. My cat woke me up, and I looked outside and saw a fight going on in my backyard. I called it in to 911."

"We're getting the tape of your call."

"Good. I recognized Spike and Katie, and it looked like they were in trouble. There were two other people out there. I went out to try to break things up."

"And you thought the knife would help 'break things up,' as you put it?"

"What? No. I didn't take any knife. I didn't take anything except my phone."

"And yet you were seen with the knife in your hand moments after it was used to stab that young man. Now tell me, Ms. Roberts, what're we s'posed to think?"

"I understand how it looks, obviously, but I was struggling with this guy who tackled me. He must've been the one with the knife. After they were gone, I felt it on the ground—the handle, I mean—and I thought it was a flashlight."

"How many other people were there, besides you and Spike and Katie?"

Rory thought for a second, picturing the scene in her mind. "Two," she said with certainty.

"Two," Opal pronounced, leaving no doubt just what she thought of the truth of that statement.

"Yes, I'm sure there were two other people. They were both males, I think, judging by their size. It was dark, and they had those hoodies pulled over their heads, so I couldn't see their faces, but—"

"I'm just going to stop you there," the deputy sergeant interrupted. "Because our only other witness has a totally different story. I just wonder if you want to rethink what you're telling me."

"Different how?" Rory asked, confused. She was telling Opal exactly what happened, so how could the "only other witness" have a different story?

"She says there wasn't anyone else out there at all—just her and Spike and you."

Rory felt her head snap back as Opal's statement and a thousand other things rushed through her brain. If she was found holding the murder weapon moments after the crime, and if the only other witness contradicted her story, and if no other evidence was found to back up her story.... Her heart rate ticked up and her breathing came short and shallow. "But ... but that's not true. There were other people out there. I saw them. They were fighting with Katie and Spike. I went to help."

"How well did you know Spike?"

"I didn't. I just met him today, yesterday, whatever. When he came with Katie to do some filming."

"You give them permission to film at night?"

"No. They didn't ask."

"You get angry when you saw them out in your yard in the middle of the night?"

"No. I mean yes, but..." Rory felt herself swimming, drowning, in a sea of words. Should she ask for a lawyer? She knew exactly what Mike thought of people who suddenly stopped cooperating with an investigation, but somehow everything she said sounded like a ridiculous fabrication, especially if it was being contradicted by the only other witness, Katie, whose friend had just been murdered.

A knock at the door stopped the interview for the moment. "Yes?" Opal called out. The door opened far enough for another deputy to stick his head in. "You're needed in room four, Sergeant," he said.

"Excuse me," Opal said as she got up and left the room.

What did that mean? On television, it usually meant that whoever was observing the interview had something to add or wanted the interviewer to take a different direction or ask a specific question. Or it meant that new information had come to light. Or it could be the interviewer's personal life intruding on the investigation, an emergency of some sort. Did Opal have a family, a significant someone who could possibly be sick or injured? Rory realized she didn't know.

She remembered one summer, when her Gramps was still the sheriff, he and Grams had invited the entire sheriff's department—deputies, office staff, and their families—over for a barbecue. Even the on-duty deputies stopped by for a burger or hot dog. There'd been games with prizes for the kids, and Grams had hollowed out half of a big watermelon and filled it with raspberry sherbet, which she then sprinkled with chocolate chips. Until you looked at it closely, it looked exactly like a regular watermelon. Everyone had marveled over it. If Rory married Mike, would she be expected to do things like that, throw get-togethers for his staff? Maybe if she started small, with one of those round, seedless watermelons hollowed out and filled with, you know, watermelon, she could build up to more remarkable things. And what would they do with Miss C during these parties? How would Mike feel about having a cat in a stroller making the rounds among his guests? Of course, if she went to prison for Spike's murder, Mike would marry someone else, someone like Seph—

The door opened, cutting Rory off in mid-thought. Opal entered again, but this time she was smiling and she didn't close the door behind her.

"Deputy, do I need a lawyer?" Rory asked before Opal could say anything. "I want to call my father."

"You don't need a lawyer, Ms. Roberts. This is all over. You're free to go."

Rory blinked back at her. "I am?"

"Mm-hmm. The other witness has changed her story, and frankly it makes a heck of a lot more sense than what she told us originally. Sheriff Davis is talking with her now, and then he's going to drive you home. You want to wait in his office? It's a heckuva lot more comfortable than here."

Rory stood, causing the chair legs to scrape against the floor. "What time is it?"

"Little after five."

"Oh no, it's time for Miss C's breakfast."

As Rory neared the door, Opal put a protective hand on her shoulder and steered her into the hall. "Don't worry about that now. I'll bet your friend Lee is taking care of it."

"Opal, I want to invite you over for dinner sometime. Do you have a family? They're invited too," Rory blurted, barely conscious of what she was saying.

That smile again. "Thank you, Ms. Roberts. We'll make that happen sometime. Now come on, there's a fresh pot of coffee on, and I know where I can snag you a doughnut that's only one day old. You see? It's just like I told you. Everything's going to be okay."

But Rory still could not help but feel that nothing was anywhere close to being okay.

Chapter 15

Rory had intended to say little or nothing to Mike as he drove her home in his department SUV, his smokey bear hat lying on the seat between them. Stiff silence during the twenty-minute ride would be a start on the payback she planned to dish out to him for allowing her to be taken away in handcuffs with half of Brooksford watching. But as she watched the farmland slipping by, she found that her anger was too strong to keep quiet. "You had me arrested?" she asked, and not for the first time.

"Again, you were never arrested. We brought you in as a person of interest. I had to, hon—"

"Don't 'hon' me."

"Sorry. Anyway, you were found holding the weapon used to kill that boy, and the only witness we had told us that you stabbed him. Until we found other evidence and she changed her story—"

"What was her story, anyway?"

"She said that she and Spike were out there filming—trespassing, I pointed out to her—and you came out and confronted them, whereupon a physical altercation ensued and you stabbed Spike."

"Is that the speech you rehearsed for your press conference later?"

"What do you mean by that?"

"'Whereupon, a physical altercation...'" Rory mocked. "C'mon, you only say stuff like that when you're talking to the press. You're giving me a canned speech."

Mike took a breath before replying. "No, that was not any kind of rehearsed speech. I'm sorry if I sounded formal. I was just trying to tell you what happened from a law enforcement perspective."

"Forget it. So you believed her story, about me running out with a small sword to stab her cameraman?"

"Of course not. Of course I believed you from the start, but we had to check out both stories."

"And mine checked out and hers didn't? Was it because of the video? Spike must have been taking video with his phone. That's the only reason those two had to be out there."

Mike shook his head. "There is video, but it's not very useful. Spike caught some sounds from the bushes but then stopped recording. Still, the sounds do back up your story."

Not as much as a video of the attack would, Rory thought.

Mike went on. "We found another witness, though, who heard a car leaving the scene, and we've got footprints in the bushes behind your garage. When we confronted Katie with all that, she changed her story."

"I don't understand. Why would she lie in the first place?"

"Said she was scared that whoever killed Spike would come for her."

"And having me take the fall would keep her safe? That's ridiculous. This whole thing is ridiculous," Rory said, as confusion and anger filled her.

"It doesn't make a lot of sense. But, hon—"

She shot him a look. "Don't call me hon. In fact, don't even talk to me right now, okay?" Rory snapped.

"But—"

She held a hand up to stop him, and he swallowed whatever he'd been about to say.

Mike pulled into the driveway behind the evidence techs' van. Yellow crime scene tape stretched from the corner of her garage all the way to the maple tree, supported along the way by thin metal stakes that had been driven into the ground for just that purpose. A deputy stood guard near the garage while two techs crouched in the middle of the yard, studying something on the ground. Mike cut the engine and started to take his seat belt off, but Rory stopped him. "Don't bother. I can walk into my own house by myself."

He continued removing the seat belt and opened his door. "Good. Meanwhile, I've got a crime scene to check out, if you don't mind." Placing his hat on his head, he stepped out onto the driveway.

Rory got out and slammed the door, only regretting that she hadn't managed to slam it a little harder. She was aware of Mike watching her retrieve the hidden extra house key from under a rock near the garage, waiting to see that she got inside safely before he turned his full attention to the scene of the crime. Such a gentleman. Well, she didn't care. Let him stand there all day if he wanted to. Not bothering to even glance at him, she opened the back door and walked into the cottage, where she found Miss C fairly frantic.

The cat circled her legs, meowing loudly. *"You have been gone for hours and hours ... half the night."*

After kicking off her boots and sliding her feet back into her slippers, Rory scooped up the cat and carried her into the kitchen. "I know, Cuddlywumps. It was scary, right? You had to be here all by yourself."

"No, it was not scary. I was just worried I'd run out of food before you got home," Miss C lied. Although Professor Eleanor had told her to always speak truth, a lie seemed more appropriate under these circumstances. She nuzzled her face against Rory's neck and purred as Rory sank her fingers deep into her fur.

"Well, I see nothing's changed since I've been on the inside," Rory said, glancing around her home. "I've got to make some decent coffee. Here, down you get, Cuddlywumps."

"I would not mind a tasty morsel, as long as you're home."

"Lee fed you this morning, didn't he?" Rory checked her watch. He'd be in class by now, so no point in texting him right away, but...

Behind her, she heard her back door open, and she stiffened. Mike—couldn't that guy take a hint? She started to wind herself up to hit him with some really good shouting, but then she heard Lee's voice saying, "Ror? Can I come in?"

"Yes. Lee, criminy, it's good to see you," she said as she went to meet him. Today there were no fist bumps or other buddy-like greetings between them. They just embraced like the old friends they were.

"You okay?" he asked when she held on longer than was usual.

"Fine," she lied, releasing him.

"She is lying," Miss C meowed. *"Also, I would not mind a little morsel."*

"Thanks for taking care of Miss C."

"Pepperoni neutrons. Sounds like she's happy to see you."

"I could take it or leave it," Miss C lied again. *"About that tasty little morsel?"*

"You fed her, right?" Rory asked, looking down at the cat.

"Yeah, I gave her a shrimp something or other."

That stopped Rory in her tracks. "And she ate it—for breakfast?" she asked incredulously. In the past, Miss C had always refused seafood for breakfast. For whatever reason, breakfast to Miss C meant chicken-dinner cat food and nothing else.

Lee shrugged. "She dug right in."

"I was desperate," the cat explained.

"Unbelievable," Rory said. "Okay, cat, I'll give you a little more. Just give me a break here. Let me start the coffee first. That stuff they had at the jail was vile."

Lee watched as she started the coffee and fed the cat again.

"So what happened last night? Mike wouldn't really tell me anything," he said.

Rory told him the story of how Miss C had woken her up, how she'd gone to the back door and had seen some kind of fight happening in her backyard. "I called 911 and went out to see if I could help."

"Ror..."

"I know, I know. I shouldn't have done that. But it was Katie and Spike getting attacked by someone. I just don't understand why Katie would point the finger at me."

Lee made a "huh" sound that caused Rory to stop what she was doing. "What?" she asked.

"Well, it does make you wonder, doesn't it? Maybe this whole thing was a setup to get rid of Spike."

"You mean you think Katie was involved?"

"It just makes you wonder."

Chapter 16

The next day, Rory sat at her desk staring out at her backyard where Spike had been killed. A soft, cold rain had fallen for hours that morning, and she hoped it had washed away whatever blood had been left on the grass. Mike had released the scene yesterday, after his deputies and the county's crime scene techs had been all over it looking for clues. They'd found the knife, of course, and the footprints that backed up Rory's story and helped convince Katie to tell the truth.

Of course the whole town knew what had happened, or, more accurately, they'd heard rumors of what had happened. Rory hadn't been able to leave the house the day before, not wanting to face her neighbors, many of whom probably believed that she had killed that boy. She hadn't even tried to work, preferring to lie on the sofa with a blanket and her cat, reading, napping, and periodically sitting up to mess with her jigsaw puzzle. The only person she'd seen other than Lee had been the UPS guy, delivering her new computer monitors. Today she was determined to start moving forward. For one thing, she had a business to run. If she spent too much time lazing about, one day she'd wake up and realize she had no grocery money. Plus, it just felt better to be moving. It kept her mind off other things, like the memory of Spike lying dead in her yard, and also the way she'd slammed the car door on Mike and gone into the house without looking back at him, not to mention how he'd left her to stew in an interview room like a criminal while he tried to figure out if she was telling the truth.

But mostly her mind kept bringing up the image of Spike dying right next to her. Yes, she'd been closely involved in the aftermath of other deaths in town, but this one was harder. This time she hadn't just heard about a death or stumbled across a body. Spike had still been alive when she threw herself into the fight. She could still feel his sweater pulling out of her hand as his body slumped to the ground. He'd been, what, twenty maybe? Just a kid.

She answered email and took care of some recordkeeping in the morning. Rory kept all of her business's financial records in both electronic and hard copies, with multiple backups, hoping that, should disaster strike, at least one copy would survive. She was also meticulous about keeping those records up to date, something that could not be said about the rest of her life. After the recordkeeping, she edited and returned a set of short business letters from a longstanding client. She sent the invoice for that job and then took a quick lunch break, during which thoughts of Spike began to intrude again, so she cast about for her next task and decided she might as well get those new monitors up and running. Best to do it now, when there wasn't much else going on.

Under close supervision from Miss C, she spent the better part of an hour unpacking and assembling the dual monitor arms. The two arms went into a single mount that attached to the desk. The whole assembly was a fairly heavy affair that would allow her spiffy new monitors to float above the desk at any height or angle. Not that she planned on moving them around much, but it would be a nice feature to have. She could not wait to try out the monitors. Here, she'd splurged on twenty-four-inch, high-definition screens. No more squinting at one crappy little screen for her. Miss C took a keen interest in the goings-on, especially since the operation required the temporary relocation of her desk bed. The cat stepped into the bed where Rory had placed it on the floor. *"I do not care for this new location,"* she meowed. *"My bed belongs on the desk, near the window, where I can observe the backyard."*

"Settle down, cat. As soon as I get everything hooked up, I'll put your bed back. I just have to release the tension on this arm so it will swing. I hope," she added under her breath, looking nervously at the left-hand monitor and having visions of it crashing to the desk and shattering. She was not at all sure that she was doing the right thing by turning and turning and turning that Allen wrench in the "loosen" direction. It would be just great if she destroyed hundreds of dollars' worth of new equipment before she'd even gotten a chance to use it. But then with one last turn, the arm swung free so Rory could adjust it. "There, see. I do know what I'm doing. Sort of. Now for the cords. And the driver."

After another thirty minutes of hassling with cords and the installation of an external driver for the second monitor, Rory turned the computer and both monitors on. She'd arranged them side by side in a shallow V formation. The left-side monitor came on just fine, but the right side remained dark. "Criminy. Okay. I think I just have to—"

Her thought was interrupted by knocking from the front door.

"Company," Miss C meowed helpfully from her bed.

"Dang. I don't guess you'd want to go see who that is while I stay here," Rory said to the cat.

"I could do that, but you would not bother to listen to me when I announced who it is, so you should do it yourself."

Already on her way toward the living room, Rory said, "I didn't think so."

She opened the door to find Mel Scott, reporter for the *Westbrook Examiner,* standing on the doorstep. "There you are," Mel said brightly. "I was starting to think you weren't home."

Really? You mean I was that close to having you just leave? Rory thought.

Mel was shorter than average, and a little overweight. She wore multiple silver studs in her ears and a silver ring on each finger and thumb of both hands. A knit hat covered her hair, and Rory couldn't help but wonder what color the hair underneath would be. Mel was known for having brightly colored hair, so wouldn't it be a shock to see her with brown hair, or blond? Not for the first time since she'd met Mel, Rory considered shutting the door in her face, but decided against it. Instead, she invited the reporter in and offered her tea.

"I'm surprised you weren't out here yesterday," Rory said as she watched Mel remove her coat and hang it on the tree by the door. She pulled the knit hat off to reveal short blue hair. Normally it would be arranged into spikes on top, but the hat turned them into more of a woven mat. Mel teased her fingers through it, and a few spikes sprang to attention, though most of them stayed flat and tangled.

"Can you believe it? I go to a conference for three lousy days, and something big happens on my beat while I'm gone. What are the odds, right?"

Ever since she'd made a name for herself in the county by covering Brooksford's very first modern murder, Mel had considered the little town her "beat." When anything out of the ordinary happened, she was sure to turn up sooner rather than later.

"Yeah. What are the odds. Have a seat here by the fire, and I'll get that tea started," Rory offered.

"Thanks. Sounds yummy." Mel removed her big blue purse from her shoulder, but not before she'd reached into it for her trusty digital recorder and a note pad and pencil.

Rory left Miss C to watch over the reporter while she went to put the kettle on the stovetop.

"So," Mel started when she returned, "about this thing that happened the other night." She'd installed herself at Rory's favorite spot on the sofa. Miss C sat next to her, meowing.

"I'm not sure I can tell you much. The sheriff asked me not to give out too much about what happened," Rory lied, though it made sense that Mike might not want too many details to get out—details of the sort that only someone who'd been there would know. She sat in the rocking chair near the window, keeping an ear out for the tea kettle that was heating on the stove.

"I understand you were questioned as a person of interest."

"I gave a statement, yes."

"And you were right there when it happened, when this young man, Reginald, was killed?"

"Yes, I was right there."

"I was also there," Miss C meowed.

Mel looked over at the cat. "I don't suppose it was your cat who woke you up again and let you know that something was wrong?"

"As a matter of fact, it was," Rory said shortly, determined not to give the reporter too much.

"And then...?"

"I can't really talk about that part," Rory lied.

"Right.... So the victim, Reginald—"

Rory interrupted, "Spike. He went by Spike." She didn't think she could stand to hear anyone call the boy in the knit cap "Reginald" again. It seemed disrespectful, somehow.

"Oh, so you knew him?" the reporter asked innocently.

Kicking herself inwardly, Rory said, "Not really. He was here yesterday filming interviews for this documentary thing."

"Documentary?"

Rory waved one hand in an "it's nothing" gesture. "It's a student film about the Woldwomper and Brooksford, Mel. Don't pretend you don't know about it."

"He was a modern mythmaker, akin to Hesiod or Homer. Or more accurately, Hesiod or Homer's secretary," Miss C meowed. *"Although I do not expect you know who Hesiod was. Perhaps you have heard of Homer?"*

"Right. So he was here?"

"He was doing the camera work, like I said, while this girl Katie did the interviews. I got the impression she was in charge." It wouldn't hurt to put that out there, since Rory had her suspicions about Katie, especially since the girl had apparently been content to let Rory take the heat for Spike's death.

"He was a film student?"

Rory considered that. "I don't really know what he was, other than he was working with Katie."

"I wonder if I could get my hands on any of that footage?" Mel thought out loud.

"I wouldn't count on it. It's evidence now, since Spike was filming when they were attacked."

"Yeah..." Mel sounded wistfully disappointed. "How did that happen anyway?"

"Quickly," Miss C meowed.

Rory answered, "I don't know. I was asleep for that part. The first thing I knew was Miss C here waking me up."

"Miss C again, huh?"

"Yes. She would know nothing if not for me," the cat meowed. Rory shrugged but said nothing.

"What time was that?"

"About one, one thirty, I think."

"And you ran right out there into the thick of the fight? Why didn't you just call 911?"

"I did call 911, but how long does it take to get help out here? It was obvious that Katie and Spike were in danger. I thought I could help." *A lot of help I did them though,* Rory thought.

"There's a lot of talk, you know, about how you must've had something to do with it." Something buzzed from within Mel's purse. She dug inside it and came up with a cell phone. "Sorry. That's my editor. I've really got to take this," she said. "Hey, Greg. What's up?"

Rory took that as her cue to go check on the tea. It seemed like that water was taking forever to boil, but she hadn't heard any of the telltale gurgling sounds of a kettle on the stove. When she got to the kitchen, she discovered she'd forgotten to turn the burner on, so the kettle and its water sat as still and cold as when she'd first set it there. "Criminy," she breathed as she reached to turn on the burner. She could just microwave a little water, but somehow microwaved tea never tasted right to her. If the kettle didn't whistle, it wasn't tea, her Gram used to say.

While Rory was in the kitchen fussing with the tea kettle, she could not help but overhear part of Mel's conversation. There was an excitement in the reporter's voice that made Rory nervous and anxious to get back into the living room.

"You're kidding. It's on YouTube?" Mel was saying. "How many views? Holy cow! Yeah, yeah. I'll take a look."

"What's on YouTube?" Rory asked when Mel ended her call. Somehow, she knew she was not going to like the answer.

"What is this u-tube?" Miss C meowed.

The reporter was already opening a browser on her phone. "My editor says it's a video from the other night, from out here." She gestured toward the back of Rory's house. "It's supposed to be showing the attack. Dang it. I've only got one bar out here. I can't get online." Mel turned a hopeful eye to Rory.

"You are not using our computer," Miss C meowed from where she stood on the sofa. *"Play with your gadgets on your own time."*

"It's supposedly got a hundred thousand views already," Mel teased.

A video of the attack? That was perfect, right? Irrefutable video evidence was all Rory needed to clear her name once and for all and to identify the actual killer. And wouldn't Mike be surprised? She could already feel the satisfaction of presenting the video to him and saying, "There, mister."

"All right," Rory gave in. "Come on into my office, and we'll find it on my computer. It'll be better to see it on a bigger screen anyway." Plus, it would be a great way to test out her new monitors—or at least the one that was working.

Miss C gave a sharp *mrrip* that indicated disagreement.

After a detour into the kitchen to turn the stove off again, Rory led Mel down the hall and into her office, with Miss C following. Sitting in her office chair with Mel hovering over her shoulder and Miss C prancing in front of the screen, Rory opened a browser window and navigated to YouTube, a site she usually only visited when she needed a quick how-to video. She could probably find one that would show her how to work her second monitor, in fact.

"Okay, what am I looking for?" she asked.

"Just try searching 'Brooksford,'" Mel suggested. "Sweet monitors."

"Yeah. I just got them. The second one's not really set up yet."

"Ah."

Rory plugged the town's name into the search bar. Twenty-seven hits came up, but only one of them had been posted in the past twenty-four hours and had 150,000 views. "Terror in Brooksford," it was titled. The comments section below was filled with things such as "This almost made me pee my self!" "Scaaarrry!!!" and "This is the real deal. Do not watch unless you want to be scared out of your mind."

Not liking where this was going, Rory clicked on the video and hit play.

"Can you make it full screen?" Mel asked.

"Yes, do that," Miss C meowed from where she now sat next to the screen, not sure at all what she was looking at.

Rory obliged, though she wasn't sure making the frame larger was going to make it easier to make anything out in the dark, jerky picture. For the first few moments, she didn't know what she was looking at, as the scene jumped from one thing to the next, each time with the frame jittering as if it had been shot by an amateur movie maker who was too spastic to keep the camera still.

That sounded familiar, she thought.

Then, she recognized her own garage. It jerked into the frame momentarily, as though someone walking up her drive had raised a camera for two seconds and then quickly lowered it.

"Hey, that's my place," she said. "This must be from the idiots who attacked Katie and Spike last night."

"Shh. I want to hear," Mel admonished her, though there wasn't much to hear. There was no dialogue, no voice-over, no music. The only sounds were the breathing of the camera operator and at least one other person with him.

Suddenly, the scene cut to a shot of Katie and Spike standing under the maple, doing their own filming. In the grainy green and white of night vision, they were clearly visible, looking up into the branches. The light of Spike's viewfinder showed up bright white on screen. In the dead quiet, Katie spoke. "Are you getting that, those branches against the sky?" Her voice was hushed.

"Shut up. I'm getting it. I know what I'm doing," Spike answered. His voice was not hushed, and it boomed out of the speakers.

"Quiet!" Katie said. "And try to hold the camera more still, would you? I'd like for this project to not suck."

"For God's sake, how many times do I have to tell you? This is a style. I know what I'm doing."

Then it seemed that one of the people behind the other camera, the one secretly filming the filmmakers, moved to deliberately make a sound from where they were hidden near the garage. Katie's head snapped toward their camera, her eyes shining eerily into it.

"Shh. Did you hear that?" she whispered.

"Hear what?" Spike said normally, still pointing his camera up into the tree.

Another sound, this one louder. It was like a shuffling among the dead leaves, the ones that accumulated in the corner where the back wall of the garage met a tangle of poorly maintained holly shrubs covered in honeysuckle vine.

"That!"

Now Spike turned as well, so that he too was looking straight into the camera they did not know was there. "It's just an animal or something," he insisted. "What'sa matter? You afraid the Woldwomper's gonna getcha?" Then he laughed, but his laughter was soon stopped as a great flurry of activity sounded from the area near the hidden camera. More rustling, only much louder than before. On the screen, branches moved. It appeared they were being deliberately shaken.

Spike cursed, and Katie queried, "Who's there? Ms. Roberts?"

Her voice sounded tight, not intimidating at all. It was the voice of a terrified person. Much as Rory wanted to believe that Katie had been in on the plan to kill Spike, the young woman looked and sounded genuinely scared and confused. Spike's hand, the one holding his phone, was not raised but was lowered at his side. Rory knew from what Mike had told her that the phone's camera had already stopped recording.

"Hello?" Katie said into the night. Silence. Katie grabbed Spike's arm and pulled him to the left of the screen, which would be toward the house. She said, "C'mon, let's get out of here. It's probably nothing, but..."

"Yeah, we're done here," Spike agreed.

Then there came an explosion of sound from near the camera, growling, leaves rustling, and a movement forward, in the direction of Katie and Spike, whose eyes widened. They screamed and turned to run. The screen went to black then, and words appeared: "The mutilated remains of a young man were found in this spot along with a smart phone that contained this video. The girl remains missing, and the legend of the Woldwomper remains unsolved." Then, in silence once again, the video ended.

"Whoa," Mel said.

"Criminy. I wonder if Mike knows about this." Rory went to the living room to get her cell phone. If those idiots had been dumb enough to film their attack on Katie and Spike, it should be easy to track them down, she was thinking. Carrying her phone back toward the office, she navigated through her contacts and hit the button to dial Mike's personal number. Sure, she was still ticked off at him for having treated her as a "person of interest," a.k.a. "criminal," but she was bigger than some grudge-holding, insecure young girl, wasn't she? Maybe. Besides, this video would further prove exactly what she'd been telling everyone all along.

"Hey, hon," he answered, sounding worried. "Everything okay?" She did not often call him in the middle of the day like this.

"Mike, there's something you've got to see—a video on YouTube. It looks like it was made by whoever attacked Katie and Spike the other night."

Meanwhile, Mel had helped herself to Rory's chair and started up the video again.

"She is touching our stuff," Miss C meowed.

"It looks like these guys snuck around my garage and shot some video of Katie and Spike before they jumped out at them. That would match up with those footprints you all found."

"Really? You can identify them?" Mike asked.

Rory hated to dash his hopes of a case solved that easily. "No. You never see their faces, but all you have to do is find out who posted the video, right?"

He made a thoughtful sound and said, "We'll see. I'm not really up on YouTube."

Mel turned in the chair. "This would make a pretty good horror flick if, you know, it weren't real."

"Who's that?" Mike asked.

Letting out a breath, Rory answered, "It's Mel Scott. This video is going to be hitting the local paper tomorrow."

"Oh no," Mel interrupted. "This video is hitting the website today. We can't sit on this. Now, Rory, can you confirm with absolute certainty that this was filmed on your property?" The reporter had her notebook on the desk, her pencil poised above it as, on screen, the video was just reaching the point where Katie heard the first sound.

"I've got to go, Mike. There's a … situation here," Rory said into the phone, not bothering to respond to Mel for the time being.

"Right. Try not to give her too much, though if this is already on the internet, it may not matter how much you give her," Mike said.

"Read you loud and clear. Um … we'll talk later?"

"We will. Love you."

After a moment's hesitation, Rory replied, "Yeah, same here."

She ended the call and set her phone on the desk.

Mel proceeded with her questioning. "So, this is your property? You recognize it?"

"Yes, Mel, I recognize it. That is my garage, and that is my tree, and those are the people who were in town making a student film about … a local legend."

"The Woldwomper." Mel gave a low whistle. The video reached its end again, jumping suddenly from Katie and Spike's screams and terror-filled faces to a black screen and those stark words.

"That body they found out in your yard over the summer, that had something to do with the Woldwomper too, didn't it?"

Rory shut her eyes momentarily. "Yes," she admitted, not that it mattered. She was sure that Mel remembered perfectly well all the details of the skeletal remains that had been discovered in town during an archaeological dig this past summer.

"Wasn't that hole in almost the exact spot where Spike was killed?" Mel asked.

Her eyes going toward the big old maple halfway down her backyard, to where brown grass now covered the part of her lawn that had been dug up in a series of interconnected square excavation units, some of which had held the bones of a teenage girl who'd turned out to be a relative of hers, Rory said, "Yes, it's very close."

"Eerie."

"Coincidence," Miss C insisted. *"Let us try not to connect things that are not connected."*

"So. Mel, it's been great sharing this moment with you," Rory lied. "But I've got a lot of stuff to do, so..."

Mel pushed the chair back and stood. "Right, right, right," she said quickly. "I've got to get into the office and report this. Got to call the sheriff for comment. I wonder if Katie would talk to me." As she spoke, she was moving into the hallway, then the living room, where she collected her big blue purse and put on her coat. "Thanks for the computer and the info, Rory. I'm sure I'll be talking to you later."

And just that quickly, she was out the front door.

Chapter 17

Rory waited until she saw Mel's lime-green Beetle drive past her house on the way out of town. Then she said, "Miss C, we're going to Gunther's." Never mind that it was after three o'clock, hours past her usual coffee-and-gossip time. She pushed the cat stroller into the center of the living room and lifted the waiting cat into it.

"*I suspected as much,*" Miss C meowed during this process. "*I do not know what this u-tube is, but I see that it has provided unexpected evidence in our investigation. Do you suppose Hesiod would have put the story of Kronos devouring his children on this u-tube if he could? That would have been interesting.*"

"Criminy, cat, do you think you could make a little more noise?"

Miss C looked away disdainfully as Rory zipped up the stroller's front mesh panel. "*I forgot—you are mostly uneducated and are not familiar with Hesiod. What about Zeus? Have you heard of Zeus?*"

"Shh."

"*Shh yourself.*" Miss C could not quite believe she had meowed that. Professor Eleanor would never have said such a thing. The Rory person, on the other hand.... Could it be that Miss C was picking up some of her habits?

After strapping on her fanny pack and pulling on a light jacket, Rory pushed the stroller outside and headed toward the center of town. Surely the investigation would all be over soon, now that Mike had the evidence right there on video. Just find whoever uploaded it, and it would be case closed. Everyone could just forget about Rory's role in this episode. But...

Opening the door to Gunther's, she saw Liza sitting at her and Miss C's usual table, working on mug of a coffee and a blueberry muffin. It looked like she hadn't slept well. Rory knew that feeling. She wondered if her own sleepless nights showed on her face as clearly as Liza's did on hers. Madison sat on her stool behind the counter, her reading glasses perched on her nose. A magazine lay spread open before her.

Above the sound of the front door's bell jingling, Rory greeted them, "Hi, guys."

Madison greeted her by name and slid off the stool to reach for the blue-green mug on the wall behind her. "Rory, we've missed you these past couple mornings. What can I get you?" she asked.

"Coffee. Whatever's freshest," Rory answered.

"That'll be decaf. That okay? You look like you need something stronger after, uh..." Madison's sentence withered to a halt. She preferred not to ask directly about Rory's recent experience at the sheriff's department.

Rory knew exactly what she meant. "No, I'm okay. Decaf's fine." She parked the stroller at Liza's table and fished two dollar bills out of her fanny pack.

With her back turned while she filled the mug, Madison said, "I saw the sheriff brought you home yesterday morning."

This, Rory knew, was her friend's way of asking if things between them were still okay. "Yes, he did. After I gave my statement, he had to come up to look at the scene, so he gave me a ride." Her and Madison's eyes met as they exchanged cash for coffee, and Rory understood that her bright statement had been understood for what it was: a convenient lie.

"I noticed your name didn't show up in the paper," Madison commented.

Rory shrugged. "Well, I guess there is some advantage to dating the sheriff." She gave Madison a weak smile and carried the full mug back to the table while asking, "Liza, how's things down at the house?"

"Yes, how are things with the Queen of the Underworld?" Miss C meowed.

Liza rubbed her temples. "Tense. Sephie is just so ... so..."

"Underworldy?"

"Mean. At least she's leaving Gracie alone. So far."

Madison said, "I still can't believe she had the nerve to come back here, after what happened."

"Oh, she has plenty of nerve. Don't you worry about that," Liza countered. "If I can pick up another section to teach next semester, maybe Gracie and I can move, but right now, I can't afford to cover rent anywhere else. Every place down in Westbrook is so darned expensive. I'd have trouble paying for a studio apartment, and forget about a two-bedroom."

So that explained the lack of sleep. A sudden worry about money would do it every time, Rory mused.

"Well, it'll work out somehow," the mayor said.

Rory said, "Yeah. Somehow it'll all come together so you and Gracie can stay right here in Brooksford." I hope, she added silently.

Liza, less worried than Madison about asking an indelicate question, said, "What about you, Ror? Have you and Mike talked, since, you know...?"

"Oh sure, we've talked. We've established that I'm mad and he's scared. At least he better be scared," Rory joked. "But it'll work out," she added with false confidence.

"Well, you look like you should be in bed, I hope you don't mind me saying," the mayor said.

Liza agreed, too quickly, making Rory wonder if perhaps they had been discussing her situation just before she walked in. Wouldn't surprise her.

She said, "Actually, I came to tell you that I got a hot tip from Mel Scott."

Madison groaned aloud. "I knew she'd be out here poking around today. You didn't give her much, did you?" There was something pleading in her voice.

"No, she gave me something. Sort of. You've got to see this. It's on YouTube, and it's going to crack the case wide open. The people who attacked Katie and Spike made a video of it. Can you believe how stupid people are?"

"It astounds me every day," Miss C meowed.

"Does Mike know?" was Madison's first question.

"Yes. I called him right away, and he said he'd look into it. But come on, you've got to see it. Can we use your computer?"

Madison sighed, as though seeing a video of the latest violent incident in her small town was the last thing she'd hoped to be doing that day. "All right. Come back in the office. Liza, you coming?"

"Wouldn't miss it," Liza said as she finished off her muffin and stood to follow Madison to the back of the store and the door that led to her office. Rory followed last, pushing Miss C's stroller with one hand and carrying her hot mug of coffee with the other. It was a tricky balancing act.

They squeezed into the office, which was the size of a large walk-in closet, with a neatly arranged desk on one side and shelves holding cleaning supplies and other odds and ends on the other. The computer currently displayed a split-screen image of the store's two security cameras. Madison pressed keys on her keyboard to bring up a web browser, and Rory guided her through the process of finding the video. They watched it in silence.

When it was over, Madison said, "That is the creepiest thing I've ever seen."

"It's like a predator filming the hunt," Liza added.

"It's a pity you never see whoever did this. There's nothing to identify them," Madison added.

Rory said, "No, but once the sheriff's department figures out who uploaded it, that'll be game over. They'll make an arrest and we can all move on. When you think about it, there aren't too many suspects. It's got to be one of those other student filmmakers, doesn't it?" She had her early money on the quarterback and his wide receiver, not quite believing that those two disheveled-looking boys would be able to work up the gumption to do anything like this, not when they were so busy working on their meta thing. Besides, it was the quarterback who'd said they were making a horror flick, which this so obviously was. They snuck into her backyard to get some nighttime atmospheric shots, ran into Katie and Spike, and things got out of hand.

"What's this number down here?" Madison asked, interrupting her thoughts and pointing at the screen.

"Oh, that's just the number of views it's gotten," Rory explained.

"Two hundred thousand?" the mayor asked incredulously.

That got Rory's attention. "What? It was a hundred and fifty thousand just a little bit ago, and I thought that was kind of a lot."

Liza put in, "Oh no, it's going viral."

"Viral?" Madison asked, confused.

"That means it's getting to be really popular online, spreading like a virus. A lot of people are looking at it and sharing it."

"You're telling me people are sharing a video linking Brooksford, the Woldwomper, and a new murder?" Madison's tension level seemed to be rising, along with her voice, so that Rory was starting to regret coming here to share her "hot tip."

"Looks that way," Liza said regretfully.

Madison turned in her chair to look up at Rory. "You've got to tell the sheriff to shut this thing down. If this goes too far, we could be done for."

"I knew all along it would be something bad, this u-tube," Miss C meowed.

Rory rocked the stroller back and forth to try to quiet her cat. *"Stop moving me,"* the cat commanded.

"It probably won't be that bad, Madison. I'm sure Mike can get it taken down, since it shows a crime being committed," Rory tried to soothe her.

"I wouldn't be so sure," Liza said. "This doesn't actually show any crime, except maybe trespassing. But it's not illegal to jump out of a bush and scare somebody. That's all this video really shows."

Rory fretted. Could it be possible that this video would be not Brooksford's salvation but its downfall?

They were still discussing the video's implications when they all heard the front door's bell jingle.

"Someone is here," Miss C meowed helpfully.

"I've got to get out there. Customer," Madison said, weariness in her voice.

But then a voice called, "Mrs. Gunther? Liza?"

It was Grace. Lee must have dropped her off here after school.

"Gracie, honey, we're back here in the office," Liza called to her. "Come here and see this and tell us what you think."

Grace shuffled into the back saying, "S'up?"

Liza threw an arm around her and kissed her on the forehead, an action Grace struggled against, but not very convincingly.

"Stop. Jeez. Not in front of people."

The door's bell jingled again, and Madison stood. "I've got to mind my store. Here, Rory, you sit down and take the controls. Show them the video again. I'll just be right out here. Grace, you want a hot chocolate?"

"Yes, please."

"With extra whipped cream. Coming right up."

While Madison returned to the front of her store to greet her customer, Rory queued up the video again. "Okay, here we go." She hit play and sat back so Grace could lean in closer for a better look.

"That's your place," the girl observed when the garage came into view.

"Yes," Rory affirmed.

They watched to the video's end in silence. Then Grace muttered, "So whoever killed Spike filmed it?"

"Looks that way, honey," Liza said, putting a comforting hand on Grace's shoulder.

"But the sheriff knows all about it, and he's going to find whoever put this up on the internet, and then it'll be all over for them," Rory said reassuringly.

Grace shrugged and said, "If it's the same person."

"What do you mean, honey? It must have been shot by one of the people who were out there that night," Liza said.

"Yeah, but might have been uploaded by someone else," Grace observed.

Miss C purred. She wasn't sure what *uploaded* meant, but Grace surely did, and the confidence with which she said it told the cat that this half-baked girl was coming together nicely.

Worry began to niggle at the edges of Rory's mind. Could that be right? Could this great clue take them to a dead end?

Grace's soft voice intruded on her thoughts. "Eeks. Four hundred thousand views already. It's blowing up."

"Four hundred thousand...?" Rory looked at the counter and saw that the number had indeed passed that number.

"Refresh it," Grace instructed.

"Uh..." Rory said, moving the mouse randomly as she searched for whatever Grace wanted her to do.

Finally Grace just reached to take the mouse from her. "Up here," she said, clicking on the browser's refresh button. "Wow. Definitely viral." She pointed to the counter, which had gone up by another fifty thousand. "And the comments..."

Grace scrolled down through the latest comments, which were along the lines of "Where's Brooksford? Must be the spookiest place in America" and "Woldwomper? What the heck?"

Rory was aware of things slipping out of control, and mentally she reached out to try and bring them back, but there was nothing to grab on to, nothing to hold. The very thing they had all feared, that Brooksford would become forever linked in the popular imagination with the legend of the Woldwomper, was happening right before their eyes.

Chapter 18

They'd all been so engrossed in the video that they hadn't paid attention to what was happening out front, which was an impromptu argument between Sephie Rennsfelder and Frank Laser, owner of the Brooksford Inn. It was Sephie's voice that carried to them first.

"You'll thank me for it one day," she was saying, to which Frank replied, "Fat chance."

In the office, Rory muttered, "I see we're having another useful and intelligent discussion out there."

Grace sniggered. Rory queued up the video again. They were about halfway through it when Madison appeared in the doorway, Frank and Sephie trailing behind her. "You'll see what I mean in just a second. This town's got bigger troubles than yours. Oh, Rory, could you just start that again, please? These two need to see it."

Rory could understand why Madison would want Frank to see the video. He stood to either gain or lose business, depending on how this played out in the online world and beyond. Sephie ... well, she wasn't sure why Madison wanted Sephie to see it. Just to shut her up for minute, maybe.

Not worrying about the mayor's reasoning, she paused the video and set it to restart from the beginning.

"What is it I'm supposed to be looking at here, Mayor?" Frank asked as he squeezed in close to the desk.

"It was recorded in Rory's yard the other night, the night of the attack."

Sephie, still in the doorway, complained, "I can't fit in there, not with this cat stroller in the way."

Rory gave up her spot at the desk. "Here, someone else can sit down. I'll take Miss C out front so there's more room." Truth be told, she was glad for an excuse to duck out so she wouldn't have to stay in the room with Sephie, who seemed to have completely recovered her brash, overconfident, and extremely attractive self. It was all just a little too much.

The woman was partially blocking the doorway though, and refused to step aside, forcing Rory, and Liza after her, to squeeze by. Miss C hissed at Sephie as they went. Sephie gazed down at her and said, "That is a mean cat, Ms. Roberts."

Rory kept her few choice words to herself and pushed the stroller out into the main café area, not realizing until it was too late that she'd left her coffee behind. Well, there was no way she was going back in after it. No way, no how. Fortunately, Madison saved her, coming through the door with the blue-green mug in her hand.

"Here, Rory, looks like you left this behind," she said.

"Thanks," Rory said as she took the mug. She and Liza resumed their seats at the table, while Madison went back to her stool behind the counter.

"You're leaving those two in your office alone?" Liza asked, voicing the thought that had been on Rory's mind as well.

"That seems unwise," Miss C meowed.

Making a dismissive gesture, Madison said, "Grace is with them. If she comes out here with a worried look on her face, we'll know something's wrong."

Rory and Liza both nodded. Grace had worked part-time in Gunther's for a while now, stocking shelves and cleaning, doing just about everything except serve customers. Rory had never bothered to ask about the legality of it all, and she supposed the girl was paid in cash under the table. If Grace and Liza were happy with the arrangement, she was happy too.

"I wonder what Frank's going to have to say about that," Madison broke in on Rory's thoughts, with a head bob in the direction of the office.

"I'd say that's pretty predictable, wouldn't you?" Rory asked.

Liza soured her face and said, not too loudly, "'It's bad for business!' That's what he'll say."

The other two women laughed. They didn't have long to laugh though, before the trio who'd been watching the video returned from the office. Grace went straight to Madison and said, very softly, "I switched the computer back to the security system, Mrs. Gunther."

"Thank you, Grace. Oh, I completely forgot your hot cocoa. You sit down and I'll get that up for you right away." Madison stood and reached for a glossy black mug on the wall behind her.

"I ordered a coffee some time ago, Mayor," Sephie complained.

"Rude," Miss C observed. *"Do they not teach basic manners in the Underworld?"*

"It'll be right up," Madison said. "Now, tell us what you thought of that video. It's gone viral, Gracie told us."

Sephie seemed to be considering what to say, but Frank started right in with, "I'll tell you what I think. I think it's going to be terrible for business." Rory had to stop herself from laughing as she and Liza exchanged a look. "Just one more negative thing about Brooksford to hit the airwaves, and it'll drive people away. Nobody wants to visit a town where people get murdered left, right, and center. I hate to say it, Mayor, you know I hate to say it, but we might need to drop this whole Historic Brooksford thing. It's just not working out."

Madison set the mug of hot chocolate on the counter and added a generous shot of whipped cream to it, saying, "Hand this to Grace, would you, Frank?"

He obliged, and then opened his mouth to say more, but Sephie talked over him. "This is exactly why you need me," she said, adding, "Coffee?" quietly to Madison, who, in her thoughts about Frank's pronouncement, seemed to have forgotten the woman's order.

"Oh, right," the mayor said. She grabbed a to-go cup and filled it with dark brew.

"What do you mean, we need you?" Frank scoffed. "This town's gotten along for two hundred years without you."

"Yes, and just look at the state it's in. You're always reacting to something, when what you need to do is get out in front of things."

"You don't know what you're talking about," Frank dismissed her.

Madison shushed him and asked, "What do you mean, Sephie? How could we possibly be in front of this? We never expected anyone to kill that boy. We couldn't have predicted this video. And once the sheriff makes an arrest, this whole thing will blow over."

"It can't take long," Rory added. "Just round up those two other film crews and question them."

With a frustrated sigh, Sephie said, "You are all completely missing the point. It's time for Brooksford to really own its heritage, and it can start with that video, as disturbing as it is. Frank, you're complaining that it will be bad for business, but did you bother to read the comments section? People were saying they want to come here. That could be money in your pocket. It could be money for the town, but we're not ready for it." She pointed toward the office. "That video you're all complaining about is going to drive people right to this town, but we need to plan now if we're going to benefit from them."

A silence fell over the group. Could it be that Sephie knew what she was talking about, that people would flock to Brooksford just because of a weird three-minute internet video?

"I do not believe it," Miss C meowed loudly. *"Also, where were you when this video was being made, Queen of the Underworld? I ask because you seem to have a plan to profit from it."*

Finally Madison said, "I don't know, Sephie. What can we do?"

"Stop acting helpless," Sephie snapped at her.

Madison narrowed her eyes but said nothing.

Then Sephie visibly collected herself and apologized. "I'm sorry for my tone, Mayor, but not for my words. This isn't a time for saying 'What can we do?' like there's no good answer. This is a time to say, 'What can we do to turn this to our advantage?' You see what I'm saying?"

Rory suddenly understood just how it was that Sephie Rennsfelder had gotten so far in her career. She'd been a bank vice president before she'd lost her mind over Brooksford and tumbled from her throne right into the county jail. But she didn't see adversity as a setback; instead she saw it as just one more opportunity, one more thing to turn to her advantage. And surely the woman's supermodel good looks didn't hurt, either.

Madison seemed to be thinking over what Sephie had said. They all were.

Surprisingly, it was Grace who spoke. "We should reply to the comments. If people say they want to visit, we could welcome them, tell them about the inn and stuff." She mumbled her way through what Rory was pretty sure was the girl's longest speech since her arrival in Brooksford. They all heard her loud and clear though.

The look on Frank's face said that he was completely stunned. "You can do that?" he asked, as though asking if Grace could spin straw into gold.

Grace shrugged one shoulder. "Sure. You just do it."

"You see," Sephie took over again, "we need a plan and someone in charge of it. Someone to get in front of this story and own it." As she said this, she raised one hand to shoulder height and formed a tight fist as though she'd just grabbed something out of the air.

"But who could we get to do that? We'd need a public relations person, wouldn't we, someone who knows how to do this sort of thing?" Madison asked, looking around at all of them.

Sephie sighed again. To Miss C, it sounded like the breath of the Underworld rushing into this world to some nefarious end. "Me. You've got me. I know how to do all this. I know how to spin something negative into a positive." She pointed a thumb toward herself with each "me" and "I."

"We have to call a town meeting so we can decide what to do and who should be in charge of it," Frank said. "Now the earliest we could probably do it would be—"

That was when Sephie grabbed her head in both hands and made a strangled screaming sound. "No! There's no time to call a meeting in forty-seven days or however long it would take you people to do anything. Don't you understand? We need to take action now. Right now. Now."

She might have said "now" again, but Madison stopped her. "I think we understand what you're saying, Sephie. And since I'm the mayor of this town, I appoint you to be in charge of handling our response to this ... unfortunate event."

Frank protested, "Mayor, you can't just do that. This is a democracy, and I remind you that your position is mostly ceremonial."

Madison held up a hand to stop him from going further. "As mostly ceremonial mayor, I hereby appoint Sephie as mostly ceremonial head of PR. There's no pay, Sephie. I hope you understand."

Waving off that comment, Sephie said, "Of course I understand. I'm not worried about pay. My only concern is the future good of Brooksford. Now, Grace, tell me more about adding replies to these comments. How do you do that, exactly?"

Grace shrank into herself under Sephie's gaze, but she managed to say, "You just do it," with a shrug, as though someone had asked her how to breathe.

"I'm going to need you to work on that with me," Sephie pronounced.

That prompted Liza to throw a protective arm over Grace's shoulders. "You'll need my permission before she can help you with anything, Sephie. And of course Grace will have to agree."

"Oh, settle down, Liza. I'm not going to eat her."

"You look like you might eat her and enjoy cracking her bones to get at their marrow, Queen of the Underworld," Miss C meowed. *"Are you acquainted with Kronos?"*

Sephie chuckled at her own comment, which she'd apparently meant as a joke. Then she said, "I just need her to help come up with responses to these people. Obviously Grace knows more about YouTube than any of us, right?"

Liza relaxed almost imperceptibly, and Grace said, "It's okay. I'll help. For the town."

"Excellent," Sephie said. "I suppose we'd better work on your computer back at the house." She turned to Frank. "Mr. Laser, you'd better get that inn polished up, because you're about to have a whole lot of business."

Chapter 19

By the time Rory and Miss C got home, the Brooksford bells were tolling a quarter after four. Rory wandered into the office, intending to work for an hour or so before dinner, which she had earlier decided would be a delicious chicken pot pie, pulled from her freezer and warmed in the microwave. She could already taste the golden crust, the creamy gravy, the chunks of chicken and vegetables. And for dessert she had fresh chocolate chip cookies she'd just bought from Gunther's. Between her fantasies about food and her worries over how easily Sephie had created a new position for herself as Brooksford's head of PR, Rory did not manage to get a single thing done. Instead she pushed the computer monitors aside so she could stare into the backyard, adding thoughts of Spike and questions about what had happened to him into her mental mix. Well, if this was all she was going to do, she might as well stop and eat.

"Come on, Cuddlywumps," she said to the cat as she pushed her chair back and stood. "Let's eat early tonight. I'm hungry, and we're not accomplishing anything."

"I am accomplishing something," the cat meowed. *"I am thinking about our case."*

Still lying down in her bed on the desk corner, Miss C stretched, letting her limbs spill over the bed's edges, then she slowly stood and stretched some more.

"You're turning that into a project, cat," Rory said, leaving the room.

"Stretching is a project. You should pay more attention to it. Perhaps then you would be more agreeable."

The cat jumped to the floor and trotted after Rory.

They were in the kitchen, Miss C eating and Rory waiting for her pot pie to heat, when Rory's cell phone rang. "Lee calling," the screen told her.

"Hey, what's what?" she answered.

His reply, "Did you know there's a film crew in front of your house?" made her forget all about eating.

"A film crew? You mean like more students?" That was all they needed, more kids to get involved in trying to make arty videos at their town's expense. Leaving the pot pie to take care of itself, Rory headed into the living room and went straight to the front window, Miss C at her heels.

"What film crew? More Hesiods?" the cat meowed. The addition of more mythmakers would certainly add a new wrinkle to their case. *"Ah, a development develops,"* she added, quoting what Professor Eleanor always said when they reached a surprising twist in whatever mystery they were reading aloud together. The cat ran to the window and jumped onto her condo in anticipation.

There, just across the street, was white a van with a huge 3 painted on its side in two shades of blue. Atop the van was a satellite antenna. Nearby, a man stood with a large camera perched on his shoulder, and there right outside Rory's window stood a blond woman, her back to the cottage as she seemed to be speaking into a microphone toward the camera across the street.

The cameraman took his eye away from the camera and said something to the woman, prompting her to turn and look into the window. At first glance, she did not look pleased to see a woman and a cat in her shot, but a heartbeat later, she managed a smile and moved toward the front door.

"Criminy, Lee, you won't believe who's out here. I've gotta go. Call you back soon," Rory said, speaking quickly into the phone. She ended the call and opened the door before the woman could knock.

"Hello. I'm Jacey Jones, Channel Three News," the blonde said with a big smile as she extended her right hand. She was shorter than Rory might have expected, but also thinner. *I guess the camera really does add ten pounds,* Rory thought.

She stammered, "Yes, I know. I've watched you for years. Your channel, I mean. The news." Words failed her at that point, and she decided she'd better let Jacey talk for a moment. Criminy. Jacey Jones was an institution, a personality. She had been the star reporter for Channel Three News for ... for ... well, since Rory was in college, at least. It was surreal to see her right there on the steps, in her trademark blue trench coat with the Channel Three pin on the lapel.

"Oh, is your cat supposed to be getting out?" Jacey asked, with a glance toward Rory's feet.

"Cat?" What cat? For the moment, Rory almost forgot she had a cat. She used one foot to shoo Miss C back inside.

"I want to see!" the cat protested. *"I must see this new Hesiod."*

"She's really cute," Jacey said, and she crouched down to pet Miss C. "I just adore cats. What's her name?" She smiled back up at Rory. Tiny lines crinkled around her eyes and mouth. She looked older than she did on TV, but prettier too.

"Name? Oh, uh ... Miss C. Her name is Miss C."

"That must be short for something."

"Yes. Cuddlywumps."

Jacey chuckled as she straightened up again. "That's adorable. You must be Rory Roberts."

"Yes."

If Jacey noticed that Rory seemed to have forgotten most of the English language, she didn't show it.

"I guess you know why I'm out here."

"Um.... No."

"Oh!" Jacey sounded surprised. "Well, this is where that poor boy was killed the other night, isn't it? This is where that video was made?"

"Oh, that," Rory said, and then kicked herself mentally. Criminy, she was making it sound like murder was so routine in Brooksford, she'd forgotten about the latest one. "Um, yes."

"Would you be willing to talk to me about that? On camera? I wish I could have gotten here earlier to get more on film before it gets dark, but I'll be doing a live shot for the six o'clock show."

"Live?" Rory squeaked.

"Or maybe we could tape something just real quick. If it makes you uncomfortable, I could just interview you off camera. That would be okay, wouldn't it?" Jacey was smiling again, as though it would be impossible to refuse her.

And Rory found it was impossible. "Yes, that'd be fine." She heard the microwave ding, signaling that her pot pie was ready, but she did not care.

"May I come in?"

"Oh! Of course. I'm sorry. I don't know what I'm thinking. Long day."

"Well, I can't imagine how you can sleep very well, what with everything that's happened," Jacey suggested as she entered Rory's cottage.

"Yeah, it's got everyone on edge."

"So, I understand you had Katie and Spike right here in your home the day before the incident. I don't suppose you'd mind if we shot a little bit in here, just for some atmosphere? Were they in this room?"

And just like that, Jacey Jones talked her way into Rory's home, cameraman and all. Rory stood back in the hallway and watched as the small scene developed, Jacey standing near the fireplace, in the same corner Spike had stood in, as her camera guy panned slowly around the room, starting with Miss C sitting regally in the window and ending on the reporter. Jacey said a few lines. Then stopped and said, "No, no, that's not right. Let's do it the other way. Get some shots around the fireplace and then get me standing over here by the cat."

They shot it that way, trying half a dozen different takes until Jacey seemed satisfied, and then she said, "Would you mind taking us out back to where it happened, Ms. Roberts?"

Rory obliged, taking them through her kitchen and then the laundry/mudroom, down the back steps and toward the garage.

"This is the garage that can be seen in the video, isn't it?" Jacey asked.

"Yes. Katie and Spike were out there under the tree." Rory pointed into her yard where, in the failing light, the tree and its fallen leaves could still be seen.

"We're going to need lights back here, Ron," Jacey said to her camera guy. "I want to do the live shots there, near the tree. If we open on the garage and then zoom in to me back there—you think?"

"You got it, Jace."

Before she knew it, Rory had told Jacey the whole story, while they watched Ron set up lights at the garage and near where the reporter planned to stand.

"I'll have to walk it toward you, Jace," Ron said. "Maybe get some shots in the grass, you know?"

"Yeah, yeah, that's great. Let's move it though. We're running out of time."

Rory saw that she would mostly be in the way, so she went back inside and called Lee, who answered on the first ring. "Ror, what's going on back there? What's with the lights?"

"Lee, you'll never guess who's just been in my house, who's in my yard right now," Rory said breathlessly. Not waiting for Lee to make any guesses, she added, "Jacey Jones."

"No. Really?"

"Yeah. You want to come over? Oh, and tell your mom that they're doing a live shot at six."

"You mean a live shot from here? Are you going to be in it?"

Rory explained, and Lee agreed to be at her back door in two minutes.

He arrived right on time, a plastic container in his hands. "Mom sent you some brownies, and some for Jacey too. I'll get to meet her, won't I?"

"I guess you will. Come inside so we're not in the way. She's only got about half an hour until her shot."

They took the cookies into Rory's bedroom, where Lee sat in the chair at the bedside while Rory switched on the television and turned it to channel three. Miss C leapt onto the bed and sat in the center of it.

"Why are we back here?" she meowed loudly. *"Why are we not keeping an eye on this Jacey so-called Jones who is doing strange things in our yard?"*

"Shh. I know it's not time for bed, but we're just going to watch this one little thing," Rory comforted her. The cat eyed her disdainfully. "I want you to be real quiet, okay?"

"We'll see," the cat meowed.

Lee watched from the chair, smiling and shaking his head. "It's cute how you two understand each other."

"Shut up." Rory would have given him a friendly punch on the shoulder, but she couldn't quite reach him.

They watched the tail end of the five o'clock news and then the beginning of the six o'clock show. Rory hadn't watched that much television news in years, preferring to get most of her information from newspapers and websites these days, though she still caught the Channel Three News on occasion. The anchors talked about weather, traffic, and politics, and then a shooting down in the city. Then one of them said, "And now Channel Three's Jacey Jones brings us an exclusive look into a small Maryland town that's suddenly an internet sensation for all the wrong reasons. Jacey?"

The shot cut to Rory's garage, and Rory pointed at the television, saying stupidly, "That's my garage!"

"Shh," Lee quieted her.

"This garage in the tiny hamlet of Brooksford, Maryland, has become a familiar sight on the internet in the past twenty-four hours, just days after a horrific crime was committed here—a crime that was apparently filmed by the perpetrators." The camera was moving now, so they saw Rory's lawn going by as the cameraman approached Jacey. "Just two nights ago, someone ran across this lawn, someone with nefarious intent, someone with murder on their mind. They ran right up here, to where two local college students were filming for a class project." The camera was on Jacey now, and she stood in the pose that was so familiar, with a microphone in her left hand and a yellow legal pad in her right. On that pad, Rory knew, were the notes Jacey had scrawled during their interview. "Before it was over, one of those students would lie here dead, and the other was so terrified she could hardly speak. But it turns out that was only the beginning."

Here Jacey paused, and the recorded package began. It opened on the Historic Brooksford sign at the south end of town, then came up Main Street, ever closer to Rory's house, and then into the living room and those lines Jacey had recorded there. It mentioned how the homeowner who'd gone to render aid had first been accused in the crime, only to be fully cleared when the accuser changed their story. Police had yet to identify a new suspect. "Spike spent part of his last afternoon here in this room, working on that project with his friend Katie. Now it seems that the legend of the Woldwomper has been loosed on this village. The question is, how far will it go?"

Rory's cell phone rang as soon as the story ended. "Madison calling," the screen told her. Criminy.

Chapter 20

The mayor sounded frantic. "Rory, what is going on? Why has Jacey Jones been reporting live from your backyard?"

"Well, Madison," Rory said and then paused to think of what to say that might calm her friend. She could think of nothing, so she tried the truth. "She just showed up here this afternoon, and I guess things might have gotten out of hand."

"Oh, you think so?" the mayor said sarcastically. Rory could picture her shaking her head and tugging at her earring. "It is bad enough to have Mel Scott get hold of a story out here, but to have it broadcast to most of the state..."

Rory's phone made another sound. "Dad calling," the screen told her. Uh-oh.

Her parents lived in a comfortable retirement community over on the Eastern Shore. Surely they didn't get the Channel Three News, did they?

"Listen, Madison, we'll talk in the morning, okay? My dad's calling now." With some quick thinking and lucky jabbing at buttons, Rory managed to get from Madison's call to her father's without hanging up on the wrong one.

When she greeted him, her father said, "Rory, what is going on up there? We just saw on the news that some boy was murdered in your backyard and it has something to do with the Woldwomper?"

Okay, so they did get Channel Three News. Great.

"Yeah, Dad. A boy did die, but no, it had nothing to do with the Woldwomper, at least not directly."

"Your mother and I think you'd better pack up and come here for a while. Bring your cat, that Mrs. K."

"Miss C," Rory corrected. She knew what was happening. Mom had decided that their daughter needed to get out of Brooksford until it was safe to walk the streets again, and she'd recruited Dad into convincing Rory to come. "And do you really think I need to come over there? I mean, I've got a lot of work to do here, and I don't want to just leave when there's so much going on right here on my property." That would sway him, because "her property" had been in her father's family for generations, since the late eighteenth century. In a way, it was his property too.

When he didn't reply right away, she knew she had him. "Dad?" she prompted.

His voice was hushed when he answered. "Okay, Ror, I don't really think you should leave either, but your mother's in a bit of a state over this. Just be careful, okay? Is Mike there?" he asked hopefully. Because having her sheriff boyfriend there would make everything better.

"No. He's kind of busy these days, what with a murder to solve and everything."

"Are you sure you're okay? It said you were a suspect."

Hearing the worry in her father's voice, Rory said, "Oh, that was nothing. Katie was just kind of confused, and things got overblown." It was probably best not to mention that she had been handcuffed and taken to the station. She was just thankful that that particular detail hadn't come up in Jacey's story.

"Of course." Then her father's voice rose to a normal level suddenly, and Rory understood that her mother had come into the room. "Well, we're not happy about this, not happy at all. But as long as Mike's keeping a close eye on things..."

"I'll be fine, Dad."

Rory heard her mother's voice in the background, and then her father said, "Uh, are you sure you don't want to come here for Thanksgiving?"

"Mike and I are planning on going to Madison's. She's fixing a big dinner. Besides, I thought you guys were eating at your community center."

"We were, but your mother says she can cook if—"

"No," Rory interrupted, knowing how much her parents had been looking forward to a no-muss, no-fuss holiday. "There's no reason to change plans now." She was going to say more, but someone knocked on her front door, while at the same time, someone else knocked on her back door. Miss C meowed. "Criminy. Listen, Dad, I've got to go. Things are crazy around here right now. We'll talk soon, okay?"

She ended the call without waiting to hear whether it was okay. Her parents were just going to have to deal with it.

"Lee, would you mind getting one of those?" she asked as they left the bedroom together with Miss C leading the way up the hall.

"Sure. I'll get the back," Lee replied, a little too quickly.

Rory had to laugh. "You're just hoping it'll be Jacey Jones, and she'll take one look at you and fall madly in love."

"A guy can hope, can't he?" Lee said as he walked into the kitchen.

Shaking her head, Rory went through the living room to the front door. When she opened it, she wished for a moment that she'd sent Lee to get this one. "Sephie. What a nice surprise," she lied. There the woman stood wearing an above-the-knee skirt with matching blazer and a blouse unbuttoned a little too far, which undoubtedly meant she'd just come from meeting a man. Wasn't she cold out there in that get-up? "Um... You want to come in?"

"Indeed I do, Ms. Roberts. I've just returned home from an important meeting, only to find that you let a television reporter onto your property without consulting me first.

Why?" she demanded as she burst into the living room. Her hair was arranged in her usual messy bun. Perfume wafted in after her—a little spicy, not too flowery, not the sort that got up your nose and made you sneeze. It was nice, Rory admitted. And were those earrings real diamonds? "This has an effect on our Historic Brooksford efforts, you know."

"Well, Sephie, as you yourself pointed out, it is my property," Rory shot back. This woman might turn out to be some kind of PR genius, but all Rory knew about her at the moment was that she was a cat-hating, self-concerned, as-yet-to-be-reformed criminal.

"I thought we all agreed this afternoon to let me handle the PR parts of this effort."

"No, we agreed to let you handle the response to the YouTube thing."

"And what do you think that reporter was doing back there? That was part of the 'YouTube thing.'" Sephie's tone put quotes around the words.

At that moment, Lee appeared, standing uncertainly in the kitchen doorway. Jacey Jones stood behind him.

"Uh, Ror ... Jacey wanted to thank you for, uh..." He seemed as star struck as Rory herself had been.

Sephie, however, was not star struck at all. She put a big, welcoming smile on her face and stepped forward before Rory could collect her thoughts enough to realize what was happening, much less form a verbal response. "Ms. Jones, what a pleasure to meet you. I'm Sephie Rennsfelder. I handle PR for this little town." The two women shook hands.

"I didn't know Brooksford had a PR person," Jacey said.

Sephie waved the comment off. "Oh, it's a brand-new thing. We felt we needed some strong guidance to get us through this little ... incident."

"Of course."

"Listen, I don't even have a card to give you, my position is just that new, but"—Sephie had somehow produced a small pad of paper and a pen from her purse, but Rory couldn't recall seeing her reach for them—"I'm going to write my cell number and email down for you, and if you have any questions at all, or if you'd like to set up further interviews, just give me a buzz, will you? Maybe I could set something up with the mayor for you. How does that sound?"

Jacey accepted the piece of paper, glanced at it, and slipped it into the pocket of her trench coat. "We'll see how this story goes. If we need more, I'll give you a call."

"Good, good. No, you don't need to scuttle out through the back door. You go right out through the front. I know your van is just outside," Sephie said, guiding the reporter through the living room, past Rory, and out the front door. When she closed the door again with Jacey Jones on the other side of it, she turned to Rory and said, "And that, Ms. Roberts, is how you deal with reporters."

"But she wanted to thank me for—"

"That's no matter now. What we have to do now is think about how this is likely to affect us. She made the story seem pretty dark."

"Well, it is dark."

"Right, but she drew it all right back to this Woldwomper business. It might turn out okay for us, but in future, it's very important that these sorts of things be handled by someone who knows what they're doing. I just hope you haven't done too much damage. No lone guns in future, Ms. Roberts. We sink or swim together on this."

"Yes, but—"

"No buts. Say, are you sure you wouldn't want to turn this place into a little antiques shop? It would take some investment up front of course, but—"

Rory interrupted her, "No. We've been through all this before, remember? I live and work in this house. No room for antiques, no time to run a store."

Sephie made a face. "Minor issues, which I think we've also talked about before. You could convert the garage to living and working space. Surely you and your little cat would be very comfortable there."

"No," Rory said flatly.

"Absolutely not. Classically educated cats do not live in garages," Miss C added.

"Okay, point taken. But just think about it, would you? It would mean so much for our plans for the town. Now, I have a lot of work to do, so ta-ta!" And with that, the woman was out the door.

"What just happened here?" Rory asked as she stood, bewildered, in the center of her living room.

"I think Sephie Rennsfelder is your boss now," Lee told her.

Making a move toward the window, Rory reached it just in time to see the Channel Three van pulling away from the curb. "But I didn't even get Jacey's autograph," she lamented.

Chapter 21

Contrary to what Sephie or Frank or Madison or any other Brooksfordian thought might happen, the town did not fall to pieces overnight. In fact, the remainder of that evening and the night passed peacefully. The only thing that changed was the rising number of views on their viral video.

The next day, Rory and Miss C woke at their usual time, Miss C had her breakfast of chicken-dinner cat food, and the two of them settled onto the sofa together for a look at the morning news on Rory's tablet. There was nothing surprising in the *Brooksford Examiner*'s front-page story, which was titled "Viral video lands tiny Brooksford on bigger map" and featured the tale of how the video none of them had known even existed had suddenly turned up on the internet and garnered 1.5 million views and counting. Mel's story contained a few quotes from Rory and told how she, the local sheriff's longtime girlfriend, who had initially been questioned as a person of interest in the case, had been the one to alert him to the video. It made no mention of how Mel had alerted Rory to the video. Investigation was ongoing. There was a whole separate story, also under Mel's byline, about Jacey Jones's visit to Brooksford. Rory had to wonder how Mel felt about another reporter moving in on her beat.

"You think she likes that, Miss C?"

"About as much as Prometheus enjoyed having his liver eaten," the cat meowed back at her.

"Yeah, you're probably right. I'll bet she'd wet her pants if she even got to be in the same room as Jacey. Hey, it'll be neat if Channel Three comes back to do another story, won't it?"

Miss C pointedly got to her feet and went to her condo to look out the front window.

After her own breakfast of several handfuls of sugary cereal eaten straight out of the box, Rory settled in to work for a couple of hours, first tackling her monitor situation. It would not do to have these two beautiful monitors and only be able to use one of them. A brief search on YouTube led her to a video that demonstrated exactly how to configure the computer's display settings, and voila, her second monitor lit up, doubling her screen space. Relieved to be reminded that the video site wasn't just for exploitative shorts made by criminals, she did an email check, answered a few messages, and prepared a price estimate for editing a short novel for a new potential client who'd been referred by an old client. It would be a nice week's work, if the author accepted her price.

By then the Brooksford bells were chiming ten. Break time. Her plan was to hit the post office to fetch the day's mail and stop by Gunther's on her way back, but as soon as she opened her front door, she knew things were going to go sideways. She knew this because there was a young woman standing on her top step, striking a pose while a friend on the sidewalk snapped a picture with her phone.

"Excuse me," Rory said to the woman's back.

"Yes, excuse us. You are on our step," Miss C added from inside her stroller.

It seemed that the cat's meowing had more effect than Rory's words. The young woman turned, delight on her face. "April, it's the cat that lives in the Woldwomper house. Get a picture of me with it." And she sat down on the step and smiled toward her photo-snapping friend.

"Hey, would you mind getting off my step?" Rory asked, trying hard to control herself and not say anything stupid that might get recorded on that phone and broadcast to the world via social media. That was all they needed.

"Yes, move," Miss C meowed.

The woman stood, huffing, "Okay, okay, I'm moving. Jeez. Crazy old bat." She stomped to the sidewalk and went off with her friend. "Can you believe how rude she was?" the friend asked.

"You're rude," Miss C meowed.

But if Rory thought she was done after those two were out of her way, she was sadly mistaken. The day's cold weather didn't seem to be deterring anyone from coming out. Main Street was unusually busy, as were the sidewalks, particularly the area near her house, which was attracting mostly college-age visitors like a beacon. "That's the house," Rory heard more than once as someone suddenly pointed toward her little stone cottage. She and Miss C had gotten used to some level of attention after they'd been featured in several of Mel's stories over the past couple of years, but this seemed different, less friendly. Didn't these people have anything else to do on a Wednesday morning? She wondered if someone had put the word out that she was giving away free pizza and beer.

The smell of wood smoke tickled at her nostrils, and she imagined the warmth of a bright, crackling fire. That would sure be a lot more pleasant than this walk through a crowd of gaping twenty-somethings.

They made their way into the south end and to the post office, where there was less of a crowd. Rory pushed open the glass door and maneuvered Miss C's stroller inside. Mrs. Crabtree, the town's postmaster, as well as Rory's next-door neighbor and nemesis, stood leaning on the front counter, scowling. She did not bother to say anything, but the sign reading No Animals Allowed still hung on the wall next to the counter. The postmaster's eyes went from Miss C to the sign to Rory, who ignored the look.

"Morning, Mrs. Crabtree," Rory said in the friendliest voice as she could muster.

Mrs. Crabtree grunted something that might have been a hello, though Rory would not have put money on it.

"Any idea what's going on out there?" Rory asked as she made her way to the wall of antique brass-fronted post office boxes and inserted a key in hers. It was stuffed with catalogs of exciting Christmas gifts she wouldn't buy. Still, it never hurt to have a browse through them. She stuffed them into the handy carrying pouch on Miss C's stroller.

Mrs. Crabtree said nothing. Unusual. She always had some rude retort, especially when Rory had Miss C along.

"Mrs. Crabtree? Are you okay?" Rory asked, against her better judgment. Still, if a person acted out of character, you did have to check and make sure they weren't having some sort of medical emergency, didn't you? She looked at her neighbor's face and saw more than the usual scowl. There was a droopiness to the eyes, her mouth had a more pronounced downturn than usual. Was she ... sad? "Um..." Rory hovered, feeling she should say something else but unsure of what that might be.

Finally Mrs. Crabtree spoke. "Would you go on and get that cat out of here?" Then she pointed to her No Animals Allowed sign.

"Medusa," Miss C hissed, using the name she'd bestowed on this unpleasant woman who hated Rory, hated cats, and had a mess of curly hair like a writhing snakes' nest atop her head.

"Sure," Rory said meekly and hurried back to the sidewalk.

Something was definitely up with that woman. Maybe Madison would know what it was.

But when she got to Gunther's, Rory started to have doubts about whether she'd be able to have her usual relaxed chat with the mayor. The place was busy with customers who were roaming through the sparse convenience store–style shelving, standing at the counter to order drinks ... sitting at her table. Both Madison and her usual helper, Laura Williams, were being kept busy behind the counter. Rory stopped short just inside the door, wondering if perhaps she should try back later, but Madison caught her eye and pointed toward the back door that led to the office. "Meet me at the back," the look said. As Rory turned Miss C's stroller to wheel it outside again, she saw the mayor pull her blue-green mug from its peg and heard her say, "You can hold down the fort for a few minutes, can't you, Laura? I need to talk to Rory."

After walking down the narrow alley that led to Gunther's back door, Rory waited no more than two seconds before she heard the door unlock from inside. She scooted in with the cat stroller while Madison held the door open. On the desk sat her mug, full nearly to the brim with coffee. The computer monitor displayed the feed from the two security cameras out front. There must be twenty people out there, Rory estimated—a huge crowd for this store.

"I got you a pumpkin spice. Hope that's okay," Madison said, her voice sounding brighter, more energized than usual.

"That's fine. Thanks. What's going on out there?" Rory replied, pointing to the monitor.

Madison removed her reading glasses from where they perched on her nose, letting them dangle from the light chain around her neck. "The best day's business I've had in years, that's what's going on," she said. "It's all down to that video, and then that story on Channel Three News last night. I already talked to Sephie, and she said we should all just brace ourselves for the weekend, when more people will be off work and school. These people"—she bent her head toward the front of the store—"are mostly college kids ditching class for the day. Some of them drove over an hour to get here."

"Well, some of them were on my front step when I opened the door this morning."

"Oh, that's not very nice. You might have to put up a sign or something, at least until this dies down."

Something in Madison's voice made Rory think she wasn't eager to see any of this die down. "Don't tell me you're enjoying this. Your place is a madhouse, and you think it's going to get worse?"

Madison shrugged. "Well, a few days' good business never hurt anyone. Maybe Sephie was right, and all this mess we've been through will turn into a positive."

"I would not count on it," Miss C meowed. *"Let us not forget that one person has already died. And we now have both Medusa and the Queen of the Underworld living in our town. Surely that is a negative."*

Rory shushed the cat and said, "A positive? Yesterday you were wringing your hands over it, and today you think it's going to be positive, all because you're making a few bucks? Madison, this is the future of our town we're talking about."

"Yes, think of the future. Think of innocent people being turned to stone or dragged to the Underworld."

Madison looked down at Miss C. "My perspective has evolved. We have to be realistic. That video is out there, and there's no way we can stop these people from coming here. Might as well make a tidy profit while they're here, you know?" she added in a whisper.

Miss C meowed again, and Madison said, "Uh, Rory, after you came in the front a little bit ago, I heard some people complaining about there being a cat in the store…"

"You're not seriously telling me you're going to ban Miss C, are you?" Rory asked indignantly. "Because if she can't come, I'm not coming."

That brought a new, worried look to Madison's face that reminded Rory of one of the things she meant to ask her. "Nobody's banning anyone. It's just that if someone complains to the health department, I could get shut down. Maybe we three could meet back here."

"You want me to come through the back door, like some kind of riffraff?" Rory tried to sound hurt, but considering the crowd out front, the back door sounded like a nice alternative.

"It's not that I want you to—"

"Forget it. I don't care. Back door, front door ... it doesn't really matter, does it? As long as I get some good coffee and get to talk to you." Rory went for a quick change of subject. "I wanted to ask you about Mrs. Crabtree. Do you know if there's anything going on with her?"

"No, why?"

"I don't know, she just seemed kind of sad or something this morning. It was weird."

"I haven't heard anything. Although come to think of it, I haven't seen Mr. Crabtree in several days. I do hope they're okay. It's very neighborly of you to care so much about her, given how she's treated you over the years."

Rory shrugged that off. "I probably imagined it anyway. Who can tell with her?"

"Yes, gorgons are inscrutable," Miss C meowed. *"Perhaps she has finally turned her husband to stone. Have any new statues appeared in town?"*

Madison was about to say something more when there was a knock at the door and it opened. Laura stuck her face in and said, "Madison, Sheriff Davis is out here to talk to you."

"Oh, send him back here, would you? And get him a coffee or something on the house if he wants it. By the bye, Rory, yours is on the house too—to make up for the inconvenience."

A moment later, Sheriff Mike Davis strolled through the door carrying a to-go cup with a lid on it.

"Morning, Mayor," he said, adding, "Rory," as he bent to kiss her on the cheek. It was the first time his lips had touched her since the "person of interest" incident, and it felt nice, she decided, although she was still a little ticked off at him.

They both mumbled greetings to him, and he went on, "Mayor, I see you're getting some benefit from Brooksford's latest misadventure."

"Well, we've got to take any advantage we're given," she said. "I don't expect it'll last once things die down after this murder."

"Poor choice of words, unless you were trying to be cute, in which case, poor choice of words," Miss C meowed, drawing Mike's attention to her.

"Is Miss C here helping with your security?" Mike asked, indicating the computer screen and its split view of the sidewalk outside the café and the front of the store.

Madison shook her head. "Oh, no. Rory and I just came back here to get away from the crowd."

"I hope you're here to tell us you've caught whoever put that video up," Rory put in.

That led Mike to shake his head. "Unfortunately, it's not that easy. We did find the person who uploaded the video to YouTube. He's some fifteen-year-old kid in California who I guess is kind of known for editing these creepy-type videos. Local law enforcement talked to him, found out he got the raw video from someone else, anonymously, and he edited it into something 'sick,' I believe is the word he used, and put it up there. Claims he never knew there was anything criminal involved. The person who sent it to him said it was video of a prank among friends."

"But surely you, or someone, can just track it back through the person who sent it," Rory suggested.

Another head shake. "Again, not that easy. This California kid has some kind of online mailbox that's open to his subscribers, so they can just leave video in it, and he'll take it and try to make something of it."

"You know who we need on this case," Madison said.

"Who?" Mike and Rory said together.

"Grace." The mayor nodded her head as though there could be no further word on the matter.

Mike said, "With all due respect, Mayor, I don't think a fourteen-year-old—"

"Fifteen, I'm pretty sure she's fifteen now," Rory put in.

"A fifteen-year-old girl then."

"And you did just say that the kid doing the video uploading is fifteen."

"Regardless, I don't think getting Grace involved would be helpful. We've got experts on this, both here and in California, and the kid that edited the video is cooperating. Besides, there's been one murder already, and we don't know that things won't get dangerous. We don't want Grace in the middle of something like that."

Madison shrugged noncommittally. "Well, is the video being taken down?" The way she asked the question, Rory couldn't tell what answer she hoped to hear—yes or no.

"No. I've been told that there's not much use in that, because it's already been shared so much, a lot of people already have it on their own computers. It doesn't show anything illegal. Law enforcement out in California did seize the raw footage and are going over it. Apparently, the kid was telling the truth. There's nothing in it that suggests a crime was committed."

"So this isn't likely to stop anytime soon?" Madison asked with a gesture toward the front of her store.

"Well, it's not for me to say, of course, but I'd guess not."

Madison smiled.

Chapter 22

When Rory went into her office to work for the rest of the day, Miss C, oddly, chose to stay in the living room, watching the goings-on outside from the comfort of her condo. Well, there were more people out there than usual, so Rory supposed the front must be more interesting. Probably a good thing—Miss C was a pretty good watch cat. At least for the balance of the day, their visitors had been better behaved than that girl this morning. Rory had half expected to see people wandering up her driveway to get a good look at her now famous garage, but so far none had. They stayed on the sidewalk snapping selfies.

A newish client had sent her a paper to edit, saying there was no rush, but his deadline with the journal that was publishing his work fell in four days. "Needs to be APA style but I can't remember what style I wrote it in ... Harvard?" he'd written her. Glancing through the paper and its citations and reference list, Rory could not determine what style it had been written in either. Something the author had made up as he went along, apparently. It would take a bit of wrestling to get it ship-shape before that deadline, but she had some open time, so she answered the author, saying she'd be happy to work on his paper and the time frame was fine—then she quoted a price that included a rush fee and enough to cover the extra hours she'd spend sweating over his reference list. He agreed to the price and paid the deposit, so after lunch she started right in, tackling the references first.

As she worked, she kept imagining she felt the light pressure of Mike's lips against her cheek from that too-brief kiss in Gunther's. Did that mean they were all right? That he'd accepted that she would get involved in odd sorts of things—such as the occasional murder or murder investigation—and she had accepted that he might have her handcuffed and transported to the station once in a while? Maybe. The real question was, how sustainable could a relationship like that be? Rory's mother kept hinting at marriage; she said she was only joking, but Rory knew that her mother wanted nothing more than for her daughter to be settled and happy, and in her book, that meant married. Mike had hinted at marriage too, asking just a few weeks ago if Rory had ever considered it. Her answer had been flip: "Sure, when I was twelve." The joking reply had stung him, she knew, but she didn't know how to take it back. The thing was, her answer hadn't entirely been a joke. When the topic of marriage had come up with other guys in her past, she'd known it wasn't right and she'd walked away. But she felt her throat tighten when she imagined herself walking away from Mike.

The Brooksford bells were chiming four, and Rory's eyes and brain were feeling tired when she heard Lee calling at her back door. "Ror, okay if we come in?"

"Sure," she called back, wondering who "we" could possibly be. Lee's mom hardly ever came over here, busy as she usually was with cooking up something scrumptious. Rory saved her work and stood up, rolling her head from side to side and feeling tightness in her neck and shoulders. If only Mike could come loosen them for her. But that wasn't likely until this murder case was wrapped up. She heard her back door close and footsteps coming through the laundry/mudroom into the kitchen. Miss C meowed, and a voice said, "Hi, cat." Grace.

As she entered the living room to find Grace on the floor petting Miss C, Rory said, "Hey, Lee, Grace. What's up?" She knew that Lee gave Grace a ride to and from school because there wasn't a bus that would take her from Brooksford to the county's largest high school, where the computer arts and sciences program was taught. But she was pretty sure he usually dropped her off at home.

"Liza's at work this afternoon, so she asked me if Grace could hang with me until she gets home," Lee answered.

Grace added, "Sephie."

"Oh..." Rory nodded in understanding. She wouldn't leave a child, not even a teen, alone with the Rennsfelder woman either. "Well, you're welcome to visit with me, and with Miss C too."

"What's with all the people in town?" Lee asked.

Rory rolled her eyes. "It's that video, plus the news broadcast last night."

"Yeah, that was cool," Grace added.

Rory went on, "It's actually quieted down. You should have seen Gunther's this morning. It was mobbed. Madison was having a field day though. I'll bet she raked in some serious cash today."

"Don't forget to tell them about the rude girl on our step," Miss C added. *"I wonder if Hesiod and Homer had to deal with these things. Do you think they had fans waiting outside their door?"*

"Oh, and I almost forgot," Rory said. "This morning when Miss C and I went out, there was this girl on our front step having a friend take a picture. Can you believe she got upset with me when I asked her to move?"

"So rude. Speaking of rude, you are ignoring my dinnertime."

"Jeez, cat, give it a rest, will you? I'll feed you in a second. Lee, you want tea or anything? Grace, you want some tea or hot chocolate?" Rory offered.

They both accepted the offer of tea, and Rory went into the kitchen to heat the water and feed the cat. She returned to find Lee and Grace at work on her jigsaw puzzle.

"Tea's coming up, guys. What time does Liza get home?" Rory—and all of Brooksford—had learned early not to refer to Liza as Grace's mom. There was some history there with her biological mother that Grace preferred to keep Liza totally separate from.

"Dunno exactly. Five? Five thirty?" Grace guessed.

So ... Mike had told them not to get Grace involved in any sort of little side investigation, and he was right about that. She wouldn't put Grace in a dangerous situation. No way, no how. But just asking a couple of questions wouldn't be getting her involved, would it? If she asked for informational purposes only?

"So, uh, the sheriff was telling us that they found out who uploaded that video," she began.

"Oh yeah? Did they arrest them?" Lee asked hopefully.

She shook her head. "No. Turns out it's some kid in California who makes videos out of raw footage people send him. He has some kind of mailbox or something that they just leave the stuff in, so he doesn't even know where it comes from, I guess."

"Pivver," Grace said.

Rory tried hard to make some sense out of what the girl had said, but she couldn't. Apparently Lee couldn't either, because he asked, "What?"

"Pivver," she repeated. "His name. The video guy."

"You know of him? That's his name?" Rory asked, wondering what kind of name "Pivver" was.

Grace shrugged. "Screen name. Sure. Everyone knows Pivver. Genius."

This was exactly why Rory thought it wouldn't be such a bad idea to get Grace's thoughts on the investigation. This girl knew stuff. "So you knew right away that the video was from this Pivver person?" she asked.

Grace shook her head. "Uh-uh. Wasn't uploaded under his usual name. We figured it out at school, a bunch of us. He left clues."

"Clues?" Rory asked, feeling old and rather stupid.

"In the name. Viper V. Anagram." She rolled her eyes, though whether the eye roll was for the stupidity of using a simple anagram or the stupidity of the adults who couldn't figure it out, Rory didn't know.

"Well, anyway, the sheriff said that this guy in California wouldn't have known that there was a murder or anything. They're trying to trace who sent the video to him in the first place."

Grace made a sound that Rory could not decipher.

"He also said that they couldn't really just take the video down. Is that right, Grace?" Might as well find out from the true expert, she figured.

"Uh-huh. Can't get rid of it. It's everywhere already—'s on my laptop."

"But surely there's a way to trace it back to whoever sent it, isn't there?"

"Dunno. Might be."

Rory hated to think it, but she had to wonder if Grace really didn't know the answer, or if she just didn't want to share that answer with an adult. Too bad she couldn't get Miss C to talk to Grace. That girl would say anything to Miss C.

"Are you still working on that superhero cat comic, Grace?"

At that, Grace's expression opened. "Uh-huh—'s going good."

Lee put in, "She showed me some of it this afternoon, what she did on the computer. It looks awesome. Some of her panels are going into the all-county art show next month." Grace wasn't even his student, but Rory could tell he was proud of her and the creative work she was doing.

A siren suddenly blared from within Grace's backpack. "'S Liza," she said before looking at it. A text, Rory guessed, since she just tapped at the screen a few times before dropping the phone back into her pack. "On her way." She gave Miss C another pet on the head and stood.

A minute later, three knocks sounded from the front door. When Rory answered it, it was indeed Liza. She came in looking tired. "Hi, guys. Gracie, did you start your homework?"

"Uh-uh. They kept asking me stuff about that video," Grace said unapologetically.

Rory felt a surge of panic. Had she contributed to the delinquency of a minor by distracting Grace from her homework? But Liza seemed unfazed. "Okay. Well, I guess you're the person to ask about that," she said. "Lee, thanks for bringing her up here. I just don't feel right leaving her alone with Sephie."

"Hey, no problem. We enjoyed visiting with her, didn't we, Ror?" Lee replied. He'd gotten to his feet and now stood with them in the middle of the room.

Rory added, "Yeah, and she helped with my jigsaw puzzle."

"She was of much less use in solving our mystery though," Miss C meowed.

Liza gestured with a thumb over her shoulder toward the door. "Listen, I'm sorry to dash off, but I just collected a ton of papers to grade, and..." Rory couldn't help but notice that, though they were all standing in *her* living room, Liza was talking to Lee.

"Oh, sure," he answered. "No problem. I mean I've got the same problem. Grading." He smiled lopsidedly.

"Well..." Liza backed toward the door.

Grace swung her backpack onto her shoulder. "C'mon, let's go." She was first to the door and opened it, but before she went out she took a moment to say, "Thanks, Mr. Cooper. Thanks, Ms. Roberts." To the cat she whispered, "Bye, Miss C." And then she was outside and jumping from the top step down to the sidewalk.

Meanwhile, Liza continued backing out, repeating her own thanks, as Lee told her again that it was nothing, he was happy to do it. Rory was starting to wonder if perhaps she herself had become invisible, because Liza seemed to have forgotten she was there.

When the door closed, Rory punched Lee playfully on the arm. "Criminy, you like her!" she practically squealed.

"What? No. I do not."

"Lee loves Liza," Rory intoned in a singsong voice.

"Shut up."

She couldn't help but notice that he was blushing, his ears turning a fiery red as he stared intently at the floor.

"Have you told her?"

"Told her what? There's nothing to tell," he continued to protest.

"Aw, Lee, c'mon. We're old buddies. You can tell me. You gonna ask her out?"

"No. Stop." He sat on the sofa and began to move some puzzle pieces around at random. Rory sat next to him, much closer than usual, and threw an arm over his shoulders.

"Pretty sure she likes you too," she whispered.

Then he turned to look at her, hope in his eyes. "You think? Really? You're just saying that."

"You kidding? She's completely into you. Didn't you notice how she just totally forgot I was here while you two were talking? If you could call that talking. It was sort of like a middle school dance."

"You were here? I didn't notice," Lee joked.

"Shut up." Rory pushed at his shoulder and scooted to a more comfortable distance. "You should really ask her out though. Pepperoni neutrons and all that. Tell her I volunteer to have Grace stay here while you two go out and … grade papers together or whatever teachers do for fun. And you know, Grace adores you too, so you wouldn't have to worry about impressing your new woman's kid."

Lee said nothing, but Rory knew from the dumb grin on his face that he was thinking about it.

Chapter 23

The next day, Rory and Miss C went on their usual trek to the post office. The sky was overcast, the air even cooler than it had been the day before. Rory wondered how much influence the weather had on dampening some of the excitement over the video. There was less of a crowd this morning, and not one person on Rory's top step. But when they got to the post office, Rory saw that something was still not right with Mrs. Crabtree. The woman did not bother to even scowl at Miss C when the cat hissed at her. Yes, something was wrong with this woman. Could it be a health issue, with her or perhaps her husband? Rory realized with a start that she could not remember the last time she'd actually seen David Crabtree. Was that it, Mr. Crabtree had some devastating diagnosis that was keeping him homebound?

She went through all this in her mind while she retrieved the mail from her box. A couple catalogs and the cable bill. It all went into the pouch on Miss C's stroller.

Well, there was nothing for it but to ask. She cleared her throat, causing Mrs. Crabtree to glare at her. "You got a problem? Need stamps or something?" the woman spat. Customer service was not her strong point.

Rory swallowed. It hadn't been too long ago that her very own mother had charmed this woman into having a normal conversation. Well, that was beyond—way, way beyond—Rory's conversational skills. Might as well just ask.

"I was just noticing, Mrs. Crabtree, that, um, you haven't seemed quite like yourself these past couple of days. And I was wondering, just neighbor to neighbor, if everything's okay. Are you and your husband doing okay? I haven't really seen Mr. Crabtree in a while."

Mrs. Crabtree turned an expression on her that Rory could not read. Rage? Grief? Happiness that was so well suppressed it looked like its opposite? Perhaps Rory was about to make a breakthrough in her relationship with her unpleasant neighbor. Perhaps Mrs. Crabtree was not an old bat at all. She was just misunderstood. But then she spoke, saying, "Are we okay?" as though the concept of her and her husband being okay was the most idiotic thing she'd ever heard. "After you let that boy get himself killed? Course we're not okay. Haven't you seen that video, those idiots wandering all over town? This place'll never be the same. Crowds. Traffic. Husband gone."

What was that? "You mean Mr. Crabtree's gone?" Rory asked, bewildered. Had the kindly gentleman finally snapped and left his horrible wife? Well, you could hardly blame him. It was a miracle he'd lasted this long, really.

"Did you turn him to stone?" Miss C meowed, earning a scowl from Mrs. Crabtree.

"Went to take care of his sister."

"Oh, is she unwell?"

"Not 'nymore. She's dead. Huh," Mrs. Crabtree added, in what Rory supposed was meant as an expression of merriment.

Forcing herself to keep calm and avoid expletives, Rory said, "I'm sorry to hear that."

"I'm not. Couldn't stand her. Meanest woman I ever met."

"Have you ever met yourself?" Miss C meowed.

Rory was searching for something appropriate to say, when Mrs. Crabtree saved her the trouble, growling, "Get that damn cat out of here." Then she reached up and pulled down the folding metal blind that separated the public space from the sorting office, though it was nowhere near time for her to close for lunch. It shut with a metallic bang, and then Rory heard the latch click home, locking her out.

"Good thing I didn't need stamps," she said to Miss C under her breath before pushing the stroller toward the door.

So much for starting a new chapter with Mrs. Crabtree.

Outside the post office, Rory was surprised to run into none other than Katie. It seemed odd to see her alone, without Spike, and Rory questioned herself at first, thinking that she must be mistaken. Surely Katie wouldn't show up here, not after what happened. But there was no mistaking that long, orange-red hair. Plus, the bright red lines of a cat scratch marked where Miss C had clawed her on the cheek a few nights before. She was getting out of a compact car that Rory guessed must be her own.

"Katie?" She said the young woman's name as a question.

Katie startled, as surprised to see Rory as Rory was to see her. "Oh, Ms. Roberts. Hi," she said listlessly, crossing the street toward them.

"Do not forget that this is the person who falsely accused you of murder," Miss C meowed. She followed the warning with a low growl aimed at Katie.

Rory didn't stop her. The cat was a reliable judge of character, and if she gave a warning about Katie, Rory intended to heed it. Still, it wouldn't hurt to probe a little, would it?

"What brings you out here? I wasn't expecting to see you."

Hands in the pockets of her ragged coat, Katie looked up and down the street before answering. "I have to finish my project. Wanted to shoot some new stuff. You know, after Spike..." She shivered, brought a bright yellow knit hat out of her coat pocket and pulled it onto her head.

"Oh, right," Rory said, nodding as though she understood when in fact she had no idea what the girl was talking about. Finish her project? The same project her friend was killed while working on? Was this some sort of tortured-artist thing?

As Katie continued to stand there looking around, her eyes darting from one thing—house, person, car, Miss C, Rory—to another, Rory considered that perhaps the best person to talk to about that video was standing right in front of her, and if she happened to find out why Katie had tried to pin a murder on her, so much the better. "Hey, you look cold. I don't suppose you'd like a coffee or anything, would you? We're just on our way up to Gunther's, and you could come along, get good and warmed up before you go out to film."

That seemed to catch Katie's attention. She stopped the movement of her head and eyes, settling her empty gaze on Rory. "Sure. Whatever, I guess. Oh, I don't have any money," she added, as though she suddenly remembered that she was broke.

Rory waved it off. "It's okay. My treat." Miss C growled again.

They walked together, and totally silently, up to the stop sign and into the north end, but when they reached Gunther's front door, Katie took one look at the small crowd inside and balked. "I can't go in there. Too many people," she said.

"I bet the owner will let us sit in her office, or we can go to my place and I'll make us some tea or coffee," Rory said, wondering what Mike would think of her inviting Katie home. Well, he'd just have to deal with it.

After considering those options, Katie pushed the door open and walked into Gunther's. Though she'd thought it was crowded, there were actually far fewer people inside today than had been there the day before. Rory's favorite table was even open, not that she and Katie would be able to talk there, not when the other tables were occupied and so close by.

Madison, behind the counter, was already reaching for Rory's blue-green mug on the wall. Her excitement today was more cautious than it had been the day before.

"Rory, what can I get you?"

"Regular coffee, please, and I'm paying for whatever Katie's having."

Katie also got a coffee. After Madison served up the coffees and collected Rory's four dollars, Rory said, "Mayor, do you know Katie? She's been in town working on a school project." She tried to be a little cryptic to avoid drawing attention. It was unlikely anyone would recognize Katie in the light of day, but there was no point in really testing it by just coming out and saying, "She's the girl from that video."

For a moment Madison just nodded and smiled, not catching on, but then her face changed, and Rory knew she'd gotten it. "Oh, Katie, of course. How nice to meet you. Rory, why don't we three go visit in my office, away from this crowd."

"Make sure there are no knives," Miss C meowed, drawing stares from some customers.

"Laura, take over for a minute, will you?" Madison said, and Laura Williams stood up from among the store shelves, where Rory guessed she'd been restocking junk food. Everyone might recognize Rory as the lady with the cat in the stroller, but Laura was the town's biggest cat lover. She took a moment to greet Rory and a longer moment to say hello to Miss C, calling her Cuddles and directing a string of baby talk at her. The cat stared back unresponsively.

Madison led the way to the back and into her office, where they crowded into the small space. She offered the one chair to Katie, who practically fell into it. Rory guessed the girl must not be sleeping very well, not after what she'd been through, and not with the whole ordeal being splashed over the internet for all to see. She found that she had no idea what to say, but Madison started with, "We're all so sorry about what happened to your friend, Katie. You must be having an awful time of it."

Rory fidgeted and bit her tongue. It hadn't been a picnic for her either, and largely because of Katie's accusations. The fear she'd felt as she sat alone in that interview room at the sheriff's department bubbled in her chest and threatened to turn to rage. Best to keep quiet.

Katie nodded and blew into the hole in the lid on her coffee. "Yeah. But I want to finish my project. Our project." Her free hand went reflexively toward her belly, resting there. Rory imagined the girl probably felt sick to her stomach, which wouldn't be any great surprise. Maybe coffee wouldn't be such a great thing for her right now.

Madison, though, said gently, "Katie, forgive me for asking, because of course it's none of my business, but are you pregnant, by any chance?"

Warmth blushed across Katie's cheeks. She nodded shyly. "Not many people know. Besides Spike." Her eyes filled with tears, but she blinked them back.

"Oh dear," Madison said.

"So you and Spike were a couple?" Rory asked, forgetting her emotions for the moment.

"Try to ask intelligent questions, please," Miss C meowed.

Rory caught the weird look Madison gave her, the look that told her that was a stupid question. But she felt vindicated when Katie said, "Not officially. Sean and I just broke up, like, a few months ago, and he would freak out if he knew I started going out with someone so soon." Rory smiled at Madison but said nothing. Miss C fell quiet for the time being.

Madison asked, "Had you and Sean been together long?"

Katie sniffed loudly, prompting Madison to pull a box of tissues from a shelf and plunk it on the desk in front of her. After taking a tissue and wiping her nose with it, Katie said, "I don't know. Like, a year or something."

"This Sean, have you seen him recently?" Rory asked.

"Oh, yeah. He's in my film storytelling class. Saw him a few days ago. In front of your house. He was there when that cop came and broke us all up, made him and Corey go film somewhere else."

Rory nodded and exchanged a significant look with Madison. Yes, once Mike got hold of this information, it would be game over for Sean and Corey.

"Which one was Sean?" she asked. "I didn't catch any names."

"The real tall one. His hair's, like, sort of sandy, and he has hazel eyes."

Quarterback. The cocky pretty boy had lost his girl and his filming chances to Spike, so he'd taken revenge. Case closed, Rory thought. Well, almost.

"Is he a football player?" she asked.

Katie looked confused. "What? No. There's not even a football team at our school."

Well, you can't win 'em all, Rory thought. Still, the guy did something to stay in shape. Even when you're young, you don't just come out with a body like that, do you?

"I guess he used to play in high school. He talks about it, like, all the time, how great he was." Katie rolled her eyes so hard, Rory almost expected them to spin completely around.

"Was he a quarterback?"

"No, some defensive thing. Now he's in the gym all the time to keep in shape, 'cause he's, like, so vain about his looks. He gets his hair done at this salon every week—his mom pays for it. It's kind of embarrassing."

"Narcissus," Miss C purred, pleased that she'd once again hit the mark in her judgment of human character.

Game, set, and match, Rory thought, even though she'd been wrong about Sean being a quarterback. A guy who lived in the gym and at the hair salon, so concerned about appearances, must have been livid to have lost his girl to someone like Spike. "He seemed pretty mad at Spike the other day. You're sure he didn't suspect anything?"

"No. How could he? We've been so careful. We never told anyone, and we tried not to be together on campus. Well, except for the classes we have together."

"He must have found out, don't you think? I mean, Katie, he was pretty upset. You don't get like that just from a little dispute over who's going to film where and when, do you?"

Katie set her coffee on the desk and let her hands fall into her lap. She looked down at them sadly. "Oh, but you don't know Sean. He gets mad about *everything*."

"Um, Katie," Madison ventured, "how much of this does the sheriff know?"

That caused Katie's head to snap up, a horrified look on her face. "You don't think...? Uh-uh. Sean would not have done anything to Spike, not like that. He couldn't have. I mean yeah, he yells and stuff, but he doesn't *do* anything— nothing that might mess up his hair, anyway."

"Nevertheless, I think you will find that murder is committed for the most banal of reasons, often for this so-called love, and often by so-called nonviolent people, just like Narcissus," Miss C informed them. Rory shushed her.

"Well, if you really think about it, it had to be someone else who was out here filming. How many people in your class were filming in Brooksford?" Rory asked.

Katie thought for a second and then said, "Just three groups, I think. Me and Spike, Sean and Corey, and Dan and Eddie."

"Dan and Eddie are the ones doing the meta thing?"

Katie's eyes rolled toward the ceiling again, and she made a huffing sound that Rory took for a laugh. "Yeah. They're kinda weird. Always doing something dumb. Meta," she added disdainfully.

"Well, it's just that ... I can't really picture those two sneaking out here at night to ... you know," Rory said, her words petering out before she could directly mention Spike's murder.

"You're right. Those two losers couldn't do anything like that. They don't have the guts. They did say they'd help me so I can finish Spike's and my project though."

"You've really got to tell the sheriff about your and Spike's relationship, and about Sean. It sounds like he probably got Corey to help him out to get one over on Spike, get a little revenge, you know. Maybe things got out of hand, it went farther than he meant it to...."

"Or maybe it went exactly as far as he meant it to," Miss C finished for her.

With a sigh, Katie said, "You're right. The sheriff gave me his card so I could call if, you know, I thought of anything."

"So you'll call him, right?" Rory asked, thinking, *Because I sure as heck will be calling him, just as soon as I get home.*

"Yeah," Katie said simply. "Listen, thanks for the coffee. I should go, do some filming to finish up. Everything we got the other night is evidence now, so..."

Madison opened the door as Katie stood. "Well, we're so glad you visited with us, Katie, and again, we're sorry for all that's happened. You have someone to help you with"—Madison nodded vaguely, Rory supposed to avoid mentioning the baby out loud—"don't you?"

Something like a smile played over Katie's lips as she said, "Yeah, I've got help. I'm not worried about that." And with that, Katie left. Rory and Madison waited in the office doorway, watching as, head down, she threaded her way through the small crowd in the café to the front door.

"See, Madison, this is all going to be cleared up real soon. Once Mike gets hold of this information, he'll get the truth out of Corey, even if Sean doesn't fess up. A little bit of divide and conquer, and this case is over, and Brooksford can go back to being Brooksford."

The mayor made a noncommittal sound. "You're going to tell him, aren't you? Somehow, I don't quite trust that girl to come through."

"Oh, I'll tell him." Rory drained the rest of her coffee and handed the empty mug to Madison. "Thanks, Mayor, but I've gotta run."

It was up to Miss C to ask the one nagging question: *"If Sean and this so-called Corey attacked them that night, why didn't Katie recognize them? Or why didn't she admit to recognizing them?"*

Chapter 24

Mike was surprised to learn that Katie was pregnant, but less surprised that she claimed Spike was the father. He wasn't even all that impressed when Rory reminded him of the confrontation between Spike and Sean just hours before the murder. But all he would tell her was, "We're following up on several leads." He was tight-lipped beyond that.

"So, did you find anything from the raw video you got from the YouTube guy?" She refused to say either of the names Pivver or ViperV aloud.

"Unfortunately, no. There's just more shots from behind your garage, but they were really careful not to show their faces or to have their voices recorded. It's looking more and more like a setup, not like they were just pulling a prank and things got out of hand. Somebody wanted Spike dead," Mike told her. "Oh, and there was a couple minutes of film from around the bridge, but again, no faces, no voices."

"But, Mike, it was Sean and Corey who were going to film over by the bridge right after the fight. Ask Opal. That's where they said they were going after she told them to stay out of Katie and Spike's way. You've got to lean on those guys hard," she insisted.

Mike chuckled, and she asked, "What's funny?"

"Oh, it just sounds like you've been watching cop shows on TV again. Hon, we've got no physical evidence. So far, we've got no way to tie any of that video to Sean and Corey, and frankly—and by frankly I mean confidentially; this information is not to find its way to Mel Scott or any other reporter you might happen to talk to—I have my doubts about whether either of those guys is smart enough to have pulled off something like this. They're not very savvy."

Rory sighed. "Maybe they're just playing dumb."

"No, I think they really are dumb. Look, just sit tight, okay? We'll get to the bottom of it. Until then, try to limit the amount of private snooping you do."

"Snooping?" she asked, all innocence.

"Yes, you know, that thing you do that tends to get you into trouble more often than not?"

"Oh, that. Well, sure, I'll try," she promised, fingers crossed.

Gazing out her office window, Rory spotted movement toward the back edge of her yard, where her property nudged up against the bank of the West Brook. She recognized the same bright yellow hat Katie had been wearing earlier. The young woman was standing there beside the brook, gazing into the forest on the other side. Then she slowly began walking to the left, upstream.

Rory casually ended her call with Mike. No harm in doing a little bit more snooping, right?

"Miss C, want to go have another chat with Katie?" Rory asked, intending to stroll right out there, but something stopped her from leaving the window. There was more movement down by the brook, from behind Katie. Someone was following her, keeping low, their head just popping above the edge of the bank while Katie walked unaware above them. It could be that whoever had killed Spike always planned on killing Katie too, and now he'd come to finish the job. Rory tensed. Beside her, Miss C hissed. "Sorry, Cuddlywumps, there's no time for the stroller right now," Rory said as she grabbed her phone and headed for the back door at a run. No time for 911 either. Whoever was behind Katie was following at a distance just far enough to be unobtrusive but close enough to reach her quickly when they saw a chance. There could be no time to lose. She made sure the back door was shut tight and jumped down the two back steps, landing harder than she would have liked on the concrete patio slab. In her younger years, she might have taken off at a sprint across the lawn, but given her age, her state of being seriously out of shape, and the fact that she seemed to have mildly sprained her ankle on that landing, she opted for a somewhat fast walk.

Ahead of her, Katie had stopped walking and stood gazing across the brook again. Now Rory could see that there was not just one person but two following her, down by the water's edge and mostly concealed by brush. She couldn't make out who they were, but they looked big.

As she drew even with the bare sugar maple, Rory decided she had to act now to warn Katie. There was no way she could fight off two attackers by herself, but maybe with a little warning, Katie would be able to get away. In the loudest voice she could manage, she called out, "Katie, behind you!"

At that, Katie turned, startled. But she seemed startled only by Rory's shout, not that there was someone following her. Then, "Cut!" Katie yelled. Rory saw one of the figures following her throw up his hands in disgust.

Rory continued toward the brook, but more slowly now.

Katie did not look happy. "What did you do that for? Can't you see I'm filming?" she demanded before Rory got much closer.

Rory still had her phone in her hand, ready to call for the help she was so sure she was about to need—or to take a picture of whoever it was following Katie.

"No—I just saw someone following you." Rory pointed downstream, to where two guys were standing partially in the shallows of the brook.

"Yeah. It's Dan and Eddie. They're helping me, and I'm doing some stuff for their meta thing. Come on, you guys. Why are just standing down there in the water? Idiots," she added under her breath.

"Oh." Rory watched stupidly as Dan and Eddie struggled onto the bank and then got tangled in some brush. Athletes they were not. "But you really should have told me you'd be back here. I just saw them following you, and I thought—"

Katie cut her off. "Never mind. Thanks, I mean, for trying to help. I appreciate it, I guess."

"So those guys are helping you?" They both looked toward where Dan and Eddie continued fighting against the brush. *They should bill themselves as the Two Stooges,* Rory thought.

"Um, yeah, sort of. They said they'd help me if I'd let them shoot me for their project, that meta thing they're doing. Dan knows way more than me about the editing program we're using, and I guess he's better than me at special effects and stuff." In a whisper, Katie added, "He's not as great as he thinks, but I kind of have to go along, don't I?"

Rory mumbled in the affirmative. She apologized again—not meaning it at all, and adding a reminder to ask permission before wandering onto someone else's property—and left them to their filming.

Chapter 25

Things in Brooksford were relatively normal for a whole day after that. Rory spent that day working steadily on her project while Miss C napped on the corner of the desk, waking periodically to *mrrp* at a bird that alighted at the feeder in the window. Chickadees, titmice, nuthatches—Rory had learned the names of their most frequent feathered visitors from a book Mr. Crabtree had given her. He'd given her the feeder too, to entertain Miss C and keep her from wanting to get outside to chase the birds at his wife's feeders. Rory felt bad for him, having lost his sister. If she could find out when he'd be home, she'd arrange to have flowers delivered—just a little something to let him know she'd thought of him. She told herself she would just casually ask Mrs. Crabtree when she expected her husband home. But once Rory and Miss C entered the post office only to find that the postmaster was in the back instead of at the counter, it was so much easier to slip in and out quietly, without even speaking to her.

Even Madison didn't have much to say when they stopped in at Gunther's for a quick late-morning coffee. There was less of a crowd, and the mayor seemed sad that her bump in business was dying down. Rory reminded her that they still had the weekend to look forward to, but that brightened her only marginally.

Things didn't really open up until later that afternoon, when once again Lee brought Grace over to Rory's after school. They'd agreed in advance that this would be a good idea, as Grace liked Miss C so much. It was about four when Rory heard them coming through her back door, and she shut down her work for the day. Miss C preceded her to greet their guests.

Grace had dropped her backpack near the sofa and was on her knees petting the cat. "Hey, Ms. Roberts," she said when Rory entered.

"Hey yourself. You guys want something to drink?" Rory asked. She was all set to have a nice sit-down with Lee and Grace, maybe do some puzzling in front of the fire, when someone knocked on her front door. "Hang on. Who could that be?"

"Can't be Liza," Grace muttered, stealing a look at her phone. The way she said it gave Rory the distinct impression that she did not want to go home just yet.

Rory opened the door to find none other than reporter Mel Scott smiling on the other side of it, her blue hair looking especially bright. "Mel," Rory said unenthusiastically. "What brings you here?"

"I was hoping to get a quote from you," Mel said, craning her neck to look past her into the house. "Maybe from Lee and Grace too, as long as they're here." She wore no hat today, so her blue hair seemed extra pointy, and her eyes sparkled in a way that told Rory the reporter was up to something.

"You should let her in. She seems to have knowledge that we do not," Miss C meowed from atop the back of the sofa, where she'd jumped to get a better view of coming events.

Pulling the door wide, Rory said, "Sure, come on in. But I can't imagine what you want to get quotes about."

Mel bustled inside, and as she went past, Rory counted six silver studs tracing an arc from her right earlobe to the top of her ear. Rory caught Grace also studying the reporter's ears and wondered how long it would be before she talked Liza into letting her get her ears pierced.

"You mean you all haven't seen the new video?" Mel asked.

Rory swore she felt her inner organs freeze. "New video?"

"Just went up this afternoon. It won't be as big as the last one, but..."

Already moving toward her office, Rory cut her off, saying, "Come on, let's look at it back here."

In her office, Rory settled herself in her desk chair and pulled up a browser window while the others crowded in behind her. Miss C arranged herself in front of Rory, where she'd have the best view. "Cat, I can't see what I'm doing," Rory complained, moving her head from one side to the other in her attempts to see around the cat's head.

"But I can see perfectly. Please proceed," Miss C meowed.

Rory went to YouTube and plugged "Brooksford" into the search bar. The first thing that came up was the old video, and there were now several versions of that—some of them shortened, some that were obviously knock-offs and parodies.

"How do people do this stuff so fast?" Rory wondered aloud.

"S'what they do," Grace answered simply. Rory couldn't see the teen's one-shoulder shrug, but she knew it happened.

About five or six videos down, she found the new one. It was titled "The Truth About Brooksford." She clicked on it.

The video opened on a daylight shot of the approach into town from the south. It was taken from inside a vehicle, and judging from the assortment of junk piled on the dash, she guessed it to be Spike's minivan. Light, new agey guitar music played. Instead of text on the screen like the first video had had, this one had a voice-over. The voice was Katie's, but distorted, nasal, like she'd had a cold or been crying a lot.

"We came to Brooksford on an overcast autumn morning," the voice intoned. "We were on a quest of sorts, to find the source of an ancient terror. Little did we know we were about to meet our own worst terror. This is our story."

Leaving out most of the bits that were true, as Rory couldn't help but notice, the video went on to tell in short terms the story of the Woldwomper, the terrifying vampire believed to haunt the forests around the tiny colonial village of Fording. The beast would drop from a tree while unsuspecting innocents rode by in a carriage or wagon—or later, a car—and rip them out and kill them. Fording grew into Brooksford, and the Woldwomper became just a story told to frighten the children around the campfire. Until last summer, when the remains of three of the Woldwomper's victims were discovered buried in backyards around town.

"And that was when the terror began anew," the voice said.

Rory rolled her eyes. "This is ridiculous."

"Shh," everyone behind her said.

"*Yes. Shh,*" Miss C meowed.

Chastened, Rory quieted.

They were now looking at a shot of the outside of her house.

"One of those victims was found behind this house. It was here that we met Dr. Liza Cunningham, an expert in local legends."

The video moved to inside Rory's living room, to the footage Katie and Spike had taken just a few hours before the attack. It was jerky, just as Spike had said it would be. Well, this may be a "style," Rory thought, but it was making her seasick.

The interview with Liza had been cut in an "interesting" way, with most of what she'd said edited to snippets of sentences and focusing on what was likely to be most alarming to viewers. Anything she'd said about uncertainty or the possible truth behind the legend was cut out, so it sounded not like the area had been the hunting ground of a murderous highwayman—the truth—but that there had actually been a supernatural beast lurking in the woods.

"Liza is not gonna be happy about this," Rory said, not caring if anyone wanted to hear her opinion or not. They were in her office, after all.

It seemed that Grace, for one, didn't mind, as she agreed, "Yeah."

Lee also jumped in with, "It sounds like they totally twisted her words. Liza wouldn't say stuff like this."

Rory turned to him, over her left shoulder, and smiled. If they'd been alone, she would have teased him, but she sure didn't want to say anything about his attraction to Liza in front of Grace, so she held her tongue. For now.

The video also included a few sentences of Rory's interview, but hers was cut the same way Liza's had been, so she came out saying not quite what she'd said at all—or at least not what she'd meant.

"The current homeowner is descended from that victim. It's ironic, and more than a little disturbing, that as a child, she was frightened by the tale of the Woldwomper as she and her family and friends sat right atop the unmarked grave."

Here, Rory's voice sounded at low volume in the background as she told the story of the barbecue, after which some scary stories had been told, including that of the Woldwomper. "It just about scared the pants off me," she said in the video.

In her office, she complained, "She took that totally out of context. Criminy."

"Shh!" the voices behind her said.

"Listen to your Greek chorus and shh," Miss C meowed.

Now they were looking at Rory's backyard, at her garage and her maple tree, in that same jerky style. "We came here looking for the Woldwomper," the narrator said. "We never thought we'd actually find him."

Suddenly, the video's character changed. They were looking at a night shot, and the deliberate jerkiness was gone, replaced by moments of steadiness interspersed with a sudden move from one clear shot to another. They were looking at Spike with his camera, shot from a low angle.

"I didn't realize there was so much moonlight that night," Rory said.

Miss C added, *"And that the Katie person had a camera of some sort."*

"Does the sheriff know that Katie has footage from that night?" Lee asked.

"I don't know," Rory said. "He hasn't mentioned it to me."

On the screen, the shot panned from the tree, past Spike and his camera, to the house and finally the garage.

"Did she have a GoPro?" Grace asked.

"That is what it looks like, huh, kiddo?" Mel said.

The narrator said, "It might have been on this very spot that the Woldwomper took one of his victims. Or, perhaps it's his victim who haunts this spot. We may never know. All we know is, something awful is about to happen."

Now, not in her narrator voice, Katie whispered, "Shh. Did you hear that?"

"Hear what?" Spike answered, just as he had in the first video.

There came then a distinct rustling sound, and Katie and her camera spun quickly 180 degrees toward the garage. "That!"

"It's just an animal or something. Probably that old woman's cat," Spike said.

"Old woman?" Rory complained, realizing Spike was referring to her. *That* hadn't been in the first video.

"Shh!" everyone behind her said.

"What'sa matter? You afraid the Woldwomper's gonna getcha?" Spike taunted Katie.

Then there was another rustling, louder, accompanied by an odd grunting that caught Spike's attention too. They couldn't see what he was doing, but from the first video, Rory remembered that this was the point when he turned toward the garage and slowly lowered his camera. This was when his and Katie's eyes were shining so brightly in the night vision of the attackers' camera. "Who's there?" Katie called. That was when something broke out from the darkness at the side of the garage. On the video, there was screaming, running footsteps, as Katie turned and ran away from whatever was coming … ragged breaths, another scream, a thud. Rory recognized her own voice shouting at them, and a meow.

"That's me," Miss C meowed proudly. *"I leapt into the breach of battle."*

"Shh!" everyone said.

The whole scene was confusion, just as Rory remembered it. There'd been too many bodies to sort out whose was whose. She remembered pushing and shoving, mostly, and then someone, Sean presumably, had tackled her. On the screen they saw a jumble of movement. In the dark were silhouetted faces that couldn't quite be made out. Meanwhile, the video showed a shot of the grass where Katie had gone down. Her breathing could be heard clearly. The camera stayed in the grass. "Spike?" they heard Katie ask. Then she screamed, "Spike!" and the shot went black.

The acoustic guitar music started up again, as did Katie's narration.

"My friend died that night. Did the Woldwomper claim his latest victim? It seems he did. So let this be a lesson to you: Sometimes when you go looking for something, you find it. Be careful out there."

The words "In memory of Reginald 'Spike' Johansson. The End" appeared on the screen, followed by the credits.

"That's weird," Rory said. "Katie was back here yesterday, supposedly filming some stuff to finish her project, but none of that shows up here."

"Maybe she just decided not to use it," Lee said.

"Could have two versions," Grace added.

"That's a good point," Lee agreed. "She might have made this in response to that earlier video, and maybe she's making another one for her class."

"Well, I hope so, because that was awful," Rory said. "There was hardly a single true thing in there."

"It is the stuff of myth and legend," Miss C meowed. *"One wonders where Hesiod drew his material from."*

Mel said, "I thought it was pretty good. I mean, as a short. It gets your attention."

"Made me motion sick," Grace said. "Too jerky."

Rory agreed, "Me too. That jerky thing Spike was doing was pretty annoying. He said it's a style, but..."

"The GoPro was better. Except when those guys attacked them. Too bad she couldn't have held more still. Maybe you could have made out a face or something," Lee said.

Mel suggested, "Let's take another look. If we pay closer attention to the faces, we might make something out."

Rory was queuing up the video to play again when a familiar-sounding siren sound blared from the living room. Grace, head bowed, shuffled out the door saying, "Phone. Liza."

"We'll wait till Grace comes back," Rory said, taking her hand off the mouse. "I wonder what Liza's going to make of this," she added, turning to look at Lee. In response, he blushed. Yeah, he had it bad for Liza.

"Love is an illness," Miss C observed. *"A famous philosopher said so."* Professor Eleanor had told her that once, and now that she'd had a chance to see love among humans up close, she had to agree. A human in love was a distinctly odd thing.

"I wonder if I could score an interview with Katie," Mel mused out loud.

Rory swiveled her chair to face the reporter. "Criminy, Mel, can't you give the girl a break? She's just lost her friend, and she's been through a terrifying experience."

"Yeah, but, if she's able to do this"—Mel gestured toward the computer monitor—"maybe she's ready to talk. It could be cathartic for her."

"I am surprised that you know the word 'cathartic.' Are you perhaps familiar with the genitive absolute?" Miss C meowed in Mel's direction.

"See? Miss C agrees with me," Rory said.

Miss C looked at her briefly and then looked away toward the window. But a second later, her ears cocked and swiveled, and her head turned to the door. *"More company,"* she meowed, and then they all heard knocking at the front door.

"You think Grace'll get that?" Rory asked, not wanting to get up. She did not much like the way Mel was eyeing her chair.

Lee answered, "If it's Liza, she'll get it. Otherwise..."

Half listening to Lee, Rory heard the sound of her front door opening, followed by Grace saying, "Oh. Uh."

"It is not the Liza person," Miss C informed them.

That got Rory out of her chair. "Sounds like it's not Liza." Then she called out, "I'm coming, Grace," as she made her way down the short hallway toward the living room.

When she got there, it was to find Sephie Rennsfelder standing at her front door. "This child has not invited me in. She's just standing here with the door open, letting cold air into your darling little cottage while I freeze near to death."

Rory did have to wonder how cold she could possibly be, given that it was at least fifty degrees today, with no wind, and the woman appeared to be wearing a particularly warm animal as a coat. There was something distinctly "From Russia, with Love-y" about the sleek, golden-brown fur with darker spots. What animal died for that? Rory wondered.

"That's okay, Grace. She can come in. Thanks for getting the door," Rory said, speaking directly to Grace rather than to Sephie.

"Thank you," Sephie said to Rory. She pushed the door further open and stepped in, then went to shut the door behind her, but Grace held on to the handle and would not release it. "Oh, what is it now, girl?" Sephie demanded.

Rory could understand perfectly why Liza didn't want Grace to be home alone with Sephie. But she was pleased to see Grace hold her ground. "Liza," was all the girl said, and then Rory did indeed see Liza making her way up the front steps. She greeted Grace with a smile and a kiss on the cheek as she came through the door.

"You've been waiting at the door for me?" she asked brightly, but then seeing Sephie, her expression soured. "Oh. Hi, Sephie."

"Liza," Sephie returned. She'd removed her coat and was throwing it over the back of Rory's sofa. Liza and Grace both watched this, looks of anger on their faces. "Oh, for heaven's sake, you two. I've told you a thousand times that this is fake. You don't think I'd wear real fur, do you? I adore animals."

No one said anything. Rory didn't doubt that Sephie adored animals—either on a plate or hanging in her closet. Aloud she said, "We're all in my office. There's something you both need to see." No point putting off the inevitable, she decided. Liza needed to see the new video right away because she was in it, and Sephie ... well, she'd stick her nose in sooner or later anyway.

"What could possibly be back there that I need to see?" Sephie asked disdainfully after Rory had turned and walked down the hall.

To that, Liza responded, "Just shut up and come find out, Sephie."

Yeah, it must be a real barrel of laughs with those two living under the same roof, Rory thought. She should have Grace come up more often to visit, or hang out and do homework or whatever she wanted to do. Heck, she could use Rory's computer if she needed to. Maybe she could even help her set up some better security and backup systems. But that was all just speculation. Right now, Rory had to deal with the crowd of people packed into her office. The room fit two adults comfortably, but five adults and a nearly full-grown teen was a squeeze. She noticed that Liza inched in close to Lee, though they didn't say anything other than hello. Sephie, meanwhile, had barged right up to the desk, where Mel now sat.

"Hey, Rory, this is a pretty sweet chair," the reporter said, rocking and swiveling. "Great lumbar support."

"Thanks, Mel, but would you mind moving so Grace can sit there? I need her to get that video ready to play again, and we want to see if we can slow it down enough to catch a face or something."

The reporter complained a little, claiming she could control the video just as well as anyone, but she did give up the chair, standing and pushing Sephie over a step so Grace could slide in and take over the mouse. She made two clicks and the video began playing.

"I can't see," Sephie complained.

Rory grabbed Mel by the arm and gently pulled her back. "Here, Mel's seen it before, so, Sephie, you get up front."

"But then I can't see," Mel said from her new place beside Rory and with Sephie solidly blocking her view of the monitor.

"Shh!" came the chorus.

Yes. Shh!" Miss C meowed from her spot on the desk.

Sephie said, "Rory, I can't believe you allow that beast on your desk. What if—"

"Shh!"

Rory switched spots with Mel so the reporter could look over Grace's shoulder and Rory herself could see by standing on tiptoe as Sephie bent down for a better view.

When they reached the portion of the video that showed Liza's interview, Liza made a dissatisfied sound but did not say anything. They watched in silence to the end of the video, and then Liza observed, "She was pretty selective in the parts of my interview that she used, wasn't she? She makes me sound like I'm saying the Woldwomper is real. And Rory, yours is even worse."

Rory felt a warm wash of appreciation for her own situation, but it was quickly doused by Sephie, who said, "Yes, you sound like you're descended from monsters and you're terrified of your own backyard." She laughed, but no one else joined her.

"How's this one doing, Gracie?" Liza asked.

Rory didn't understand at first what she meant, but Grace immediately answered, "Only fifteen hundred so far. Only been up a few hours."

"Does that mean it's not going to go viral?" Rory asked hopefully. Because if this other video was out there but never caught on among the video-watching, vampire-chasing public, they had nothing to worry about. Well, they had some things to worry about, but distinctly fewer things than whatever might be inspired by a second viral video.

Grace shrugged, with both shoulders this time. Did that indicate a higher degree of doubt, Rory wondered? "Could still catch on, if the right people see it," she said.

Sephie asked, "Do you know any of these 'right people'? How can we make sure they see it?"

"Sephie, what are you talking about? We don't want this to get too far," Liza said to her. "The town is just now starting to calm down a little bit after that other video."

"Exactly. The first video was fine, but it doesn't seem to have any staying power. People move on so quickly these days. That's why we need to push this one. Why, you should be thanking me. This little video wouldn't even have the views it has if it weren't for me."

Mel pushed in to ask, "Are you saying you had a hand in promoting this video, Ms. Rennsfelder?"

Sephie scoffed. "Promoting? Dear me, no. I do not *promote* things. I encourage things to happen."

"You mean you got Katie to finish this video and post it?" Rory asked.

In response, she got one of Sephie's more condescending smiles. "I believe that's what I just said. I encouraged her to finish."

"Encouraged her how?" Mel asked.

Sephie hesitated. Rory sighed and, against her better judgment, asked, "Criminy, you didn't pay her to do this, did you?"

"Well, you could hardly call it paying her. The poor girl's a starving college student. Five hundred dollars is a fortune to her."

"Five hundred...? You're telling me you paid her five hundred dollars to post this video?"

Sephie sounded taken aback when she said, "Well, I was just helping her to finish her little school project. I don't see what your problem is. This will help Brooksford, provided we can nudge this video into taking off like the last one. I do hope I can get some reimbursement from the town coffers though. Money's rather tight these days, since my last job ended."

Rory's fingers grabbed at her own hair. She wanted to yank it out, or better yet, yank out a few of Sephie's blond locks. That would be mild, compared to what Madison was likely to do to her once she found out about this.

The adult humans fell into a melee of discussion about who had done what, what was good for the town, and whether it was ethical to pay a college student to finish a class project so that you could use the result for your own purposes. Then Miss C yowled, *"You are all missing the point, which is that we should be examining the evidence for clues."*

That stopped discussion long enough for Grace to say, "Don't you think we oughta look at this video some more? See if we can recognize anybody?"

Lee came to his senses first. "Grace is right. We should be looking at this more closely. Whoever attacked Katie and Spike is right there. If we could somehow get a better look..."

"Gracie, can you get it to where the attack starts? Maybe if we see it one more time," Liza asked.

Reluctantly, Grace said, "I can. But s'better t'do it at home. Got the software."

"Well, but maybe you can just humor us so we can all look at it now. Then later this evening you can work on it some more, after your homework."

Grace started the video again, fast-forwarding to the point where Katie and Spike heard the first recognizable noise while they stood underneath the maple tree. A stick cracked, they turned and froze. Through the camera, though there'd been a full moon that had cast its silver light over the scene, the viewers could see nothing more than shadows at the back of the garage. For some seconds the shadows seemed completely still, then the camera suddenly turned away, and when it turned back, the shadows were already bursting across the lawn directly toward them, only the camera was now pointed toward the grass, and then as Katie turned to run, they again saw the grass and her running feet.

"No, we're not going to see anything out of that," Liza said.

"Not yet," Grace added. Looking at the girl, Rory could see the wheels turning in her head. She had plans for how to enhance just the right parts of that video. But was that a good idea?

"After your homework," Liza reminded her.

Lee added, "Yeah, I hear you've got a big calculus test on Monday, and Mrs. Neidermeyer said she's making yours extra tough so you can't score over a hundred again."

Recognizing his teasing tone, Grace muttered, "Teachers." She smiled as she said it though.

Time to get this crowd out of her office, Rory thought. She said, "Okay, everybody out. You can all look at the video some more on your own time. C'mon, Grace. Mel, Sephie, let's go."

"Yes, please go. I have work to do," Miss C meowed.

"That cat is awful. So mean," Sephie said with one last look toward the cat bed and the cat curled in it.

As she slunk past Sephie on her way out the door, Grace countered, "Is not. Just doesn't like everybody."

Sephie watched her go, then watched as Liza and Lee also passed her. Rory had the distinct impression that Liza wanted to get in between Sephie and Grace, for Grace's protection. Speaking of Grace's protection, she wasn't so sure it was a good idea for the girl to get too involved with this video. Walking into her living room with Mel in front of her and Sephie behind her, watching as Liza and Grace were putting their coats on, Rory decided she couldn't let it rest.

Before Rory could say anything, Mel announced, "I've got to get out of here. Unless anyone would like to give me a quote on the record about this new video? No? Okay then, I'm off to see if I can find your mayor." The reporter was out the front door in a blue blur. The Blue Blur, that would be Mel's superhero name, Rory thought, almost breaking into a smile before she remembered what she needed to do.

"Um, Liza, could you help me with something in the kitchen for a second?" she asked. It was a lame and obvious attempt to get Liza alone so they could talk in confidence, but right then she didn't care.

The look on Liza's face told her all she needed to know about just how obvious the ploy had been. "Okay, sure," she said uncertainly. "Hang tight, Gracie." When they were in the kitchen, she asked, "What's wrong? Is it something with Grace?"

Rory hesitated. Maybe it wasn't her place to tell Liza what was and wasn't good for Grace. "Well, sort of. I'm just not sure she should be messing around with this video. Maybe we should just let the sheriff's department handle it. They'll bring in specialists or something."

Liza's eyes darted back toward the living room, where Lee and Grace seemed to be in some sort of mock wrestling match. Grace was laughing hysterically.

Lowering her voice to the barest whisper, she said, "I thought the same thing. But if I don't let her do it under my supervision, she'll just go behind my back later. Besides, I'd stack her up against any expert the sheriff's department can bring in. I think the best I can do is to keep a close eye on her."

"Maybe. But I'm calling the sheriff as soon as this crowd clears. This is really dangerous business, Liza. One person's already been killed." Rory adopted her most serious tone.

"I know," Liza said, and Rory had the distinct impression that she was afraid.

When they returned to the living room, Liza brightened and said, "Okay, Gracie, let's get out of here. Sephie, I guess we'll see you at home later?"

Smiling, Sephie said, "Oh, yes, but not much later. I thought perhaps we could all have supper together this evening. Doesn't that sound fun? I picked up some delicacies in town that just need reheating."

With a forced smile, Liza said, "Great. Thank you." And she shepherded Grace outside.

That left Sephie, Lee, and Rory. Rory suspected that Lee was itching to head home to fill his mom in on the latest happenings, but he seemed reluctant to leave her alone with Sephie. Finally she said, "So, buddy, I guess your mom's probably waiting on you."

"Yeah, she must be. But if—"

"You go on. I'll call you later."

"Okay," Lee said reluctantly and left through the back door.

"My goodness, it's been just like New York's Grand Central Station here, hasn't it?" Sephie remarked when he was gone.

"Terminal," Rory corrected her. "It's Grand Central Terminal. To be really accurate about it," she added when Sephie just stared at her.

Finally the woman said, "Well, whatever you call it, it certainly was very busy. So many people." She cast her eye around the living room.

Fearing that Sephie was having more fantasies about turning her house into a "darling little antiques shop," Rory said, "Well..."

But Sephie interrupted, saying, "Do you really think that odd child will find anything in that video?"

That wasn't what Rory had expected. It caught her flat-footed, but she did manage to say, "Um…"

Sephie charged on. "I mean, do you think it could be dangerous if she does find anything? That's what you and Liza were whispering about in the kitchen, wasn't it?"

"Well, yes."

"If you ask me, that odd little Grace should just keep her nose out of it, let the authorities handle it from here. You are going to talk to your sheriff about this, aren't you?"

"Of course," Rory answered, wondering if what Sephie had said about Grace had been a statement of concern or a warning.

Chapter 26

Rory fed the cat and stuck a frozen fried chicken dinner in the microwave for herself. The chicken came out crispier in the regular oven, but she was much too hungry to wait twenty minutes, plus time for preheating. The few minutes it would take to heat her dinner in the microwave would give her just enough time to call Mike and tell him about the new video, assuming he didn't already know about it. She looked forward to eating dinner on the sofa, holding the handy microwavable tray on her knees, a kitchen towel folded underneath it to shield her from the heat. Rory flopped onto the sofa, phone in hand. The gas fire blazed in front of her. Miss C, her own dinner finished, followed her to the living room and jumped onto the incomplete jigsaw puzzle, sending a piece or two over the edge.

"You are calling your pet sheriff, aren't you?" the cat meowed. *"I believe he should be informed of this latest development."* She experimentally pushed a puzzle piece about with one paw.

"I need to call Mike. You think he's heard about this video yet?" Rory asked the cat.

"How should I know?"

"How would you know? You're a cat. Stop messing with that puzzle." She scrolled through her contacts to find Mike's personal cell number, knowing he would not be pleased to hear that Grace was getting involved in the investigation in Brooksford. And indeed he was not.

"Don't tell me you've gotten Grace involved in your all's amateur hour out there," he complained when Rory raised the subject after a minute of small talk. It turned out that he already knew about the video and had viewed it several times.

"Well, it was sort of her and Liza's idea. Mostly Grace's idea, I guess. Liza said she'd keep an eye on her. I did warn her," Rory said.

Mike sighed loudly. "We have people with the state police who can take care of this sort of thing, you know. People who've gone through specialized training, who have years of experience and aren't unknowingly putting themselves in danger."

"I know, but Grace is ... well, she's just Grace. She's brilliant at computers and stuff."

"You see, hon, that's just the problem. If she turns something up and the wrong person finds out about it, she could be in danger. Whoever killed Spike set him up, and that means that we're not dealing with a nice person here."

"Have you heard anything about Sephie Rennsfelder?" Rory asked out of the blue.

"No," Mike responded, sounding as though the question had caught him off guard. "Why? Has she done something?"

"Not that I know of. It's just the way she is, pulling strings all the time." After a moment's thought, she said, "She told us she paid Katie to finish this latest video. Well, she told us she 'provided the needed funds' to finish it." Her voice put air quotes around the phrase Sephie had used. "That's suspicious, isn't it?"

Mike thought for a moment and then said, "Maybe. But honestly, hon, my impression of Sephie is that she's got some kind of obsession with this whole Historic Brooksford thing. She could be just out to make a load of money for herself, but whatever her motive, I don't think she's up to doing anything dangerous. Not after her recent stint in the county lockup."

Rory made a sound that was neither agreement nor disagreement.

"Look, we've got people working on this new video. Thank you for the information, but we don't need you all to go looking into this any further," Mike said. Rory couldn't help but note that he was careful not to say, "I don't want you looking into this." At this point in their relationship, he knew better than to try to tell her what to do.

She made another noncommittal sound, and he added, "At least, if you and Madison and whoever else won't keep your noses out of it, don't get Grace involved. I could charge you with endangering a child."

"Charge us? But what about Sephie? She's the one who's threatening," Rory could not stop herself from saying.

"I'm going to say this again. Sephie might be a bad influence on Grace, but I really don't believe she's dangerous. You may find this hard to believe, but law enforcement has resources beyond the reach of a high school student."

"You mean you've already found something?"

Mike sighed, sounding frustrated with her questions. "There is something in the newest video that we're looking at very closely. That's all I can tell you. Look, hon, I've gotta go. We'll talk more tomorrow."

Feeling unsatisfied with how the conversation had gone, Rory said, "Yeah, okay."

"Have a good night. Stay out of trouble." His words sounded rushed, tacked on like an insincere afterthought.

"You too." Rory ended the call nervously. Over the past couple of months, Mike had been in the habit of ending their evening chats by telling her he loved her. Now she wondered if that was a habit he was trying to break.

Chapter 27

Saturday morning, Liza called Rory early and asked her to join a meeting at Madison's apartment above Gunther's General. Basically everyone who had crowded into Rory's office the previous afternoon would be there, minus Mel and plus Madison. Grace had something to show them all, Liza said—something big. And so as the Brooksford bells chimed ten o'clock, Rory was pushing Miss C's stroller down the narrow alleyway that led to the back of the Gunther's building, with Lee at her side. She'd just finished updating him on everything Mike had told her the night before.

"So it sounds like he's got something already," Lee said as they reached the back staircase. "Here, I'll carry her," he added when Rory moved to hoist the stroller for the trip to the second floor.

"Thanks. Yeah, they've got something, but he wouldn't give me any clue what it was."

"I wonder if Grace might have found the same thing."

"I'll bet you anything she has. She's pretty brilliant. Why aren't you out of breath?" she asked as Lee lightly set the stroller on the second-floor back porch.

He grinned and pounded his chest with a fist. "Running. Keeps the heart and lungs strong. You should try it. You could be strong like me."

"You are such a goober. Better be careful that Liza doesn't see you acting like a goober."

Lee blushed, and Rory thought, *Mission accomplished.*

Rory tried the door, found it unlocked. She cracked it open and peeked in. Seeing no one but noticing a pile of jackets on a living room chair, she called out for Madison. The mayor walked through the kitchen doorway and hurried toward the dining room area of her open-plan apartment. "Come in, you two. The others are here already," she said. "Lee, would you be a dear and carry that tray of mugs into the kitchen? Thank you."

It looked like she'd brought everyone's personal mugs up from the café. Well, everyone except Sephie, who didn't rate a mug yet. Madison was still waiting to see how their new neighbor would work out, and a lot of that hinged on how she treated Liza and Grace. If things soured there, it was doubtful she'd ever get the chance to choose her own mug; it would always be a paper cup for her, no matter how many decades she lived in Brooksford.

Women's laughter sparkled from the kitchen. Liza and Sephie seemed to be hitting it off all of a sudden, and Rory thought she heard the stifled snicker that was Grace's laugh as well. So maybe Sephie would be getting her own mug soon. Who knew?

"Sounds like a party," she commented to Madison, adding, "Is it okay to let Miss C out?" The cat was pushing at the mesh of her stroller's front panel and meowing loudly.

Madison said, "Yes, you'd better. Otherwise we'll never have a moment's peace. Everyone seems to be in a good mood today, considering what we're here for."

"Ebullient," Lee said, holding the tray of mugs. His was a deep red with gray speckles.

"All right, Mr. Walking Thesaurus," Rory teased. "Just carry the mugs, and try not to do anything stupid in front of Liza." She unzipped the stroller, and the cat jumped out and to the floor, heading immediately for the kitchen.

To Madison's puzzled look, Rory added in a whisper, "Lee and Liza have a thing, only they haven't told each other yet."

"Ooh..." Madison smiled knowingly, and Lee blushed a deeper red and retreated to the kitchen.

"Any idea what we're here to see?" Rory asked as she tucked the cat stroller up against the wall.

Madison shook her head. "No. Just that Grace found something in that video. Liza said it's pretty upsetting. What has the sheriff had to say about it?"

"He says they found something too. Also he says we shouldn't let Grace get too involved. Something about endangering a minor. He said he could charge me."

"He was joking, wasn't he?"

"Um, yeah, I'm pretty sure he was."

"Well, you ask me, I say it's better that we all know Grace is involved. That way, if things get dangerous, we'll be around to keep an eye on her."

Rory nodded. "Exactly."

"I'll get your coffee. Make yourself comfortable in the office area," Madison said, gesturing toward the corner of her living room that held a small desk with a computer. Currently, the monitor showed the security camera feed from her store.

Minutes later, morning greetings exchanged, they all gathered around the computer and Liza said, "Okay, Gracie, you're on."

Grace, seated at the computer chair, pulled a thumb drive from her front jeans pocket. When Miss C complained that she could see nothing, Rory bent to pick her up. She held the cat in her arms and watched Grace.

"Isolated something from that dark part," Grace explained quietly.

"This is absolutely amazing. This child is a genius," Sephie turned to say to everyone. As proud as she sounded, you'd have thought *she* was the girl's stepmother, Rory observed to herself.

On the short-haired side of her head, the top of Grace's ear could be seen turning red. So that was something she and Lee had in common. Could that be a strong foundation to a father-daughter relationship? Rory wondered. She'd tease him about it later, she decided.

Meanwhile, Grace was quickly clicking through menus on the screen, until she pulled up a series of thumbnail images. They seemed to be still shots from the latest video, all taken from Katie's camera as it was focused on the darkness near the garage. Grace clicked on one image from the middle of the series. "Here. S'hard to see, kinda."

The image was a still of the rear half of Rory's garage. The grass showed up silver green in the moonlight, but the corner of the garage where the attack had come from was dark. Grace pointed to that dark area. "S'in here. I enhanced it."

She minimized that image and opened another version of the same image, but this one had some changes, notably to the dark area that held all their attention. A moment later she'd zoomed in on that area. It was noticeably lighter than the original. Light enough that they could make out two human shapes crouching there in the darkness.

Madison gasped at seeing them.

Sephie turned and smiled at her. "This is nothing. Just wait. It gets better."

Grace did her one-shoulder shrug. "That's the easy part. Now…" She zoomed in further to the figures.

"Is that…. Can you see a face?" Madison asked, leaning in closer to the screen.

"Uh-huh," Grace confirmed, and then she opened a third image, this one even further enhanced and centered on the face of one of the figures in the darkness.

Those who hadn't seen it before sucked in their breath. Whatever Grace had done to that image had been brilliant, because they could all clearly recognize the facial features of one of the people hiding there, despite the hood surrounding his face. The features were handsome in a pretty-boy sort of way, with light-colored curls spilling onto the forehead.

"That's Sean," Rory said. Punching Lee with the hand that was not busy supporting Miss C, she added, "I knew it. Didn't I tell you?"

"Do you think this is what the sheriff has too?" Madison asked hopefully. "Maybe he'll be able to make an arrest. Maybe..."

Liza stopped her. "Hold on. There's more. Gracie, show us the next part, honey," she said, adding an encouraging hand on Grace's shoulder.

"'Kay. Well, thought it was weird that the face was so good." She opened another file, this one zoomed in tight on Sean's face. Only now, something about it didn't seem quite right. Rory couldn't put her finger on it, but something about the face was just ... off. "Hafta look close," Grace said, pointing to the face on the screen. "Lighting's wrong. Shadows on the face are different."

Yes, that was it. The shadows on the hoodie around the face were at a different angle than the shadows on the face itself. Also, the color of the light seemed different.

Lee asked, "Couldn't that be because he was holding a flashlight or something? Or if he's holding their camera, maybe the light from the view screen is causing that effect."

Grace shook her head. "Thought of that. But only the face is different."

"Another light would show up on other parts of his body, His shoulders, his chest," Liza explained further.

Confused, Madison asked, "Well then, what does that mean?"

"S'not his face. Was pasted in," Grace said.

"Wait, are you telling us that this isn't Sean?" Rory asked, dumbfounded. She continued to stare at the face, at everything that seemed wrong with it, and yet she still wanted it to be Sean, because that would give them the easy answer they needed.

"Could be him, but this face doesn't go with this video," Grace said.

"So someone went to the trouble of doctoring this video to make Sean look guilty?" Madison asked.

"Didn't I tell you?" Sephie said triumphantly. "This girl is a genius."

Rory could only wonder if anything besides Grace's work on this video had happened between the previous afternoon and this morning to make Sephie change her opinion of the girl from "odd child" to "genius."

"Who could do this?" Lee asked.

Shaking her head, Grace answered, "Someone good but not too good."

"Was it posted by the same person who did the last one?" Rory asked.

"Naw. I dunno this one—TeamK19 somebody."

"Katie," Rory said. "It's got to be Katie. She's realized that Sean must have murdered Spike, and she's trying to give the sheriff's department enough of a reason to arrest him. It is her video. Plus she just told me the other day that she knows how to do special effects stuff."

"But why 'TeamK'?" Lee questioned.

"She probably got help from someone, and my money's on those jokers in the army jackets."

Madison asked, "Do you think this is what your sheriff found?"

"I don't know. Looks like I'm going to be calling him again," Rory answered, somehow not looking forward to that conversation.

Chapter 28

As it turned out, Rory didn't have to call Mike. She was pushing Miss C's stroller home after the meeting at Madison's, when she heard a car horn tooting behind her. Glancing over her shoulder, she noticed an extended-cab pickup pulling to the curb next to her. Mike. The passenger-side window lowered, and Mike smiled out at her from behind the wheel. He was in civvies, which would normally be a good sign, meaning the case was wrapped up and he could relax and spend some time with her, but today it only told her that he had no idea there was a problem with that video.

"Hey there, pretty lady. Where you headed?" he asked, still smiling.

Rory couldn't help but smile back. Before Mike, it had been years since anyone had bothered to tell her she was pretty or even moderately attractive. The best part was, he not only told her, he seemed to genuinely think it was true. Which meant they were okay, right?

"I don't talk to strangers," she joked and continued walking.

"You won't be smiling soon. Not after we share our news," Miss C meowed at him.

The truck kept pace with them. "I brought lunch. I have corned beef." As he mentioned the corned beef, he held up a white paper sack that Rory recognized as being from her favorite deli in Westbrook. Her mouth watered.

"Well, I guess you don't look *that* strange. Meet me up at my house," she said. "But I better warn you, my boyfriend's the sheriff in this town."

She continued up the sidewalk, perhaps a step faster now, watching as the truck pulled into her driveway. Ah, Mike's home, she thought. Only this wasn't his home, just as his rowhouse in downtown Westbrook wasn't her home. She spun off into imaginings of where their home would be if they made one together, and by the time she turned the stroller's wheels up the drive, she'd decided that it would have to be here. This was her ancestral home, of sorts. And surely Mike wouldn't look half so gorgeous anywhere else as he did leaning there against the tailgate of his pickup in his leather bomber jacket and blue jeans. Okay, he probably would, but that was totally beside the point she was trying to make to herself.

"You forgot our lunch date," he accused good-naturedly as she approached.

"We did not forget. We just disregarded it because we had more important things to do," the cat meowed.

Oh, their lunch date. The one they'd set weeks ago for the one day in the near future when neither of them planned to be working. Rory realized she had forgotten all about it. "No, I didn't," she fibbed, stretching up to kiss him. A little kiss could make up for any myriad of wrongs, she'd found. "Well, I mean I did forget, but you usually cancel dates when you're working a case."

"So I do. But this time I've got good news. We've made an arrest."

"You have?" Rory asked in surprise, with a sinking feeling in her stomach. She pushed the cat stroller toward the back door, Mike following.

"Don't sound so surprised. The Monocacy County Sheriff's Department does have its moments, you know."

"They are small moments, but I suppose you must take what you can get," Miss C meowed.

Rory said, "Sorry. So, the arrest?"

"Yeah, that second video did it. We could make out an ID on one of attackers. It was clearly Sean. We brought him in last night."

"Really? Has he fessed up?"

"Not yet, but we're pretty confident that he will. It's not like he can deny that he was there. Not when we've got his face clearly showing up on video. I got you chips and a garlic pickle too."

"Um..." Rory's hand was on the doorknob, but instead of opening the door, she looked back at Mike.

"What's wrong?" he asked, confused.

"You might want to hold lunch and get back to your case."

Mike put his hands on his hips in that alluring way he had. "What are you talking about?"

"Well, it's just that ... um, Grace took a look at that video—"

"Rory—"

She turned to face him and held a hand up to stop whatever he'd been about to say. "Just wait. Liza agreed to let her do it, and Liza's been with her the whole time. It's better that she does it under some kind of supervision than sneaking around behind everybody's back, which is exactly what she'd do."

Mike's voice took on a resigned tone. "Okay. Tell me what she found."

"Well, it's just like you said, she did some enhancements and zoomed in and isolated Sean's face. And there it was, clear as day. We all saw it—you should have heard the gasp."

"Wait, how many people are we talking about here?" Mike asked.

Thinking, Rory listed off the names. "There was me and Lee and Madison. Grace and Liza, of course. Oh, and Sephie. Miss C."

"Yes, do not forget my invaluable contributions," the cat meowed.

"So whatever Grace found, the whole town probably knows by now."

Rory thought about that too. If Madison had mentioned it to Laura, Laura would have mentioned it to nearly everybody who set foot in Gunther's and had a second to chat. "Probably. But listen. We figured out that it wasn't Sean. I mean, it could have been Sean, it must have been Sean, but that face wasn't right. The shadows and lighting and everything were off, so it was obvious that the face had been added to that video. Somehow you might be able to use it to get him to talk, but the video won't hold up at trial."

Mike rubbed a hand over his chin. Rory hadn't expected her announcement to throw him off balance, but it clearly had.

"I see you were not prepared for this," Miss C meowed. *"You should read Marcus Aurelius. Then you would know it is ridiculous to be surprised by anything."*

"He claims to have an alibi, but so far we haven't been able to confirm it," Mike said.

"Well, you've probably got the right guy. You just don't have the right evidence. The only person who could have doctored that video is Katie, right? And she must have done it to send you in Sean's direction, to get him off the street. I mean, what do you think he's going to do once he finds out she's pregnant with Spike's baby?"

Mike sighed heavily. "I don't know, hon. Something about Sean keeps bugging me."

"Me too. I think it's because he killed his ex-girlfriend's new guy." Rory's voice was edged with bitterness as she remembered Spike lying in her backyard, his body still and his face ashen.

"Allegedly killed," Mike reminded her.

"Whatever."

"You claimed this guy tackled you that night—"

"No, he did tackle me," Rory said testily. If Mike thought for a second that he was going to turn their conversation into an interrogation....

But he conceded her point immediately. "Okay, he tackled you. How did he do that, exactly?"

Not wanting to think about that night, Rory said, "Does it really matter?"

"Maybe not, but we're running out of leads. Anything might help."

"It could be an important detail, revealing the perpetrator's character and physical ability. If you were a better investigator, you would know this," Miss C meowed.

With a loud, exaggerated sigh, Rory closed her eyes. In her mind, she went back to that night ... the moonlight, the fight on her lawn, the guy coming toward her. "He sort of grabbed me like he was hugging me and dragged me down."

"Threw you or dragged you?"

"Dragged. Why?"

"Because that's not really how you tackle someone. In a good tackle, you lower your center of gravity and lead with your shoulder, hitting the ball carrier in the midsection. You hit him low, not high. Then you wrap him up." Mike demonstrated, crouching and lightly planting his left shoulder in Rory's lower chest, ending with his arms wrapped around her.

"Okay, Mr. Football, but is there a point to this, or are you just questioning my semantics and trying to take advantage of me?" Rory said directly into his face, their lips inches apart.

Mike closed the distance, kissing her gently and for entirely too short a time, in Rory's estimation. Then, still holding her, he said, "With Sean's football experience, I'd expect him to be a better tackler than what you describe. So maybe it wasn't him, or maybe he was just trying to be gentle with you."

"Or perhaps he was not very good at this tackling."

"Uh-huh," Rory muttered, not very interested in having a football conversation just then. "You coming in, or...?"

Releasing her, Mike said, "Better not. Sorry, but I have to go talk to Grace so she can show me what she found in this video. And then I'll need to get back downtown. Take a rain check?"

Rory smiled, trying to look innocent. "Sure … but only if I can come along to see Grace. I promise not to interfere."

࿊

"I should be allowed to question this Sean for myself, to see how closely he aligns with the mythical Narcissus," Miss C meowed from behind Rory's seat as Mike drove them to the other end of town. *"Also I need to question Katie. And if someone could read to me from Homer, it would help me to think."*

"Tell me again why we had to bring the cat?" Mike asked as he pulled to a stop in front of the old Miller house. In the driveway, Sephie's Mercedes sat behind Liza's Kia.

Rory unbuckled her seat belt and opened the door. "Because I need some exercise and Miss C needs fresh air. It's a perfect plan. You drop us off here, and we'll walk home." She couldn't quite bring herself to tell him that she wanted the cat to be there because Grace was nuts about her and was more likely to be comfortable, and talkative, in Miss C's presence. She'd barely convinced him that she herself needed to be there because Grace would probably clam up if he went alone.

Mike said, "All right," but from his tone, she knew he wasn't buying it.

She chose to ignore that, having all she could handle wrestling the pet stroller out of the back seat.

Rory had called ahead, so they were expected. It was Sephie who opened the door as they approached across the lawn.

"Did you really have to bring that animal?" she said to Rory, but then she seemed to catch herself and she addressed Mike, saying, "It's so good of you to come,

Sheriff. I think you'll be impressed with what our Grace has found."

Our Grace? Rory thought. She wondered what Liza would have to say about that.

Mike put on his best official smile. "Well, from what Rory's told me, it's pretty impressive evidence."

Sephie ushered them inside, past the front staircase, and straight through to the house's back living room. There, Grace and Liza sat on what was obviously a fold-out sofa. A laptop computer sat open on the coffee table in front of them. Grace's face looked strained when Mike greeted her, but she relaxed as soon as Miss C let out her first meow. The girl had only mumbled a syllable or two in Mike's general direction, but for Miss C she managed to say, "Hey, Miss C." She even smiled. From the look Mike gave her, Rory knew that he now understood exactly why she'd been so insistent on bringing the cat. *Score!* she thought.

"So, Grace, I understand you've found something important," Mike said as he settled onto the sofa between Grace and Liza.

After a verbal nudge from Liza, Grace proceeded to take Mike through the same presentation she'd given earlier in Madison's apartment. Rory watched him as she pointed out the details of the face that were just wrong, how the shadows didn't match up, how nothing else but the face was lit in quite the same way. It was obvious that this information was totally new to him. He hadn't been just humoring them or letting their little investigation play out in the background while the real one proceeded way ahead of them. Rory did not much like the furrow in his brow. It meant he was worried.

"So you're one hundred percent sure that that face was planted in this video?"

"Sure," Grace said.

The brow furrowed deeper.

After some moments' thought, Mike said solemnly, "Thank you, Ms. Cunningham. You've been a great help to law enforcement." He extended his right hand. At first Grace seemed unsure of what to do, but then she met his hand with hers and they shook. To Rory, he said, "Well, hon, looks like you were right. I've got to get back to work. You're sure you don't want a ride home?"

Rory stopped him. "No, no. You go on. We'll walk. It's nice enough out."

"Rory, you'll stay for lunch, won't you?" Sephie offered, reminding her that this was not actually Liza's house. Such a complicated situation, the house left to Don Miller's mistress, the contents to his ex-wife, the ex-wife now renting rooms from the mistress. *Only in Brooksford,* Rory thought.

Aloud she said, "I wouldn't want to put you out..."

Sephie waved that off. "It's no trouble. I'll whip us up something. Sheriff, thank you for coming." She seemed intent on ushering Mike to the door and maybe seeing him off with a kiss, but Rory shoved herself between them and grabbed his arm, pulling him toward the door as he wished Sephie a good day.

"Possessive much?" he whispered to Rory as they went past the front staircase.

"Shut up and kiss me."

He did, but it was more of a friendly, see-you-later kiss than the lover's kiss she wanted. It would have to do though, and as she knew Sephie was hovering at the far end of the hall, it would do perfectly.

"Love you. I'll be in touch later. Sorry about lunch," he said.

"Me too, to all that you just said. But don't be sorry." She kissed him again, on the cheek this time, and then he was out the door.

Rory stood in the open doorway watching Mike walk to the truck. She waved as he drove away, then she closed the door. She stood for a moment with her hand on the doorknob, wishing that Grace hadn't found anything fishy about that video, so she and Mike could be back at her place enjoying their lunch date. He'd get a little mustard on his chin the way he always managed to do, and she'd tease him and wipe it off, and then....

"You make such a cute couple," Sephie said from directly behind her.

Rory started. Criminy, when had the woman snuck down the hall toward her? She collected herself enough to say, "Yeah, he's pretty great. Uh, can I help with lunch or anything?"

Fortunately, Sephie said no to that. Rory wasn't sure what she would have done if the woman had actually asked her to help in the kitchen. Maybe her culinary ineptitude was so obvious that Sephie knew better than to ask for her help. In any case, Rory sat at the table with Liza and Grace while Sephie clanged about in the kitchen.

Grace seemed troubled during lunch. Finally Liza asked her, "Is something wrong, honey? You've hardly said a word."

Rory wasn't sure what was so unusual about Grace not saying much during social occasions, but who knew? Maybe the girl could talk a person's ear off under the right circumstances. Most people could.

After a one-shoulder shrug, Grace said, "Don't know if I should've told the sheriff something."

"What is it?"

"That video. S'going viral."

Rory hadn't even thought to ask how many views the new video had gotten. The first one had been bad enough, but there had been something amateurish and college-pranky about that footage, shot as it was from the point of view of the laughing attackers. Katie's video was something different. It was more chilling, in that you as the viewer knew what was coming—at least you did if you'd seen the first video—but Katie and Spike did not. And you knew that very soon, Spike would be lying dead in the November grass.

Now she asked, "How many views does it have?"

"Like, a million," Grace answered. "S'all over social media. Twitter."

Rory's inner editor latched on to "like a million." What did that mean, exactly? A million? Nearly a million, over a million, approximately a million? Well, it hardly mattered just now. Whatever the number was, it was big.

"That's good," Sephie said. "Excellent."

"Is it?" Rory asked.

"Yes. Think of it. More views means more visitors means more business means more income." As she warmed to her topic, Sephie forgot all about the bowl of soup that sat in front of her. Or rather, she didn't so much forget about it as shove it out of her way so she could get her elbows on the table and lean forward. She reminded Rory of a kid telling an especially exciting story. Maybe this was how she kept her figure so trim. She talked business instead of eating.

Sephie went on. "As I see it, we need to attract a steady stream of visitors into this town to maintain people's interest. To keep the townspeople's interest, I mean. Otherwise, everyone will just forget about this little escapade and we'll go back to being a little backwater nobody's ever heard of."

"Brooksfordians," Rory corrected her. "We call ourselves Brooksfordians, not townspeople."

For a second, Sephie stared at her as though she'd grown a second head. Then she laughed. "Yes, of course you do. How could I have forgotten about that? Brooksfordians," she repeated and chuckled again. Then as though she'd pressed an off button, the laughter stopped and she went on. "But listen, we keep the visitors, we add some little shops and whatnot for them to visit, maybe a spa"—here Rory noticed Grace and Liza look at each other quickly. What would opening a spa have to do with them? But Sephie was still speaking—"Pretty soon word gets around. 'Hey, have you heard about Brooksford? That quirky little town? You should go see it.' And we get more visitors, until finally the whole thing becomes self-sustaining. All we need is some buy-in from important stakeholders."

Sephie looked pointedly at Liza, who said, "Look, if you want to open a spa, obviously I can't stop you, but I am not going to be your hairdresser."

With a pout that Rory imagined was much more effective when she was trying to convince a male associate to go along with one of her plans, Sephie said, "Oh, but think of it, Liza! It could be our gimmick: 'The spa where the stylist has a PhD in beauty.'"

"My education is not a gimmick," Liza snapped.

"Professor Eleanor would be appalled by you," Miss C meowed at Sephie. *"So would Socrates. He never turned education into a money-making scheme."*

Sephie was undeterred. "Of course, dear," she said patronizingly to Liza. "I'm just asking you to think of the possibilities. Honestly, how much do you make teaching those little classes at that college? Enough to support you and Grace? Enough to buy yourself a house like this?" She motioned around the kitchen, which, Rory could not help but notice, was in serious need of a makeover. The cabinets looked like they'd come from a 1980s warehouse blowout sale, the appliances seemed to be on their last legs, the tile floor was worn and scuffed. If the whole house was like this kitchen, it wasn't such a great place to be able to afford. But then, maybe that had been Sephie's point.

Liza was taking the same look around and must have been having much the same thoughts. She said defensively, "Gracie and I are doing fine. I'm doing work that matters, and we are doing fine."

Sephie scoffed. "Oh, please. If you weren't living here at drastically reduced rent, where would you be? In some bug-infested studio apartment?"

"I saw a roach last night," Grace said. "In the bathroom. Upstairs."

Liza took up that thought. "There, you see, this isn't the palace you make it out to be. It's an old farmhouse."

"With roaches," Grace added.

"Be that as it may, you are both missing the point again. We all three work together, you and I pool our capital to fix this place up, and pretty soon we'll have a wonderful, inviting spa experience to offer our guests. People will pay Mr. Laser for a relaxing night at his inn and pay us for a luxurious day of beauty. We'll think up some special mud treatment or something."

Against her better judgment, Rory said, "I think there's some kind of clay deposit near here. I remember my grandmother talking about it, how back in the day they used it to treat their skin." She shrugged apologetically when Liza turned a disbelieving stare on her. Whose side are you on? the stare asked.

Sephie grabbed hold of what Rory had said. "There, now that's the kind of initiative we need. Do you know where this deposit is? I wonder how you even make a mud bath. I've had them of course, but—"

Grace cut her off. "Don't have to do a whole bath. Just do the face." She motioned with one hand as though washing her face.

"Of course!" Sephie beamed. "We could call it the Historic Brooksford Facial. And Rory, I hope you'll think some more about—"

"I am not turning my house into an antiques store," Rory told her again.

Liza turned to her and said, "I see you're not so eager to get on this bandwagon when it's your own house that's being talked about."

Rory smiled her apologies. Of course she really had no right to stick herself in the middle of whatever negotiations were ongoing between Sephie and Liza. Especially if, as it sounded, Sephie was trying to pressure Liza to invest her talent and money into some cockamamie spa that could sink more easily than swim.

After lunch, when Liza walked to the front door with Rory and Miss C, Rory apologized for real. "I shouldn't have said anything about that clay. Sorry."

"Oh, forget it. She'd find out about it anyway. You know how she is. Give her another hour and she'll have found out where it is and have dug up a month's supply of the stuff."

"Yes, we know. She is very Underworldy," Miss C meowed.

"But still, I shouldn't have stuck my nose in."

"That is true."

After shushing her cat, Rory went on, "What's Sephie up to anyway?"

Liza guided them onto the front porch and stepped out with them. "She seems to think I have free money I can use to invest in sprucing up that old barn into a beautiful, relaxing spa. And she seems to think I would want to do all the grunt work at said spa while she provides 'management oversight.'"

Rory looked toward the old barn, now used as a garage and glorified tool shed. True, though it was a smallish barn, it might be large enough to house a business, but a spa? The floor was packed dirt, one wall had a missing board, the metal roof was more rust than metal. "Are we sure Sephie's actually been to a spa before? Because that does not look like a spa," she said, pointing toward the barn.

"Oh, it 'has such character' though," Liza said, obviously quoting Sephie again. "And she's run the numbers and decided, what with her recent, um, experience, she can't attract enough capital to build something new and grand like she'd originally planned. Now she's going for something smaller, where the average woman can come for a day of pampering."

"And if you don't go along with it?"

"Well then, Grace and I will be looking for another place to live, most likely. Sephie's thinking she'd find another live-in person to help her run the place. The thing is, she's starting to get Grace on her side, asking her to come up with logo designs."

"I'll bet Grace would be good at that."

"She is. That's the problem. Part of the problem."

"And the other part is…?"

"Well, if Sephie's right about the kind of money we could make at this, my current salary, part-time, with no benefits and no guarantee I'll still have a job next year … it just doesn't stack up. Financially, I might be better off working for Sephie."

Chapter 29

As Rory and Miss C walked home after a surprisingly pleasant lunch with Sephie, Liza, and Grace, they noticed that there seemed to be increased traffic in town once again. "I guess people are going sightseeing on a Saturday," Rory commented. "Just what we need. Although Madison's probably loving it." She wondered how things were working out for Frank and the Brooksford Inn. Seemed she'd get a chance to ask him, as she saw him and the big chocolate Newfoundland, Clementine, going into the post office ahead of them.

She guessed Mrs. Crabtree had just finished giving Frank the "you can't bring animals in here" spiel, because the old woman appeared to be fuming, and she had an especially deep glare for Rory and Miss C. No matter. They'd only be there a moment, just long enough to get the mail and chat with Frank.

"Afternoon, Rory, Miss C," Frank said absently. Clementine panted into the stroller.

"Barbarian," Miss C meowed at the dog in the friendliest way possible. Clementine had helped save her life once, after all. One should always be grateful, Professor Eleanor had taught her, even to barbarians.

Rory said, "Hi, Frank. Mrs. Crabtree." She stopped for a beat to allow the postmaster to glare some more and then went on. "Frank, I've been meaning to ask if you'd seen any uptick in business since this thing with the videos started. I know Madison has had some busy days up at the café."

Frank flipped through a large stack of mail. "No. Despite what Sephie said about this being great for the town, so far all I've seen are fools who want to tramp around the lawn and take pictures of themselves."

Rory wondered if she should mention Sephie's spa idea, decided she shouldn't. Let Sephie spread word about her own ideas.

Instead she said, "Well, maybe if the traffic keeps up, we'll get some people who want to stay for a day or two."

"Be better if they all just go away and leave us alone," Mrs. Crabtree said.

"Right. The appeal of the Brooksford Inn is to get away from any kind of crowd, to relax and experience life in a small town," Frank agreed.

That set off sparks of thoughts in Rory's mind. She knew the inn had not done well in the past couple of years, not since Don Miller's murder had started off the recent troubles in Brooksford. In the wake of that first killing, the problem had been that Frank's name had been mentioned repeatedly in relation to the crime, and who wanted to stay at an inn run by a murderer? But since then, the whole "get away from it all" shtick hadn't seemed to work. When you really thought about it, why would anyone plunk down money to stay in Brooksford, where there was only one small restaurant that wasn't open all the time, where there was nothing to do but walk up Main Street to get a cup of coffee and a pastry? True, the coffee and pastries were great, but it wasn't a big draw. Maybe Sephie was right. Maybe it was time for them to try something new.

But there was no way Rory was putting an antiques shop in her home. As Grace would say, uh-uh.

She went to the wall of PO boxes to retrieve her mail. Catalogs and appeals for charitable donations. "Maybe you should try some new marketing techniques," she suggested to Frank as she dropped the mail into the pouch on Miss C's stroller.

"What do you mean? I run ads," Frank countered. He usually wasn't big on new ideas.

"I know, but maybe it wouldn't hurt to, you know, mention the Woldwomper a little. Maybe try advertising on YouTube."

Frank gave her much the same look Sephie had earlier—like she'd grown a second head. "You crazy or something? That would just attract a bunch of nutcases. You think I want nutcases staying at my place?"

Like you haven't had nutcases stay there before, Rory thought, but she decided against saying that aloud. "They'd be paying nutcases," she pointed out.

"That's the last thing we need," Mrs. Crabtree growled from behind the counter. "Stupid idea," she mumbled, just loud enough for Rory and Miss C to hear. The cat hissed at her, and for a second Rory seriously thought her neighbor was going to hiss back.

But Rory's suggestion seemed to give Frank pause. For a moment he said nothing. Rory, having the distinct impression that she'd just become Sephie's greatest cheerleader, said, "Think about it: We get a little display about Fording and the Woldwomper in the historical society, telling the true story, not all this made-up stuff. You set up some sort of display in the inn, some pictures in the rooms or something. Pretty soon you've got a booming business." At least that was how Sephie saw it. Could it work?

"I'm surprised to hear you talk like this, Rory, given what happened in your backyard just a few days ago."

Mrs. Crabtree added, "And it'll just be more of the same if you encourage that nonsense. You mark my words. It'll be the ruin of this town."

Rory ignored that and answered Frank. "Well, Frank, when you really think about it, Sephie is planning for the future of this town in a way that no one else is. Now that the Woldwomper genie is out of the bottle, we should be the ones to benefit, shouldn't we? Because if we don't, outsiders will come in and do what we won't." She shot a look to Mrs. Crabtree, who scowled back.

"Does that mean I will soon be living in an antiques shop?" Miss C meowed. *"Because if I am, we need to schedule the shop to close when it is my nap time, which is much of the day."*

"I just don't know," Frank said, shaking his head. The Rotary logo on his blue ball cap looked dingy and sad, somehow. "It's like I woke up one morning and realized I was living in a completely different Brooksford from the one I grew up in."

Rory wondered which morning he was referring to, a morning this week or a morning two years ago, when he woke up to learn that one of his best friends had been bludgeoned to death? She searched the sudden jumble of words in her head for something comforting, came up with, "It's changed for all of us. But think of the business."

"Bah," Mrs. Crabtree said. Knowing what was coming next, Rory pushed the stroller toward the door. "Get that cat out of here!"

Frank opened the door, and Rory pushed Miss C outside as the cat meowed, *"Medusa! Get a mirror!"*

A second later, Frank and Clementine had joined them on the sidewalk. Rory opened her mouth to tell him good-bye, but before she could say anything, a car stopped in the street and the driver, a college-age woman, leaned out the window with a cell phone to take Rory and Miss C's picture. Rory was acutely aware of how her mouth had been hanging open when the picture was taken. "Thanks!" the young woman offered, waving, as she drove on toward the intersection.

"Nutcases," Frank grumbled.

"Paying nutcases. Listen, Frank, you're right. It might be a little crazy for a while. But I really think it'll be worse if we don't take control. What are you doing for Thanksgiving?"

"Huh?" Her question, coming out of nowhere, seemed to confuse him.

"Thanksgiving, that great American holiday. Is your dining room open? You serving a special meal?"

Suddenly Frank looked like a defeated old man, too tired to fight on. "We'd planned on it, but we haven't gotten a single reservation. I guess me and Betty will be having it to ourselves."

"Here's an idea..." Rory felt her mind spinning with possibilities. "What if you could get Liza to come in that afternoon and give an illustrated lecture on the real story of the Woldwomper? You serve everybody a great meal, and while they're having their coffee and pumpkin pie, they get to listen to a really interesting talk?"

"That is surprisingly not a bad idea," Miss C meowed.

"You realize Thanksgiving is five days from now? People already have plans," Frank said, but Rory could tell from the thoughtful way he spoke that she'd sparked something in him.

"Not everybody has plans."

"It being so close though. Too late to advertise."

"Get on the phone to Mel Scott. Or better yet"—Rory could not believe she was about to say this—"talk to Sephie Rennsfelder. She wants to be the town's PR person, let her earn her zero dollars. And before you say Liza probably wouldn't do it, I happen to know she's looking to earn a little extra cash. Who knows? Maybe you could make her talks a regular thing. I bet she'd jump at the chance."

Frank smiled a little, said, "You've caught the bug, Rory Roberts. The same bug the mayor's caught. But I don't know." He rubbed his chin.

"Think of the full dining room. Think of the money."

"I am. Oh, I am. More like dreaming than thinking."

"Talk to Sephie."

With a guffaw, Frank said, "She's patient zero for this bug that's going around, wantin' to change everything."

"I know, but talk to her. Frank, the town needs you to catch this bug. You need to be one of the leaders if Historic Brooksford is ever going to work."

"I think you have spent too long in the vicinity of Persephone. You are beginning to talk like her," Miss C meowed.

Frank said, "Rory, your cat's getting restless. Better get her on home. Thanks for the pep talk." But she could not tell from his tone whether anything she'd said had made a difference.

Chapter 30

Rory and Miss C continued toward home, noticing a definite increase in both vehicle and pedestrian traffic. The only problem was that these people had nowhere to go once they reached Brooksford. Many of them stopped in at Gunther's for something to drink, and some milled about outside the town hall and the historical society as though waiting for something to happen. Her own house had become a sort of beacon, where, it seemed, everyone wanted to stop for a photo. Seeing the crowd inside Gunther's, Rory decided to skip that for the time being. She was pretty sure Madison hadn't even seen her go by, what with how busy she was behind the counter.

But the little knot of people hanging around in front of her house did not look inviting either. She tried to think of a way she could get past them without drawing attention to herself, so that she could maybe get around back and get inside without being accosted. But with each step she took toward home, she knew this was impossible. There was no way a woman pushing a cat in a stroller was not going to be noticed.

She had reached the Crabtrees' house when she saw one person in the knot nudge another. Then there was pointing. None of it was threatening; in fact, the people's faces brightened at seeing Rory and Miss C. They couldn't wait to talk to her, to take selfies with her and her cat, to ask if they could maybe just go out back for a minute, to take selfies back there. This was what Rory discovered when she swallowed her trepidation and, instead of ducking up the Crabtrees' drive and hiding in the bushes somewhere—which she did seriously consider—she continued straight on and waded into the eager little crowd.

A few selfies wouldn't hurt, she decided. Put a welcoming face on the town. That wouldn't hurt either. And so Rory smiled and smiled and smiled again as, one after another, the people—mostly young people who seemed to have come from local colleges, judging by the sweatshirts they wore, but also—and this really threw her—a middle-aged couple with British accents. They were vacationing around Washington, DC, they said, and had rented a car for the day so they could come out and have a look at the home of the Woldwomper. Turned out they were fans of the supernatural who'd seen the Jacey Jones story on the news, hunted down the video online, and scrapped plans to tour a couple of museums in favor of a side trip to Brooksford. They were polite, thanking Rory for taking the time to pose with them and asking her if there were any place to get a meal. "We saw the inn, but we haven't any reservations," the man said. "Do you think we'll get in?"

"Oh, don't worry about that. I know the owner. You head on down, and I'll make a call for you. I'm sure he'll fit you in," she said, hoping she wasn't making promises that Frank would not keep.

Then one of the college girls asked, "Hey, we want to go out back to get pictures with the tree. You don't mind, do you?" She said it as though it was impossible for Rory to refuse. How could she possibly mind? But that was a bridge too far.

"I do mind, actually," Rory said, as nicely as she could while still being firm. "Out front is fine, I'm happy to meet you, but I have to keep the back off-limits. Sheriff's orders," she lied, though she was pretty sure what Mike would have to say about letting strangers wander all through her backyard. She imagined his mouth curling down into a frown. Thoughts of his lips made her knees go wobbly.

The girl pouted, and her voice became whiny. "Jeez. We just want to take a picture. Those other guys are back there."

That set off alarms in Rory's mind. "What other guys?" she asked quickly, while also thinking of whether this was a reason to call Mike, or 911, or someone.

"Those guys taking video. They just went on back there. At least we asked first!" the girl added quickly and with her voice rising on every word as Rory hurried to get her cat and herself in the house.

Inside, she shut and locked the door and released Miss C from her stroller. The cat, as though she'd understood the talk about the backyard, trotted straight for the laundry/mudroom, ahead of Rory. Uncanny, that cat.

"Forget it, cat, you are not going out there," Rory said as she looked through the glass pane in her back door and saw none other than Dan and Eddie wandering through her yard. They each held a smartphone and appeared to be filming. Working on their "meta thing," no doubt. Rory swore and opened the door, slipping through it while blocking her cat from doing the same.

This was no time for niceties. "Hey! What do you think you're doing?" she yelled.

The boys froze and looked back at her. One of them seemed to turn his camera on her, and she wondered if she was being filmed. Not acceptable, she decided, and she headed down the two back steps and across the patio, not caring if she looked like a crazy old lady, as they would surely portray her. She was not willing to be part of their meta thing, whatever that was.

"I haven't given you permission to film back here. Turn that thing off." She wondered if she looked exactly like Margaret Crabtree as she stomped across the lawn toward them. Rory realized that, although she knew them as a unit—Dan and Eddie—she had no idea which was which.

The boys looked at each other and slowly lowered their phones. "Sorry," one of them, the shorter of the two, offered as Rory came within normal conversational distance. "We thought it would be okay. Katie did it."

"Well, it's not okay, and Katie asked first. She had permission."

"Oh. So, uh, d'you think it'd be okay if we, you know, shoot back here? We're doing a meta thing for our class project."

Rory took a slow breath to calm herself. She understood now what Katie had said about these guys not being smart enough to figure out much on their own. "I know you're doing a meta thing, and no, it's not okay for you to be back here. You're trespassing, and I want you to get off my property before I call the sheriff's department. I know the sheriff personally, you know, and he will not be happy to know that you're just traipsing around back here when I don't want you here." She wondered vaguely if these boys would know what "traipsing" meant. She wondered if they knew what "meta" meant.

The taller of the two said, "Sorry. Jeez. C'mon, man." And then they stalked past Rory, headed for the driveway. They did not offer any further conversation, and she wasn't sure if she should be happy that they'd gone so easily or worried about whatever their meta thing was going to turn out to be. Worried, she decided, and she wondered how soon it—whatever it was—would hit the internet and add to Brooksford's viral moment.

Chapter 31

Miss C watched from the office window as the Rory person confronted the two young film directors in the backyard. It was so unfair that she had been denied the opportunity to be part of the confrontation and to hear exactly what was said. This Rory person had developed into a human with passable cat care skills, but as an investigator she remained rather inept. The cat thought of all the Agatha Christie stories Professor Eleanor had read to her in their years together. Poirot, now he had been a detective of the first class. Miss C wondered seriously if Rory even had any "little gray cells." Doubtful.

Outside, Rory spoke briefly to the filmmakers, who then sulked away. They looked like two people who had never won anything, never achieved anything, never been recognized for anything. Humans reserved their laurels for the few who were both talented enough and lucky enough to win them, Miss C had observed. The rest wallowed in obscurity. These two were the most obscure humans she had yet encountered. They had no business, really, trying to play at being Hesiod. But then who had Hesiod been, or Homer, or Herodotus? Extraordinary people, or just lucky to land in the right place at the right time with the right ideas? Perhaps Hesiod had, like these boys, been a sulking youth who wanted to tell a "meta thing" about his world. It did give one pause. She wished Professor Eleanor could be here to discuss it all with her. She would understand.

But that was beside the point at the moment. Deal with the circumstances in front of you, Uncle Marcus had said. What was important now was to identify for certain who that dark figure had been in the video, if it was not the Sean person. And the best way to do that would be to interrogate Katie, since it seemed she had been the one to put the evidence onto this u-tube.

Rory passed a quiet evening with Lee and his mom, while Miss C passed a less quiet evening in the living room window. One thing the cat had to admit since this whole business started: There was more to watch out the window, what with the new crop of local and not-so-local tourists that had come in. Having her cottage be the focus of much of the activity proved a bonus for Miss C, as it meant that nearly everyone who came to visit Brooksford for touristic purposes passed by her. And, as a place for clear thinking, nothing surpassed a good window.

Miss C gazed out onto the street and then, by changing her eyes' focus ever so slightly, she was looking at her own reflection. *"Just like Narcissus,"* she purred to herself. Narcissus, who had fallen in love with his reflection and been turned into a flower. Professor Eleanor had told her the story once while planting bulbs in a pot for their balcony. The following spring those bulbs had bloomed into pretty yellow flowers. Miss C had to admit the details of the story were hazy now, but she was sure Narcissus had not been violent. Then again, those who loved themselves too much could turn violent to protect their beautiful reflection. And parts of the plant that Narcissus had become were poisonous—she remembered Professor Eleanor warning her about them. But could a poisonous flower stab someone to death, like someone had done to Spike? Or was it perhaps more likely that its influence pushed someone else to do the stabbing?

"Humans...so predictable, and yet so unfathomable," Miss C meowed quietly as she considered the many questions that remained unanswered.

ʢ

"Are you still in that window?" Rory asked the cat when she came home from Lee's that night. They'd had a nice dinner and then played cards for an hour or so, before Rory decided she'd better get on home, before the evening slipped into what could be properly called the depths of the night. First of all, she no longer felt comfortable walking even the short distance between their two houses, what with all the new visitors in town, and second, she was rarely awake much past nine o'clock.

"There is still so much to see and to ponder," Miss C meowed from her loaf position atop her condo.

Rory approached quietly and reached to stroke the cat's head, scratching first behind the black ear, then behind the orange one. Miss C purred.

"Anything going on out there?"

"It has quieted considerably. Still, it will not do to let our guard down."

Rory peered out onto a darkened Main Street. Not a soul in sight. "I don't see anything."

"You wouldn't, with your inferior human senses."

Continuing to scratch Miss C's head, Rory said, "You're a pretty good watch cat, aren't you?"

"Superior, I would say."

"Well, c'mon, Cuddlywumps, let's get ready for bed." Rory stepped away from the window, giving the cat one last scratch between the ears. Miss C meowed something back that Rory would have sworn meant "in a minute."

Shaking her head, she went off to get ready for bed, slipping into her flannel pajamas, brushing her teeth. Still Miss C sat in the window. Rory crawled between the covers on her bed and adjusted her pillows behind her. This was usually when Miss C appeared, coming to snuggle with her as they watched a show or two before falling asleep. But tonight Rory flicked on the TV and scrolled through her streaming options with no input from the cat. And so she settled on old episodes of *Frasier*, a comedy she had loved years ago.

She turned off the bedside light and snuggled down under the blankets and wished the cat would show up, because reacting out loud to whatever is happening on screen just makes more sense when there is someone, even a cat, there to listen. Alone, she worried while she pretended to watch the show. She hadn't heard from Mike, which was a bad sign. It meant there'd been no significant progress in the investigation.

Rory was deep into the second episode of *Frasier* before Miss C appeared, jumping onto the bed and turning around three times before settling down next to her. The cat began to purr.

"Are we safe?" Rory asked.

"For the moment."

"That's good." Rory set the sleep timer on the TV for ninety minutes. Miss C stretched one paw out to touch her person's thigh and watched as she fell asleep.

Chapter 32

Sunday dawned bright and just a touch warmer. By the time the sun rose, a white-yellow disc shining through the branches of the maple in the backyard, Rory had been up for a couple of hours. She'd risen at five as usual, in response to Miss C's incessant tapping and meowing. After feeding the cat and skimming through the morning's newspaper, in which she learned that Sean had been detained briefly as a person of interest and then released, Rory decided to check YouTube to see if any new videos had been posted. Specifically, she wondered if Dan and Eddie might have finished their meta thing. She and Miss C went into the office, and she turned on the computer. Soon enough she had a different video playing on each monitor. There was nothing that seemed to be from Dan and Eddie, but there were plenty of new Brooksford videos. None of these added much to the story; they ran more along the lines of "My Day in Brooksford," and they were less than fascinating. Their content did underscore the fact that there just wasn't much to do in this town.

The morning progressed quietly, as Sundays usually did, with the passing time punctuated by the ringing of the Brooksford bells. By noon the sidewalks were getting busy with visitors, most of whom came to gawk at Rory's cottage and the calico cat sitting in its front window. *Yeah, this town is definitely gonna need something else to entertain people,* Rory thought the one time she chanced a look out onto Main Street, only to see six college-age kids standing with their backs to her house, snapping selfies.

She was pulled away from the window by her ringing cell phone. It was probably Lee calling to check up on her, she thought, but no, the screen showed Liza's name, and when Rory answered, the woman sounded frantic.

"Sean's in town. Grace just saw him. She was walking home from Gunther's, and she saw him getting out of a car in the town hall parking lot."

"Is she sure it was him?" Rory asked, not doubting what Liza was telling her, but then how many times had Grace actually seen Sean?

"Yes, she's sure. She recognized him from that video. Do you think we should call the sheriff?"

One down side to being in a relationship with the local sheriff, Rory was finding, was that it meant everyone felt free to come to her asking if she thought they should tell the sheriff something, or hoping that she would contact him for them. "I guess I can call him, just to let him know," she said, not wanting to bother him, especially when she knew he must be busy trying to nail down a new suspect.

Before she could get through her contacts to find Mike's number, her phone rang again. Madison this time. "I just saw Katie walk past my shop," she said. "You think we should try to talk to her about that video?"

Rory's gut reaction was yes, but she asked the obvious question once again. "You're sure it was her?"

She could almost hear Madison smirking through the phone. "Of course I'm sure. I was wiping down a table, and I looked out the window, and there she was, walking up Main toward your way."

"Okay."

"You think I should call the sheriff?"

"Well, you know what? I have to call him about something else anyway, so I'll mention it to him, okay?"

"Oh, thanks, Rory, you're the best." Madison ended the call quickly, probably anxious to get back to running her suddenly very busy café.

This time, Rory was able to find Mike in her contacts and press call. The phone rang twice before he answered, "Sheriff Mike Davis speaking." From the level of background noise, she guessed that he was driving somewhere, using the hands-free calling.

"Hey, it's me," she said as she walked through the kitchen on her way to lock the back door. Given the current circumstances, it would not do to leave it unlocked while she and Miss C went out searching for their suspects. "Sorry to call you while you're working, but people have just told me they've seen Sean and Katie in town. I thought you should know."

"They're together?" he asked.

"No. At least they weren't seen together."

"Okay, thanks. We've been looking for Katie. She's gone underground all of a sudden."

"What about Sean though?"

"Well, you said yourself that it looked like she set him up by doctoring that video."

"Yeah, but that doesn't mean he's innocent, does it?"

"No, of course not. Listen, I'm on my way up there. There's some rain heading in, so it might take me a little longer than usual. Just don't do anything, okay? Either one of them could be dangerous, so don't get involved. Please."

"Okay," Rory said, retrieving her fanny pack from the bedroom.

"You promise you won't get involved?" Mike insisted. "I mean it."

Fingers crossed, she said, "Sure, I promise."

As soon as she ended the call, Rory buckled on the fanny pack and dropped the phone into it. "C'mon, Cuddlywumps, time to take a little walk."

"But I thought you wanted to stay out of the crowd," Miss C meowed, not that she was complaining. She rather

enjoyed going into a mass of people in her stroller, watching as the crowd parted for her. What other housecat had such power?

"We'll just go down to Gunther's and get a quick coffee or something."

The cat preceded her to her stroller and waited to be lifted in. Hefting the feline, Rory said, "Criminy, cat, you're going on a diet as soon as this is over."

"What is a diet?" Miss C asked. Of course she knew the answer, but the Rory person could be distracted by the silliest things, so it was worth a try.

Before they could get out the front, though, they heard a knock at her back door. Rory tensed, hands on the stroller handles. She could just head out, pretending she hadn't heard anything. That would be great if the person at the back door turned out to be one of the pesky tourists who, after already trespassing onto her property, decided it would be polite to ask permission to just take a few pictures, as long as they were there. Or maybe they wanted to ask a few questions about the Woldwomper. Or maybe it was Lee. With the back door locked, he wouldn't be able to come right in as he usually did.

Deciding she had to check, she said, "Hold on, Miss C. I'll just see who that is, and then we'll go."

"Do not dawdle. My public do not like to be kept waiting."

Rory squared her shoulders and walked straight through her kitchen and into the laundry/mudroom. There was no point in sneaking around, really, because whoever it was would surely see her through the door's glass window panes. She let out a relieved breath when she saw that her visitor was not a stranger but Lee. She hurried to unlock the door for him, wishing they could just go back to how things used to be, when she could leave the door unlocked all day long and not worry about a thing. Well, they might not ever get back to those days, it looked like.

"Boy, am I glad to see you," she said to him.

Worry creased his forehead, and he asked quickly, "What's wrong? I tried to call you a minute ago and got your voice mail. Figured I'd better come over and check."

Good old Lee. He came in, and Rory shut the door behind him. "Everything's fine with me, but parts of the town are in a tizzy. Grace thinks she saw Sean down near the town hall, and Madison just saw Katie walking up this way," she explained, leading the way into the living room.

"Oh? Does Mike know?"

"Yeah, I just called him. That's probably why you got my voice mail. He's on his way up here, but until then, we are not to engage the subjects."

"So what are you doing?" Lee asked, watching her zip Miss C's stroller closed.

She smiled mischievously. "Well, you know, it won't hurt to take a quick walk down to Gunther's. Get a little coffee. Evaluate the situation. You want to come with?"

Lee took a look through the front window. "You know it's starting to rain, right?" he asked.

"Oh, it's just going to be a little shower. We'll snag a table at Gunther's and wait it out. Now, you coming?"

"Sure. Pepperoni neutrons," he uttered their secret battle cry without enthusiasm.

"Let me just—" Rory began, but she was interrupted by a knock on her front door. "Oh, for Pete's sake. That better not be one of these loonies." She opened the door, and there stood Katie. "Oh, hi," Rory sputtered. She'd expected to see Katie across the street, from a distance, not right up in her face on her own front step. Mike would be furious if she invited the girl in, but then Lee was there, so what could go wrong? Still, it was probably best to follow instructions as closely as possible. "I'd invite you in, but we were actually just on our way out. You could come with us, though. We're just going to get a coffee."

Katie said breathlessly, "Sean's coming. He's after me. He's following me. Please, you've gotta let me in, before he sees where I went." She'd placed one hand on the doorjamb, so the only way Rory could close the door would be to slam it on the girl's fingers.

"I would leave her in the rain," Miss C advised. *"This Katie person has proven herself to be duplicitous in the past."*

Rory found she could not refuse the frightened, haunted look in Katie's eyes. If she left the girl standing out there on her doorstep and Sean caught up with her and ... well, and did whatever he was planning on doing ... what would Mike think of her then? Rory opened the door wider. "Come on in." After Katie brushed past her, Rory stuck her head out and took a look toward the intersection. Yes, there was a small group crossing into the north end, and several paces behind them, just reaching the stop sign, was a youngish man who seemed to not be part of their group. He was the right size for Sean, but he had a hoodie closed over his head, and he was kind of hunched over against the light, misty rain. Could be him, but she wasn't sure.

She closed the door and asked, "You're sure it's him? You got a good look?"

Katie gave her a look like that had been the most stupid question anyone had ever asked. "Of course I'm sure. I know what my ex-boyfriend looks like."

Had there been something menacing in her tone? And if so, was it directed at Rory or at Sean?

"You've got nothing to worry about. The sheriff's on his way up here now, so he'll take care of it," Rory said, as much to warn Katie as to reassure her. She'd had dangerous people in this living room before and had been blindsided by them. Well, not this time. Having Lee there helped, too. Between the two of them, plus Miss C, they could take this girl if they had to, she judged. The thought reminded her that she'd better let the cat out of the stroller, just in case they needed her.

"Yes, let me out. I am of no use to you while I am stuck in this chariot," the cat advised.

As she undid the zipper and watched Miss C leap to the ground and go straight to Katie, Rory wondered what Mike would say if he knew she was relying on the cat for protection. The thought almost made her smile, but she suppressed it. This was not the time.

"So how are you, Katie?" Lee asked, and Rory recognized genuine concern in his voice. He was such a sweetheart. He'd be great for Liza—and for Grace.

"Oh, you know, sad. Scared," Katie answered.

Rory said, "Your movie turned out really good." She thought it was worth a small lie to find out if Katie was in fact responsible for the second video. "I see it's gotten to be pretty popular on YouTube, too."

The tiny smile that curled Katie's mouth was all the confirmation she needed, but the girl also said, "Thanks. Dan helped me finish it. I wasn't gonna post it yet, but after Sean did his ... well, I just had to, that's all."

"So the first one was definitely Sean's?"

"Sure. Who else would even do that? He's such a jerk. A lying, cheating, murdering jerk." Katie folded further into herself, her face threatening tears.

"Tell us why you felt you had to put Sean's face in your video," Miss C demanded as she sniffed at Katie's shoe. Katie pulled her foot back.

Rory moved to shoo the cat away. "C'mon, cat, leave her be." She caught Lee's eye, saw that they were probably thinking much the same thing: If Sean was in fact the kind of guy who lied and cheated on his girl and yet expected her to be faithful to him, who still thought he owned his ex months after she'd split with him, who thought nothing of taking deadly revenge on her new guy ... then he likely wouldn't stick at harming Katie, as well as anyone who tried to get in his way.

"Well, you don't need to worry about Sean right now," Lee reassured Katie. "Like Rory here said, the sheriff's on his way, and you'll stay with us until he gets here. You want some tea or anything?"

With another small smile, Katie said, "Sure, that'd be great," and started to remove her coat.

So, Rory guessed she would be making tea for everyone to enjoy until Mike arrived. She started to ask what kind everyone wanted, but the ringing of her cell phone interrupted her. "I'll do the tea, Ror," Lee said. Then he offered Katie a seat, and the girl perched in the rocking chair near the window, clutching her coat to her chest. Sitting there slumping forward and chewing on her bottom lip, hands clasped together around her coat, she certainly didn't look threatening.

Rory pulled the cell from her fanny pack. It was Madison calling. When Rory answered, the mayor said in a hurried, hushed voice, "He's here. Sean is in my shop." Lowering her voice further, she added, "He just ordered a coffee. What should I do?"

"Well, I guess you better make him a coffee. Katie's at my place, and the sheriff is on his way. All we have to do is keep them away from each other. As long as Sean's in a public place, I don't think he'll do anything, so take your time about getting that coffee."

"But Laura's already serving him. I think he's getting it to go."

"Do something to try to keep him there, then. Anything."

"Will do." Through the phone, Rory heard shuffling and then Madison calling out somewhat frantically, "Laura, wait! That coffee's no good. Don't serve it. We'll have to make a fresh batch." Then the call was disconnected.

Later, when Rory got the full story from Madison, she would learn that the mayor had physically grabbed the cup of coffee out of Laura's hand, spilling half of it and dumping the rest in the sink. "Poor Sean looked so confused," Madison would say, "and he said, 'I don't care if it's not perfect. I just want something to warm me up.'" Then Madison laughed, and Rory, imagining the scene, laughed with her.

But it wasn't time for laughter yet. When Rory turned around, it was to meet Katie's anxious face. "That was about him, wasn't it?" she asked, her voice high and tight.

"Yes," Rory admitted. "He's down at the café, but I told them to delay him as much as possible. And the sheriff will be here any minute now, so it's going to be okay." She hoped she wasn't telling another lie. Then she thought, *So much for not getting involved.*

Meanwhile, Lee was banging around in the kitchen, filling the kettle with water and setting it on the burner, getting mugs from the cupboard. "Ror, are you out of Earl Grey?" he asked, making her remember her shopping list.

"Yeah, sorry. I was going to get some from Gunthers' the other day, but I forgot."

Normally he'd do something helpful like offer to pop home and get some tea from his own stash. Today though, he did something truly helpful and said, "It's no matter. This peppermint looks good."

Miss C continued to sniff at Katie. *"You stink of fear,"* the cat meowed, placing a paw on her knee and preparing to jump into her lap for a better sniff.

Katie pulled back. "Get away, cat," she said.

"She won't hurt you," Rory reassured the girl as she rushed forward to pull the cat away. *Probably,* she thought. "I don't know what it is about cats, but they seem to be drawn to the one person in the room who doesn't want them around. C'mon, Miss C, come and sit in the window." Rory deposited the cat on her condo, hoping she'd get interested in something happening outside.

But the cat's attention was completely focused on Katie. *"This girl is afraid, but is she afraid of her so-called ex-boyfriend or of being caught for murder? Who better to plunge the deadly knife into Spike than the one who pretended to love him? We should question her further."*

The cat's meow caused Katie to cringe and then jump up from the chair and shuffle into the corner on the other side of the fireplace, about as far from Miss C as she could get without leaving the room.

"It's okay, really," Rory said again, feeling bad now that her cat was terrorizing Katie, who was already being terrorized by her violent ex-boyfriend. On the other hand, Miss C was keeping the girl from doing anything dramatic— well, except for standing there in the corner like she was trying to melt into the walls.

Then the cat's attention was caught by something outside. Rory tensed, watching Miss C turn quickly and look out onto the street. What if Sean had seen Katie come up here, into this house? What if Madison had not been able to keep him at the café for more than a minute or two? But the cat quickly lost interest in whatever she'd seen, and Rory relaxed. If Miss C didn't think it was dangerous, it wasn't. That didn't negate the problem of Sean though.

"Lee, we don't have time for tea. We've got to get Katie out of here. Sean will look for her here, especially if he was following her up here to begin with," Rory said.

He replied, "So we'll take her next door to my place."

"You should get her out of town completely, if you are so concerned for her safety," Miss C meowed. *"The best solution is to put her into her own car and send her on her way."* The sound sent Rory into action.

"C'mon, cat, into the stroller," she said. "Lee, we'll need your mom's minivan. Katie will hide in the back, and you'll take us to, um..." She sputtered, realizing she didn't have a plan beyond getting Katie out of the house and past Sean.

"To Liza's. I mean Sephie's. Whatever," Lee finished for her. "Coats on, everybody, and out the back. I'll just run home and grab the keys. Meet you in the driveway next door." He turned and jogged toward the back door, stopping in the kitchen long enough to turn the burner off.

"Pepperoni neutrons," Rory said to Lee's back. Katie started putting her jacket on as Miss C twined through Rory's legs, meowing. *This is absolute chaos,* Rory thought as she grabbed the cat and set her into the stroller. She zipped the stroller shut and went for her own coat. Lee should have the van open by now, shouldn't he?

"Come on. Aren't we going now?" Katie urged from the kitchen doorway. She looked close to tears, her face tense and frightened.

Rory gripped the stroller handles. "Yes, we're going. But take a look out the window before you go out there," she warned, not wanting Katie to burst out into an ambush possibly set by Sean. In the laundry/mudroom, they both peered through the panes in the door. "Looks clear, and the rain stopped too. C'mon."

Lee sat in the driver's seat of the minivan that was parked in the Coopers' driveway. The engine was running, and the sliding side door was open. He was great in a crisis. Rory would have to be sure to mention that to Liza. Katie sprinted for the van and leapt into it. Rory and Miss C were several seconds behind her.

"Why do we have to take the cat?" Katie pleaded from the very back of the van, where she'd taken refuge.

"Because we always take the cat," Rory answered.

"Yes. I am indispensable," Miss C meowed as her stroller was lifted up and in. Rory climbed in after her and slid the door home.

Lee drove sensibly toward the south end of town. The pace was aggravating but probably for the best. No use drawing attention to themselves by speeding or running the stop sign. Rory kept a close eye out for Sean, but she saw no sign of him. Maybe he was gone? Soon enough, the van turned in at the driveway to the old Miller house. Sephie's Mercedes and Liza's Kia were both there, and Sephie, Liza, and Grace all stood near the barn. Sephie was gesticulating with both hands, no doubt in the middle of some sort of informal presentation on how to turn the old place into a semi-luxurious spa. Liza and Grace watched silently, faces closed. All three of them turned to stare at the unfamiliar minivan pulling into the drive.

"I'll go explain what's going on," Lee offered. "That way we can get Katie straight inside. We don't want her to be just hanging around out here, or Sean could come by and see her."

He slid out of the driver's seat and approached the trio at the barn. When he gestured with a thumb over his shoulder, three pairs of eyes turned to the van. Concern on her face, Liza started for the house at a quick walk, beckoning to the minivan.

"Time to go," Rory said to Katie. She had already opened the side door and was backing out of it, pulling Miss C's stroller behind her.

"Is Sean around?" Katie asked. She had not moved from the cargo area.

Rory cast another look up Main Street toward the center of town. "No. I don't see him. But let's hurry. Every second we wait just gives him more time to find you." Liza had gotten up the front steps and was opening the door. Rory really wanted to get Katie inside, where she'd be hidden and safe.

"Okay, but can you let me out the back? I don't exactly feel like climbing over this seat again."

And I don't exactly feel like running all over town to hide you from your ex-boyfriend, but I'm doing it, Rory thought. Aloud, she said, "Yeah, sure." She left the cat stroller sitting in the gravel drive while she went to release the van's rear-door latch. As the door glided upward and Katie clambered out, Rory noticed a car just coming into town. There was something familiar about it, she thought, and when it suddenly veered toward them and stopped, blocking the end of the driveway, she remembered. Dan and Eddie.

"What the—" Katie started, looking over her shoulder to see the car that had stopped just feet from her.

Rory cut her off. "Go inside," she ordered.

"No, it's okay. It's just Dan and Eddie. Or ... it's just Dan."

"Right, but Sean could be coming, remember? Let's go," Rory urged.

"Some people are very unappreciative when you try to save their life," Miss C observed from her stroller.

Dan, Rory realized now, was the shorter of the Dan-and-Eddie duo. He was the one with the straight black hair. Eddie had shorter, lighter hair and a chin covered in acne. Dan was out of the car now and coming toward them. "Katie, are you okay?" he asked, with a suspicious look toward Rory. "What are you doing to her?" Katie might think he was harmless, but he sounded plenty aggressive to Rory, and as she well knew, even "harmless" people could turn violent under the right circumstances.

Rory considered the situation. It was too complicated to explain, so she just said, "Katie thought Sean was following her, so we brought her here to hang out for a while, just until he's out of town. The sheriff's on his way."

Dan took this in but didn't seem to believe it. "Sean's here?" He looked around as though expecting to see Sean materialize out of thin air.

"Last we knew, he was up toward the center of town, but he could be coming this way, so we'd really like to get Katie inside."

"Oh, okay." That seemed to take the wind out of Dan's sails, and now he stood uncertainly, just as harmless as could be. "Let's go then." He gripped Katie by the elbow and steered her toward the house.

She ripped her arm from his grasp. "Stop touching me. Jeez." Katie marched toward the house, with Dan following, looking like a forlorn puppy. This was a weirdly uncomfortable turn, Rory thought, but at least they were moving in the right direction. Meanwhile, Lee and everyone from the Miller house watched from the front porch. Lee's eyes met Rory's, and she shrugged and began pushing Miss C's stroller up the drive.

"Sorry. I just wanna help you," Dan whined as he trailed after Katie.

"Well, I don't need your help."

"But I just thought, in your condition—"

Katie walked up the first two steps to the porch and rounded on Dan, who stopped short of the bottom step and gazed up at her. "My condition is none of your business."

"But you should have a man to help you."

"You mean you? Ha," she laughed and turned her back on him.

Rory was close enough to clearly hear the change in Dan's voice when he said, "And Spike would've been your man? Get real, Katie. He didn't want that baby. He wasn't never gonna stay with you, get all tied down and stuff. He told me." The whining was over. This voice was cutting and cruel. There was something familiar about that voice, but Rory couldn't quite put her finger on it.

Katie froze on the edge of the porch. Lee was just a step away from her but seemed unsure of what to do. Rory stopped too. She ignored the horribleness of "wasn't never gonna" and realized that Katie had badly misjudged Dan. They all had. He wasn't a harmless loser at all. He was a very dangerous loser.

Dan continued to talk. "What was Spike gonna do when it came time to pay rent? Tell you how pretty you are? You need me, Katie. Spike was useless. That's why..." He stopped, and they all waited breathlessly for what would come next. Was he about to confess to murder?

It suddenly all made sense. Dan wanted to be with Katie. He could have found out that she and Spike were going to be filming in Rory's backyard that night, could have made his own plans to follow them, shooting scenes for his own little horror movie. Dan was savvy enough to send limited portions of the resulting video to Viper V. Everyone would naturally suspect Sean, because he was the one who was making the horror flick. Then Dan helped Katie create her tribute video to Spike. Dan had the skills to doctor that video so Sean's face would be found. He was good at editing a story together, and he knew a little but not a lot about special effects, so a careful look would show that the face didn't belong.

Rory heard Miss C growling in her stroller. She listened for sirens but heard nothing. Well, what better weapon than an angry cat? She quietly unzipped the stroller's front panel, and the cat leapt to the ground.

Chapter 33

Miss C felt the brittle, brown grass under her paws. She was aware of it rubbing against her belly as she crept forward. Dan's back was turned while he argued with Katie, but even if he'd seen a cat on the ground near him, he probably wouldn't think anything of it. Most people wouldn't. The cat's left ear twitched and rotated to her rear, picking up the sound of the Rory person moving the stroller aside. Rory had proven herself adequate in previous altercations, so Miss C was gratified to know that she intended to get in on this fight. If it came to that. They were all still waiting to hear what Dan would say. But it was Katie who spoke.

"That's why what, Dan? Why *what?*" She spat the words at him, her face contorted into a mask of ugliness, mouth set in a snarl, eyes blazing. "Go on. Do you have something to tell everyone?"

"What if I do? Wouldn't you just love if I told everybody everything?" Dan spat back. Miss C could not see his face, but she imagined it was as ugly as Katie's.

Katie processed that for a moment. Then she said, "You wouldn't dare..." and moved toward him. The Lee person put an arm out to restrain her, and she pushed him off and launched herself down the steps and straight into Dan. She aimed a lopsided punch at his head, but he blocked it easily. Miss C crouched near their feet, unsure if she should intervene, or which side she should intervene on.

They'd set out to protect Katie, but now it was Katie who'd become the aggressor.

It was all very confusing.

Everything became more confusing when tires screeched in the street and a voice yelled, "Hey! What are you doing to her?" Miss C did not need to turn around to know that the voice belonged to Sean, the person they were supposed to be protecting Katie from. But Katie paid no attention to him now. She just went on trying to hit Dan.

Sean's running footsteps approached from behind, and Miss C fully expected that he would attack Dan too, since he seemed to think that Dan was trying to harm Katie. But Sean proved himself more astute than Miss C would have given him credit for when he instead put himself between the two and grabbed Katie in a bear hug, effectively stopping her from throwing more punches. Katie screamed and struggled against him, but no one moved to help her. They were all too dumbfounded to do more than watch.

The Rory person stood transfixed, as though her feet were growing roots. The others wandered closer to the scene, but staying well out of reach of any of the participants.

"I just did what you said," Dan insisted.

"You weren't supposed to kill him, you dummy!"

Sean's face went slack in astonishment. Katie was finally able to wrench herself out of his grasp. "So it *was* you," Sean said to Dan. "And Katie? You told him to? You sent this twerp to kill Spike?"

Katie transformed again, into an innocent, frightened little girl. "No, no, no. That's not how it happened. Why would I tell him to hurt Spike?"

Dan's only transformation was toward greater anger. "Yes you did! Yes you did!" he yelled repetitiously to Katie. "You said to get rid of him. You told me where you'd be!"

Miss C's ears twitched again, this time picking up the shrillness of a siren in the distance and coming closer. The humans did not hear it yet.

Then, suddenly realizing he'd just admitted in front of an astounded crowd that he'd committed murder, Dan looked desperately from one to another of them with wide-open, wild eyes, gauging what he should do next.

Grace stood a few feet from him. When his eyes fell on her, something in his expression caused her to take a step backward. The movement was like a cue, prompting him to lunge for her. Grace took another step back, but not quickly enough, and in a second, Dan had her in his grasp. A stainless steel switchblade gleamed at her throat, its point making a small depression in the skin of her neck.

Rory heard Liza screaming Grace's name, but everything else went strangely quiet. There was the look of fear in Grace's eyes, the wild look in Dan's, and, sounding somehow far-off and foreign, the crunching of gravel under their feet as Dan pulled her farther away from everyone else.

"Everyone just stay back!" Dan shrieked.

They did. They all stood motionless, unsure of what to do, seeing no way to intervene without having that blade slice into Grace's neck.

Trying to keep her voice from shaking, Rory said, "Don't make things worse, Dan." She took a small, tentative step forward, but he warned her off immediately.

"Just stay back, I said!" Then he backed down the driveway toward his car, dragging Grace with him, the knife blade still pressing on her throat.

From the corner of her eye, Rory saw Miss C crawling through the grass at the edge of the drive, keeping pace with Dan. Could the cat have a plan? Rory inched forward as well, only moving when Dan's eyes weren't on her. She sensed she needed to be close enough to help, if Miss C did try something.

They could all hear a single siren in the distance now, and the sound seemed to push Dan to move faster. When he turned his head to check their distance from his car, Miss C sprang forward, leaping into the air toward the hand that held the knife. Claws and teeth pierced bare flesh, causing Dan to cry out. Miss C snarled and growled like a creature straight from the Underworld as she shook her head from side to side, causing further injury to Dan's hand. Grace made a strangled noise, and they all feared she'd been hurt. But in the next second, she was scrambling away. She rubbed her throat with one hand, but no blood was visible.

In the moment when he let go of Grace to disentangle his skin from the cat's teeth, Rory recalled Mike's advice about making a good, solid tackle. *Lower your center of gravity, lead with your shoulder, hit him low, and wrap him up.* So, as she ran toward Dan, she led with her lowered left shoulder, which she plowed into his midsection with enough force to knock him to the ground. Then Sean was on him, followed shortly by Lee. Miss C released her hold and retreated, leaving the humans to restrain the culprit while she sat in the grass and groomed the blood from her whiskers.

Seconds later, Mike arrived, speeding up onto the lawn with siren blaring and lights flashing. There was a moment's confusion when he leapt out and found Sean sitting on Dan's chest and Lee on his legs, with Rory on the grass nearby, but that was quickly sorted. Deputies soon rolled onto the scene, blocking the street completely, and Dan and Katie were arrested without further incident. Grace was badly frightened but uninjured. She fell into Liza's embrace, and together they retreated to the safety of the porch. No one would have guessed they weren't mother and daughter.

As they watched Mike getting Dan situated in the back of a deputy's patrol car, Lee asked Rory, "Where'd you learn to tackle like that?"

"Oh, I've been watching a little football with Mike. Picked up a few pointers," she said slyly.

"That man's been good for you."

"Yeah. Speaking of being good for people..." She turned to look over her shoulder toward the porch, where Liza stood with Grace wrapped in her arms. Sephie stood a little behind them.

"What, me and Sephie?" Lee asked. "Nah, it'd never work out."

Rory punched him lightly on the arm. "You know what I mean. Just ask her. She'll say yes."

Lee might have said something more, but they were interrupted by Mike, who came up and gripped both Rory's elbows in his strong, warm hands. "You're sure you're okay, hon? 'Cause we can get you to the hospital, get you checked out, and Grace too."

She looked into his blue eyes, so filled with concern for her, and she seriously considered fainting, just so Mike would catch her. But instead she said, "I'm fine. I promise. And I think Grace is too. She's just scared."

He pulled her into him and wrapped his arms around her. "Why don't you listen when I tell you not to get involved in things like this? It's so dangerous," he said directly into her ear.

"That's part of my charm," she replied, pulling back to look into his face again.

Mike grunted something noncommittal and released her. "We'll talk about that later. Right now, I see I have the press to deal with."

Only then did Rory's ears pick up the sounds of a deputy arguing with Mel Scott, who, camera in hand, was trying to gain access to the scene.

"Yeah, good luck explaining this to her," Rory said.

Mike shook his head. "I don't even understand it myself yet."

Chapter 34

Thanksgiving Day dawned seasonably cold, with a clear blue sky. Mike arrived hours before they were scheduled to be at Madison's for dinner. It had been weeks since he and Rory had been able to enjoy any extended alone time together, and Rory, for one, was craving an afternoon with him, just sitting on the sofa doing nothing in particular, maybe putting the finishing touches on the scarecrow puzzle that lay unfinished on the coffee table. She was even open to lounging on the bed, eating chips and watching football, listening to Mike dissect every play. But it turned out he wasn't in the mood for lounging. When she went to the kitchen to fetch a couple Cokes from the fridge, he followed at her heels.

"What's up with you?" she asked, handing him a cold, unopened can.

He took it and, instead of opening it, set it on the kitchen table. "Nothing. Just … I feel like some exercise. How 'bout a walk?"

"Right now?"

"Yeah. Work up an appetite before that big dinner. You told me Madison's cooking up a feast."

Disappointed, she said, "Well, sure, if that's what you want to do. I'll get Miss C ready."

He did not bother to ask if it was really necessary to take the cat.

Outside, the sun had warmed away the coldness of dawn, leaving a chill that called for a light jacket. The Brooksford bells were chiming noon, and some people, Rory guessed, would already be sitting down to eat. Her empty stomach rumbled. She'd really been hoping for a light snack before dinner, not exercise. Along Main Street, she could smell Thanksgiving: turkeys roasting, wood smoke curling out of chimneys. She knew that all over town, women, and perhaps some men too, had gotten up long before the sun to get those turkeys in the oven, get the potatoes peeled, get their side dishes mixed up and ready to bake. She was so glad she wasn't one of them.

From one backyard came the shouts and laughter of a touch football game. "I'll bet you could get in on that game if you wanted to," Rory teased. Lately Mike had been trying to convince her that it would be fun for them to toss a football around in the backyard. So far, she'd managed to put him off. She had made one tackle recently, and that was enough sport for her.

"Uh-hmm," he muttered, distracted.

He usually had a lot more to say than that. Something was definitely up with him. It couldn't still be the case, right? Because Dan had made a full confession, and he'd spilled all kinds of details about Katie's wicked plan to get revenge on Sean by setting him up for murder. Turned out Sean had been the one to dump Katie, not vice versa, and he was a reasonably nice guy. Cocky, vain, but far from the jealous maniac Katie made him out to be. She was the crazy one in that failed relationship. Katie still insisted she had nothing to do with anything related to Spike's death, but the sheriff's department was building a strong case against her. She and Dan were both charged with first-degree murder and were being held without bond in the county jail.

Nor could Mike be nervous about having to deal with Rory's parents, because they were safely two hours away, enjoying a festive community dinner in their condo complex.

That seemed to leave Rory herself as the only thing that could be distracting him. He didn't want to be alone with her, doing any of their usual things. He didn't seem to want to talk to her. The possibilities of what could be wrong turned the hunger in her stomach to nausea.

"It's nice out," she said as they neared the intersection.

"Huh? Oh. Uh-huh. Very nice. Not too cold."

Jeez, he sounds exactly like I do when I'm flustered. Maybe her involvement in this most recent case had just been too much for him. Maybe if she'd just stayed out of it like he'd told her to.... Well, too late now.

"I think your pet sheriff is having a stroke or something," Miss C meowed. *"He has lost the ability to speak in complete sentences."*

They crossed into the south end and continued in silence past the historical society and post office, past the town hall, all the way to the Brooksford Inn, where the parking lot was full. Frank, Betty, and their chef had hurriedly dreamed up a seated dinner arrangement, and Liza had agreed to provide entertainment in the form of an illustrated lecture about the legend of the Woldwomper. They'd easily sold out two seatings and probably could have sold out a third.

"What's up with Lee and Liza?" Mike suddenly asked.

"He says he's going to ask her out, but I think he's too nervous to do it. You never know, maybe she'll ask him."

Mike chuckled. "It'd make things easier on him."

This loquacious exchange was followed by more silence as they turned for home. Rory found herself enjoying the fine day a little less with each step. It felt like things were coming to an end, somehow. Like, after this afternoon, things would never be the same between them. She quickly wiped a tear from her bottom eyelid before it could spill down her cheek and betray her. *Whatever happens, I'm not going to lose it,* she told herself.

Ahead of them, a car turned in at the Crabtrees' house. "Hey, is that Mr. Crabtree?" Mike asked.

"Looks like it."

"He's been gone awhile, hasn't he? It's good to see him back in time for Thanksgiving. Let's say hi." Mike quickened his pace toward the Crabtrees' driveway. He was normally friendly, ready with a kind word for anyone except a bad guy, but he'd never before expressed any interest in the Crabtrees. Why should he suddenly care that Rory's neighbor was home? He was definitely avoiding something, she thought as she followed him.

Mr. Crabtree was just getting out of the car. His wife stood at the edge of the driveway, and he gave her a kiss on the cheek. In return, she scowled at him. Maybe scowling was how she showed love, Rory considered. Then she thought, *If that's true, she must really love me,* and she barely managed to stifle the laugh that followed. But she still had a dumb smile on her face when Mrs. Crabtree turned her scowl on them. Instantly the woman's eyebrows lowered and the creases in her forehead and at the sides of her mouth deepened. No, that was definitely not love.

"Happy Thanksgiving!" Mike greeted the couple. He and Mr. Crabtree shook hands. Pleasantries were exchanged.

Rory offered her condolences over the loss of Mr. Crabtree's sister. In response, he frowned and said, "Thank you, Ms. Roberts. We were never very close, but still, someone had to take care of her affairs after she passed. But there is one thing I'm very excited about, and you'll be interested in this too, I expect." He held up a finger, signaling "Just wait till you see this!" and then opened the car's back door. Inside the car, something moved. Something big. Mr. Crabtree leaned into the back seat and came out holding one end of a leash. Following him, an enormous fluffy cat, an orange tabby, emerged, jumping to the ground. It was at least twice as big as Miss C. Long tufts of fur extended from the tips of its ears. There was a harness around its chest, and the other end of the leash was attached to it. The cat nosed briefly at the driveway surface and then cast its regal gaze over the assembled humans. It seemed to do a double-take at the cat in the stroller. Miss C remained strangely quiet.

"Everyone, meet Zeus," Mr. Crabtree announced. "He's my sister's Maine coon, and the Mrs. and I are taking him in."

Rory could have sworn she heard Miss C gasp. Just her imagination, probably.

Mike and Rory expressed congratulations and delight as they petted Zeus, welcoming him to the neighborhood. The cat accepted the attention as though it were his due. Rory stole a glance up at Mrs. Crabtree, who had the most sour expression she'd ever seen on a living human being. So *this* was what the old bat had been so distracted about. She'd known her husband was bringing a cat home, and she wasn't happy about it. When their eyes met, Rory gave her a knowing smile. Mrs. Crabtree quickly looked away.

After Zeus had been introduced, the conversation quickly wound down and Mike and Rory resumed their walk, leaving the Crabtrees to their own quiet Thanksgiving celebration.

"I thought she didn't like cats," Mike said.

Rory had to let out the laugh she'd been holding in. "Oh, she hates them. And now she's living with a giant cat named Zeus. That's the most hilarious thing I've heard in ages."

"Yeah," Mike replied, distracted once again.

Rory halted in her tracks and commanded, "Stop."

"Huh?" Mike shuffled forward another step or two before realizing Rory had stopped moving.

"Just stop. You seem to have something on your mind."

"Well..."

"Just spit it out. You're acting weird, and it's driving me crazy. Look, if you're still mad at me about that thing with Spike—"

Mike's forehead creased the way it did when he was worried over something. Rory wanted to reach out and smooth those creases away, but she didn't move.

"Mad at you?" Mike said, quickly adding, "No, no. I was worried about you. I worry about you all the time, hon."

"Now you sound like my mother," Rory joked.

"Please don't make jokes right now."

Now you really *sound like my mother,* she thought, but wisely kept that to herself.

Mike went on, "Sorry I'm acting so weird. I just don't know what you're going to do. I never know what you're going to do." There was befuddlement in his voice.

"Many of us feel that way," Miss C meowed.

Rory sighed. So. She'd been right. She'd finally gone too far—putting herself in the middle of the fight that got Spike killed, then nosing around in the investigation and even, at the end, managing to get young Grace involved, although she was pretty sure that last bit wasn't entirely her fault. And now Mike had had enough. Well. This wasn't how she'd planned on spending Thanksgiving, picking up the pieces after he broke things off with her. Still, better to get it over with. "Stop wasting time," she said. "Just do it."

"I wish you wouldn't put it quite that way, but you're right. We're not getting any younger."

"Speak for yourself, mister," she said testily.

"I am … I mean I'm not getting any younger … and if there's anything I really need to do … I should just do it," Mike stammered, his eyes looking into the distance over Rory's shoulder.

Criminy, the man was falling apart right there in front of her. *"I think your pet sheriff is having a stroke again. Perhaps you should call the 911?"* Miss C meowed.

Annoyed now that he was just avoiding the dirty deed and couldn't bring himself to say the words, Rory said, "All right, you want me to say it? I'll do it. Maybe we should—"

He interrupted her with a kiss, one that was far more than friendly. "Okay," she said when their lips separated. "But—"

"Shh. Just let me talk, please. Listen, this isn't quite how I wanted to do this. I don't have a ring or anything. I mean I have one, my grandmother's, but I don't have it with me. But that doesn't mean I haven't thought this through."

"What are you—"

"Shh."

"Yes. Shh," Miss C meowed. *"I am trying to hear what happens."*

Finally, Mike looked directly at her, his blue eyes pleading with hers. Rory felt something break inside her, as though something hard and impenetrable had suddenly been split wide open. It was not a bad feeling, she decided, not bad at all. And as they stood face to face on the sidewalk between her house and the Crabtrees', Mike said clearly and strongly, "Rory Meredith Roberts, will you marry me?"

She was stunned for exactly four seconds—she knew how long it was because the part of her mind that still functioned counted off, *One Mississippi, two Mississippi....* Then she said, "Huh?"

"Please don't make me say it again."

"But ... you mean you're not mad at me?"

Mike's brow creased again, this time in confusion. "Of course not. Why would I be mad at you?"

"Oh, no reason," she said quickly, because if he wasn't angry, there was no point in drawing attention to any reasons he should be, right?

"Are you going to answer me?" Mike asked when she said nothing else.

Rory had been imagining herself walking into Madison's big Thanksgiving dinner on Mike's arm, making the announcement, receiving happy congratulations from their friends, inspiring Lee and Liza to spend some time together. She snapped back to the moment. "Sorry. Yes. Of course I will. Marry you."

"I just love it when you get all eloquent," he said.

And, as the Brooksford bells began chiming, he kissed her again, neither of them caring if anyone stopped to notice.

❧

A Cuddlywumps
Classical Dictionary

GENITIVE ABSOLUTE: A type of construction in Greek grammar. For our purposes, you don't need to understand the genitive absolute or even know exactly what it is. Miss C will just think a little less of you for not being able to grasp it.

GREEK CHORUS: In ancient Greek drama, the chorus was a group of actors who commented on the dramatic action through song, dance, and recitation. They represented the general population of a story and expressed the emotions and judgment of average citizens.

HERODOTUS: Often called the "father of history," Herodotus was born in the fifth century BC on the southwest coast of what is now Turkey. He traveled throughout the Mediterranean world collecting the information he wrote down in his *Histories*. Much of this has to do with the wars between the Greeks and the Persians, but there are also many stories of the customs of the strange people he either encountered directly or heard about from others. Not all of these stories are true.

HESIOD: One of the earliest of the Greek poets (flourished ca. 700 BC). He wrote the *Theogeny* and *Works and Days*. In the *Theogeny*, Hesiod related the history of the gods, starting with how the Earth and Heavens were formed and how the different gods came to be. In *Works and*

Days, he wrote of the importance of hard work for the ordinary person, as well as advice on sea trade, some proverbs, and lucky and unlucky days.

HOMER: Greek poet of the eighth century BC who wrote the epics *The Iliad* and *The Odyssey*, about the Trojan War and the hero Odysseus's voyage home from the war, respectively. Little is known about him, though he is often thought to have been blind. Some people think that Homer did not create original epics but merely copied down poems that had been recited orally for generations. Others think there never was a real-life poet named Homer and that these epics were created by others.

KRONOS: In early Greek myth, Kronos was the youngest of the twelve Titans. He was the son of Uranus (Heaven) and Gaea (Earth). He became king of the Titans when he castrated his father, separating Heaven from Earth. His parents warned Kronos that his own children would overthrow him, so when he married his sister Rhea, he swallowed each of the children she bore him (Hestia, Demeter, Hera, Hades, and Poseidon). But when the next child, Zeus, was born, instead of giving him to Kronos to swallow, Rhea gave her husband a stone, which he (unknowingly) swallowed instead. Meanwhile, Zeus had been hidden in a cave on Crete, and when he grew up, he forced his father to vomit up his brothers and sisters. Together, he and his siblings then defeated their father in war. And so the warning from Kronos's parents proved true.

MARCUS AURELIUS: A Roman emperor and Stoic philosopher of the second century AD. According to the Stoics, life is to be lived by reason rather than emotion or passing fancies.

MEDUSA: In Greek mythology, a Gorgon with the face of an extremely ugly woman and a writhing mass of poisonous snakes instead of hair. Anyone who looked directly at her would be turned to stone. According to some accounts, the hero Perseus defeated her with the help of a shiny bronze shield; by looking only at Medusa's reflection, he was able to behead her without being turned to stone.

NARCISSUS: In Greek myth, Narcissus was a handsome youth who attracted the attentions of many young ladies, and a few young men too. But none of them interested him, and his disinterest broke many hearts. In fact, he met no one who interested him until one day he happened to see his own reflection in a pool of water and immediately fell in love with himself. Unfortunately, a reflection cannot return affection, and Narcissus spent the rest of his life (which turned out to be not very long) right there by the side of that pool, staring at himself and longing for a response. Starved and dehydrated, he soon died, and his body turned into the flowers that today are known as narcissus. In modern botany, *Narcissus* is the name of the genus that includes jonquils, daffodils, and paperwhites.

PERSEPHONE: Goddess of the underworld in Greek mythology. She was the daughter of Zeus and Demeter. Hades, god of the underworld, wanted to marry Persephone, but her parents refused him. So Hades abducted Persephone and took her to the underworld. Her mother, understandably upset, refused to allow any plants to grow on earth until Persephone was returned. Unfortunately, because Persephone had eaten some pomegranate seeds in the underworld, she would have to stay there part of each year: one month for each seed she had eaten. But every year when Persephone returned from her underground kingdom, plant life bloomed again.

PROMETHEUS: A Titan who was said to be responsible for giving humans the gift of fire. Another version of the story said that humans had fire already, but Zeus took it away from them after Prometheus played a trick on him. It was then that Prometheus stole some fire and gave it back to humans. As punishment for this, Zeus had him chained to a rock and sent an eagle to eat his liver. Every night, Prometheus's liver grew back, and every day the eagle returned to eat it again.

SOCRATES: A Greek philosopher of the fifth century BC, Socrates was known in Athens as a gadfly whose questions and answers could demonstrate that those who thought themselves wise were in fact rather ignorant. Some Athenians did not appreciate this. Socrates was convicted of corrupting the youth of Athens and not believing in the gods, and was sentenced to die by drinking hemlock. He could have escaped but chose to stay and face his sentence.

ZEUS: The chief Greek god who ruled from Mount Olympus. As the god of the sky and weather, he was responsible for thunder and lightning, and the thunderbolt was his traditional weapon. Though he was married to Hera, Zeus was known for the many amorous encounters he had with other women. His many children included Apollo and Artemis, Persephone, and Athena.

Liked the book? Please take a moment to leave a review at the site you purchased it from. Thank you!

About the Author

Roby Sweet is the cozy-mystery-writing alter ego of editor and blogger Sarah Andrews. She lives in Maryland, where she writes and edits with the help of two cats and one dog, though not all at the same time.

Keep Up with Miss C!

Miss Cuddlywumps is one busy cat. Besides starring in her very own cozy mystery series, she oversees the writing and maintenance of a blog called *The Cuddlywumps Cat Chronicles*. There, Miss C and author Roby Sweet write about cats in history, mystery, and culture, and also about older cats in shelters and in need of homes. It is great fun, and very informative.

Catch up with them at cuddlywumps.blogspot.com and cuddlywumpspublishing.com.

Lightning Source UK Ltd.
Milton Keynes UK
UKHW040559301018
331447UK00001B/258/P